THE RAGING PEACE

THE
RAGING
PEACE
Volume One
of the
THRONE TRILOGY
by
Artemis OakGrove

Lace Publications 1984

Lady Winston Series

Printed in the United States of America

First Edition

First printing November 1984

Cover design by Studio A

Lace Publications
POB 10037
Denver CO 80210-0037

Library of Congress Cataloging in Publication Data

OakGrove, Artemis, date
    The raging peace.
    (Volume one of the Throne trilogy) (Lady Winston
Series)
    I. Title. II. Series: OakGrove, Artemis, date
Throne trilogy; v.1. III. Series: Lady Winston series.
PS3565.A4R3   1984   813'.54   84-14409
ISBN 0-917597-00-1

The author wishes to thank these patient souls for their encouragement, information and instruction:
Mary Davidson for helping me get through the rough draft.
Lindsay, who helped me get through the final draft and put up with my eccentric punctuation.
My travel agent, Coreen, for booking my passage home.
Tibi and MaryLou
Special thanks to Angie Rozmen for opening the door to the inspiration for this story.

1

"I'm taking Dana to the dinner theater tonight. Do you want to come with us?" Delores used the soft-spoken manner she saved for these occasions. Luring her beautiful law partner into social settings was a self appointed, full time mission. She wasn't discouraged by the shaking of Leslie's head. "I could invite Joan; she wants to meet you."

"You're too generous Del. I really can't tonight. You have fun." Leslie's sensual voice lent an intangible authority to her dodge.

The dark eyed, senior partner frowned. "I suppose you're going slumming tonight instead."

With an icy smile, Leslie laid her pen down and replied, "I have work to do. Good night, Del."

The dismissal stung Delores. Her tightly shut lips whitened and she turned her solid, athletic frame to leave. She caught a disgusted sigh coming from Leslie's office as she walked out the front door, and suppressed the urge to slam it behind her.

It was always the same when Leslie was late leaving the law offices of Rhinehart, Benson & Serle. Delores would corner her with indefatigable attempts to introduce available women to her. When she relented and joined Delores and Dana at a party or dinner, she always had a good time, and the women she met were pleasant and respectful. She even went home with one or two of them. The earth didn't move. Delores always tried, and had done so for seven years, since Leslie had added the third name to the letterhead.

For thirty-three years, Leslie had known she was alone, telling herself that some people were meant to be that way. She had long since given up finding that special someone to rid her of her terminal loneliness. Her fantasies had been brought to their knees. She was faced with herself. Alone.

Her eyes had avoided the calendar all day. Now they rested unhappily on the page. February first. The month of limbo. A month that wasn't winter, nor was it spring. Like no other time of the year, February exemplified the desolation in her heart. She pulled away from the calendar and turned to stare into the premature darkness settling on the dusty streets below.

A tiny stir quickened in her heart. She hadn't planned on going to Cary's bar until Delores mentioned it. The bar scene was beneath her partners. "Especially Cary's," they said. They tried to shame her out of going there to no avail.

Cary's discharged excitement with the force of thunderclouds venting electrons. The variety of patrons combined and recombined in a mixture of emotions, energy, passions, and life. If she were going to be lonely, she was going to have fun doing it.

She repaired her makeup and combed her hair, then walked over to her closet and donned her grey wool coat. As she smoothed her ash grey gloves over her knuckles, the sound of loud music and the taste of scotch teased a path into her thoughts. Unbidden hope awakened her nerves. She halted in midaction; the briefcase could stay behind. She reached for her purse and walked resolutely out of the office, thrusting it into darkness behind her.

The elevator came to a floating stop at the third parking level. Her heels creased the silence in the garage, her gait becoming more lively as she approached her Mercedes 450SL. Relaxed in the tasteful confines of her auto, her mind drifted for a moment before starting the engine. A solitary dinner didn't appeal to her, so she decided to forego the meal and the trip home to change clothes. The need to outrun her blues and head directly for Cary's and a scotch took possession of her.

The distance between her office, lodged squarely in the middle of downtown Denver, and Cary's was mercifully short enough to deliver her from her solitude, and the ever present absence of a mate.

A flutter of anticipation animated her mood; this was the first time she had come to Cary's directly from work. The crowd wouldn't be large enough to shield her in a protective blanket of anonymity. She summoned her courage and went in.

The loud music assaulted her senses, enticing her nerves to loosen. She walked around the pool table that greeted all comers like a sentry. It lay dormant. The front of Cary's housed a lengthy bar, reclaimed from an abandoned goldrush saloon; the decor took its lead from there. The cluttered rustic air brought to mind bygone days. It had a curious resemblance to the westerns she had been weaned on in her youth; romantic, antagonistic ghosts reliving their colorful pasts.

A dozen or so tables competed for space nearby. The more intimate section of Cary's surrounded the rectangular dance floor. It was here that Leslie could fade into the shadows and watch life unfurl. She took a seat near the far wall. From her vantage point she could observe the whole of the bar and its inhabitants. She was glad to have come this early; it gave her the time to play voyeur instead of participant. She knew that once her presence was discovered, it would be an endless stream of women asking her to dance, robbing her of the opportunity she now savored.

The crowd had a promising look about it. The jukebox was monopolized by two women in jeans and flannel shirts. Their drinks rested on the neon display, ignored. They sorted through the selections, sporadically pressing buttons and laughing.

The pool table was pressed into service by two women who wouldn't make it through their first game before they would be checked for identification. Over near the bar Leslie recognized the face of a regular at the bar, a bleary face that hadn't recovered from the night before.

The door opened and seven women in sports silks entered. They were full of themselves, apparently fresh from a win. A middle-aged couple took to the dance floor and swayed to a blaring ballad.

She settled into her seat and sipped the drink the waitress brought her. It was here, several years ago, she first became aware of the nickname she no longer cared about shaking. The Ice Princess. She supposed every bar had at least one woman no one could get anywhere with. A private smile crept over her features.

Thursday evening metamorphosed into Thursday night. Leslie began to notice herself rocking rhythmically in her chair and tapping her foot. She looked up to see the first of many women she would dance with. The liquor started to surge in her brain, opening doors and battering down defenses. Her awareness felt heightened; she could see things around the bar and the women in it she hadn't noticed before.

The ceiling glittered, white paint blasted with luminescent flecks that caught stray light rays from the juke box and bounced them back at her like unrelenting taunts. Leslie is afraid, Leslie is too proud, Leslie is running from herself. They battered into her consciousness.

She winced to herself, then opened her eyes, seeing for the first time the woman who held her in arms that felt like fence railings in her back. She tried to see the eyes of the tall brunette and couldn't. She stiffened and began to count the seconds until the song would be over and free her of her artificial prison.

Then, out of the corner of her eye, she saw her. A lanky, dark haired woman in a leather jacket. The sight made Leslie lose her balance. Her brunette partner caught her deftly and continued dancing, oblivious to the shock wave that seared through Leslie.

Leslie tried to listen to the music and concentrate on what she was doing. "This must be the longest song ever recorded," she thought to herself. Without knowing why, she was standing outside of herself, watching her body stop cold in its tracks. Uncharacteristically, she informed the brunette that she had to sit down in the middle of the dance. She watched herself walk back to her table, alone, not caring if she hurt any feelings, only that she get a chair under her unstable legs.

Seated, she re-entered her body and looked for a cigarette. She took inventory to make sure she was whole, inhaled deeply, and looked timidly across the bar. Her eyes zeroed in on the pool table, dispensing with the customary detours.

There, directly in her sights, was what her soul recognized as her destiny, and her heart recognized as the lost longings of her youth.

At the pool table stood two women with cues in hand, watching intently as a third sized up her next shot. Leslie followed every move of the slender, boylike woman. She watched as the object of her curiosity calmly ran the table with an easy grace that seemed uniquely hers. She was spellbound as she observed the stranger, cigarette carelessly dangling from thin lips, line up and execute each shot with a studied perfection.

When the game was over, the handsome vision reached over the table and gave her opponent a healthy handshake. She retired to a stool, drank from a beer, and laughed with the others around her. She displayed no ego or pride in what she had just done, only pure joy and relaxation.

Suddenly, Leslie realized that she hadn't been breathing, nor was she entirely certain that her heart had been beating. She sat back in her chair with a deep breath, closed her mouth and placed both hands over her heart, willing it to settle to a normal rhythm. She met with partial success and decided that a trip to the ladies room was in order.

She stood, checked her legs for stability, and made her way to the back of the bar. She emerged refreshed and stopped near the cigarette machine, trying to appear casual while cruising the main bar area. Adrenalin raced through her veins, arousing the sensations she recognized from the courtroom. She smiled to herself, knowing she wasn't hiding her foolishness. "I feel like a spy in a cheap novel."

She braced herself, set her jaw and pierced the smoky atmosphere unabashedly in the direction of the lean stranger. The stranger was looking back at her. Clearly, she had been noticed, caught, she felt, and her resolve melted in a pool at her feet. She experienced a shudder, not unlike a small orgasm, rustle through her muscles. Her hand instinctively covered her mouth in embarrassment.

Her next conscious act was looking at herself in the restroom mirror.

"Leslie, get control of yourself, woman," she scolded herself. She pulled a paper towel from the holder and ran it under the cold water. "This is silly. How can I possibly be that rattled by anyone?" She mopped her forehead and began to get steady. "I must be drunk out of my mind."

She warred with herself for several minutes, debating between sneaking out the back door and boldly introducing herself. She was jostled from her dilemma by a woman who had had entirely too much to drink making her way to a stall. Leslie sidestepped the drunk to make room and sighed to herself. She was sober

13

by comparison, but fervently wished she wasn't. It would be easier to avoid responsibility for her actions if she could blame her foolhardiness on alcohol. She knew she had to meet the incredible stranger, but had no idea how to go about it.

The only resolve she could muster was to purchase another drink. She glanced in the mirror, straightened the neckline ruffles on her rust dress, combed her springy blonde curls and braved her fate, unable to decide anything.

Fate wasted no time in deciding for her. Leaning against the cigarette machine was destiny's messenger. Clad in motorcycle boots, black slacks, blue, button down shirt, and black leather vest was a woman of medium height, heavily boned and muscular. Her stance was patient and confident. Leslie noticed her sleeves were rolled part way up her forearms, which were crossed comfortably over average sized breasts.

Leslie's gaze was inexplicably drawn to the frank features of the face that housed eyes wise beyond their years. Somehow she wasn't surprised by the light brown hair, cut in the mannish style that still adorned some of the diehard butches that haunted Cary's.

She felt no threat from this person; indeed she almost hoped that they could talk.

"Feel better?" came the husky inquiry.

She knew the voice would have a deep resonance to it. What she didn't expect was her response to the genuine concern displayed by the simple question. Every muscle relaxed. She felt her diaphram tug in a deep breath, and she replied automatically, "Now I do."

"My name is Rags. Why don't you sit at my table a moment? I'll get you a drink." Rags stood straight up and without hesitation firmly grasped Leslie's elbow and guided her to a table situated about halfway to the pool table, in line with the bartender's ordering station.

Rags held out a chair for her, a gesture she accepted without reserve. Leslie noted the authority behind the gesture; no question of roles here. "What can I get you?"

"A scotch on the rocks, please." Leslie sat, rooted in fascination as she watched Rags order her drink and a beer. The bartender had stopped what she was doing to prepare the order, and no money was exchanged. Leslie knew that she had never seen, or noticed at the very least, Rags before now. Nor had she been to the bar so early on a weeknight. It was clear that Rags was a regular, possibly even a fixture. Her mind was still muddling over her lack of awareness when her drink was placed carefully before her.

She gazed into it thoughtfully, then drank fully half of it before her common sense returned, along with her manners. "Pardon me!" She extended her hand to Rags, seated comfortably across from her. "My name is Leslie."

Rags took the proffered hand solidly in hers and squeezed ever so slightly as if to emphasize the delicacy of the situation. "I am pleased to meet you, Leslie."

Leslie was instantly aware that this was a woman who was accustomed to being in control of every situation she encountered. It made her begin to feel secure as well as relaxed. She was completely disarmed. Awareness of her immediate surroundings began to seep back into her mind. She realized that she was seated with her back to the area of the pool table. Suddenly, it was urgent that she turn around to verify that the dark stranger did indeed exist and was still there. She knew that she was helpless to her own inhibitions and wouldn't make such an obvious move. Her nerves began to tangle.

Rags gently let her hand go and leaned forward slightly. "You don't really want to meet her, Leslie," Rags projected, and calmly offered Leslie a cigarette as a distraction.

One look into Rags' wrinkle padded eyes told her that the seating arrangement was by design. She ignored the cigarette before her. "I beg your pardon?" She made no effort to mask her astonishment.

"Leslie, what do you do for a living?" Rags inquired.

Leslie was nonplussed and answered without thinking, "I'm an attorney, but. . ."

"All the more reason for you to stay away from her," Rags interrupted.

Leslie raised her eyebrows. "What?"

"Surely in your profession you are aware of how some people are very dangerous to themselves and everyone around them."

Leslie nodded in agreement.

"Ryan is one of those people. She is extremely dangerous, and you shouldn't get involved with her." Rags carved each word out of stone and handed them to Leslie with all the subtlety of a dump truck.

"You don't mince words do you?"

Rags shook her head in reply. "Life is too short for anything less."

Leslie sat back in her chair and studied how Rags managed to be menacing and nonthreatening at the same time. Then the fog cleared and her analytical mind shifted gears. "Wait just a minute. How? Who? Are we talking about the same person here?"

"The tall, skinny one with the leather jacket." Rags motioned in the direction of the pool table. This freed Leslie to look over her shoulder. Indeed, the only person in the bar that fit that description was still there, and quite real. She drank in the sight for a luxurious moment, then turned to Rags.

"How did you know that I was interested in her?"

"I don't think you were aware of it, but you broadcast pretty loud," Rags supplied.

Leslie's eyes widened. "Do you think she knows?" The concern in her voice spilled out with the words.

Rags sat back in her chair with a wry chuckle. "Ryan's talents are many, but observation isn't one of them."

"But it's one of yours?" Leslie speculated.

"You might say that. I haven't much else to do, except keep Ryan out of trouble whenever I can."

Leslie's mind went into overdrive. Ryan's name began to vibrate inside it, in step with her heart. She could sense her blood travel to her feet and, for a short instant, she felt faint. The moment left as quickly as it came. She recovered, but she felt as though some outside force had just imprinted, indelibly in her being, Ryan's name. She felt a bond form in her heart, and she knew that no matter how Rags had determined her interest in Ryan, or how sincere her warnings were, she would never be able to heed them.

No sooner than the thought materialized in her mind, cognizance registered on Rags' face. Leslie began to feel uneasy; it was too uncanny to be a coincidence. She just met Rags and

16

already she felt her most private self had been invaded by her. Strings were being pulled and buttons she hadn't known existed were being pushed. She retraced her steps that evening, searching for clues that would have tipped Rags off. She couldn't find any tangible reason why Rags knew what she wanted. It would have taken a mind reader to know. . .

Leslie's thought froze when she saw Rags smile knowingly. The hair on the back of her neck rose and tingled. She shifted in her chair, stared into her drink and withdrew into herself.

Having her inner self exposed to this complete stranger both annoyed and comforted her. The back door retreat was regrettably out of reach. She knew not where she could go to shield herself from Rags' probing.

Then Ryan's image formed, with the charismatic smile and mysterious eyes that she had seen for a brief but lasting moment. She longed to kiss those lips and escape for an eternity into those eyes. She felt as though she had known Ryan for thousands of years. It was settled. She had to meet her, even if the price was as expensive as being invaded by the phenomenon seated across from her.

She decided to take the offensive, as she was wont to do in the courtroom. "Is it just my mind, or anyone's?"

Pain began to filter through Rags' resolve, sadness cast a shadow over her face. "Anyone's."

Leslie was moved by the unexpected humanness of Rags' reply. She hadn't realized that such an ability could cause problems for its owner. She scrutinized her tablemate more seriously and saw what could pass for an accelerated aging process on another woman. Rags carried her worry like a badge of honor. Here was a woman who had compassion locked away deep within the dark reaches of the soul. The otherwise fossilized armour parted momentarily to reveal a well developed sense of altruism and sympathy.

Clearly, she was being allowed to see a facet of Rags that few ever would. Her heart warmed to this enigma. She returned the compassion in kind, extending her hand reverently, offering a steady reassurance. Rags accepted the gift, one soul to another, knowing Leslie would never abuse the confidence. She took the delicate hand between her massive, square ones and caressed it

17

firmly for a long moment.

The sadness faded from Rags' face, her protective shell locked reluctantly back into place. "I wish you would reconsider meeting her." She didn't expect an answer. The Fates were crowding in around her. She knew that she couldn't prevent the scenario from playing itself out. The feeling she picked up from Leslie had grown. To repay her for the reassurance, she added, "I only listen in when there is cause."

To shift the spotlight from herself, Rags looked beyond Leslie's shoulder and waited until Ryan looked her way. She made an undiscernable signal, then withdrew her gaze.

A moment later, Ryan stood at the table, beer in hand, acknowledging her summons.

2

Rags tried to keep the introduction as inconsequential as possible. Her first instinct was to protect Leslie from the unavoidable sorrow that followed Ryan like a shadow. She wished that Leslie had shown a faint heart, an inkling of doubt about encountering her fate. She saw, in touching this new mind, a willful determination, the twin of Ryan's in intensity. Leslie showed no room for compromise, nor was it possible to dissuade her.

She knew that Ryan would be smitten with Leslie's youthful, innocent appearance, and that only a few seconds would pass before Ryan would turn on her inimitable charm.

A warm smile transformed Ryan's face. She shifted her weight to one leg and placed her beer on the table with a slow, unconscious movement.

When Ryan's eyes met Leslie's, Rags saw that their fate was sealed from that time on.

Ryan extended her hand toward the blonde. "Leslie." Her rich, vibrant voice cut through the noise of the bar with ease.

Leslie reclaimed her poise in answer to the smooth welcome. She knew she had waited for this moment all her life, and so wasted no time in taking Ryan's hand between both of hers to draw Ryan near. The hand was rough to the touch, in contrast to its suave owner. Ryan bent closer, fascinated by her nerve.

Their meeting transcended time. In the eternity of the moment, each gave the other an unobstructed view of her soul. For Leslie, it was as though a door opened and there, before her, was someone she had always known. Her uncomplicated motives and needs allowed her unconscious self to recognize the true individual behind the penetrating jade eyes. Consciously, it was just a feeling, a prickling on her skin, a muted joy in her heart. It was vital to her that she explore the essence of this person. She knew she must gain complete knowledge and understanding of this woman, whose eyes stirred her so.

Ryan experienced recognition of a different sort. For her the experience roused a myriad of carefully buried feelings. Internally, her intricate mazes and layers of need combined with her elaborate system of defense to cloud the true identity residing in the pale grey windows. Yet, she knew this was the hope she dare not have, the way out she could not take. The eyes caressing hers were the key to the oppressive bonds that held her fast, the champion of her cause. She shuddered inwardly as she saw, in her mind's eye, this quintessential beauty decompose and whither, destroyed by a malignant foe. She straightened sharply, freed her hand from Leslie's grasp and blinked back the trance.

Even if Rags were bereft of her gifts, she would have known immediately that Ryan was uncomfortable. She watched the spindly fingers make a nervous brush through the ebony mane, signalling Ryan's genuine distress clearly to anyone with a working knowledge of her habits. She searched Ryan's mind for the cause of the discomfort, but found, not the substance, but the left over residue of it. Carelessly, she hadn't monitored Ryan's reaction to Leslie, only the reverse.

She picked up the plaintive cue and sought to distract Ryan. "You could use a refill, buddy."

Leslie's heart sank as Ryan withdrew from the intimacy, becoming once again someone separate and apart. At once Ryan was reserved and collected: herself. Her eyes made a sharp movement from Leslie to her friend's impervious face to her near-empty beer. She removed her hand from her hair and signaled the bartender for another round of drinks, then straddled a chair at the table. She returned her attention to Leslie, who was boldly staring at her.

Closer inspection showed Leslie the translucent skin, the color of glazed glass, that fit tightly over the refined bone structure of Ryan's face. The sight hinted at breeding in the diminished light. The thin lips carried a whisper of flesh tone and vanished into non-color. The sovereign jade eyes were the only chromatic

20

feature about the face, indeed the person. She found herself squirming in her seat under the unsettling gaze that measured her.

Ryan could see that it would take very little sun to transform Leslie's skin into a rich bronze veneer, accenting the sensuous lips, delicate nose and high-set cheeks.

She wanted her groin to respond to the perfected beauty, not her heart. Long sequestered emotions threatened to break free in the face of Leslie's guileless, inviting eyes. She pried herself loose from their snaring appeal and scanned the feminine form. The arousal she was after was not far from reach. Charged currents flashed between her legs at the sight of Leslie's hardened nipples pouting out the fabric of her dress. Ryan's breathing quickened slightly, and the balance of power shifted to her advantage.

A calm settled over the sophisticated aura that clung to Leslie's features. She gradually surrendered to the consuming penetration of Ryan's inspection. Every woman Ryan was attracted to felt it; it devoured and savored, appreciated and owned.

Rags watched Ryan work her magic with a new interest. She kicked herself mentally for not seeing sooner that here, in the person of Leslie, was the answer to her dreams. If Ryan pursued her obvious interest in the blonde vision, she would let loose her hold on . . . the thought trailed off in a shivering spasm of pleasure.

She leaned toward Ryan. "You aren't being very subtle, my friend. You're supposed to be talking with her, not inhaling her. Leslie is an attorney. You might need her some day."

Ryan's eyebrows raised slightly and a smile eased over her features. "Well, counselor, what is your specialty, civil or criminal?"

More relaxed, Leslie produced a cigarette from her purse to accompany her answer. "I generally stick to civil cases. I find them more of a challenge. I do take an occasional criminal case, the overflow from one of my partners." Before she could make a move to light her cigarette, Ryan was poised to perform the service for her. She accepted the courtesy as a compliment, taking note of the gold lighter housing the flame.

"We don't get many attorneys coming in here — not good for the image."

"I don't doubt it. I get a great deal of pressure from my colleagues for that very reason. I like it here, so I just ignore them." She couldn't bring herself to ask a direct question of Ryan yet, so she turned to the relative comfort of Rags, surprised at herself for genuinely wanting to know. "What do you do?"

"I just work in a warehouse, running a forklift or whatever no one else wants to do. It keeps me busy and off the streets," Rags replied in a tone that let it be known that was exactly why she did it. "I don't need excitement in a job, like some people do," she added to entice the conversation toward Ryan and keep the focus off of herself.

Being an expert at dodges, Leslie recognized automatically the tactics Rags had employed. She redirected to Ryan, "I assume she means you."

Lighting her own cigarette, Ryan flashed a "thanks a lot" look to Rags. She didn't volunteer any information, and finished her beer quietly.

Leslie hated cat and mouse games. She sliced through it, "What *do* you do for a living?"

Ryan tugged at the cellophane wrapper on her cigarette pack. She wasn't used to being asked questions about herself. "I'm a pilot for a private, executive carrier."

The brief conversation drifted into the smoky atmosphere, the participants retreating into their private thoughts.

Leslie was absorbed in fascination. Everything about this person was black. The wiry hair took a forward, obstinate wave, then swept back, halting abruptly above the black leather collar. The willowy frame was coated with midnight armour. A black shirt, pants and boots protected their owner, swallowing light.

Both of her new acquaintances had a vague villainy about them, but something about them made Leslie want to trust them. They seemed to demand fealty and confidence. Singularly, they were dramatic, together an unassailable force. Leslie was drawn to them and she knew there was something beyond her insatiable curiosity that made her want to know more about both of them.

Rags' compact solemnity complemented the excitement radiating from Ryan. They appeared to exist for one another. Leslie reviewed Ryan again. The fire of intelligence blazing about the eyes was enough, by itself, to make her lonely years of waiting worth every minute.

Ryan peered inwardly and locked in combat with the painfully empty space that demanded filling. Six years had passed since she suffered the double trauma of the loss of her father and betrayal of her first love. At twenty-five, her life had caved in around her; now, at thirty-one, she grieved still, was still disconsolate.

Rags' thoughts were cut short by the appearance of a newcomer to the bar. She acted quickly, anxious to avoid a damaging scene. "Leslie, would you like to dance?" She didn't wait for a reply, but hurriedly ushered Leslie out of her seat and onto the dance floor with one fluid motion, leaving Ryan alone with her thoughts at the table.

Ryan looked up just in time to see a stunning young black woman watching her. "Who was that?" came the melodic accusation.

"You know better than to talk to me like that," Ryan answered cooly. She stood, held out a chair for her lover and changed the subject abruptly. "How was work, Sanji?"

Sanji was at once contrite, knowing that her relationship with Ryan depended on three things: beauty, sex appeal and obedience. To lose any of these was to lose Ryan. Without hesitation she accepted Ryan's gesture with the grace and allure expected of her.

She had known other women in her twenty-five years of life, but none of them had ever expected so much of her, nor rewarded her so richly as Ryan. When she first came to the United States from her native Jamaica, she was beset by a string of lovers. Her tall, dancer's physique attracted women easily, but Sanji would lose interest or get bored, and move on.

Ryan changed all that. It required every ounce of her concentration to live up to Ryan's autocratic standards. Her interest never slackened. Instead, it grew daily.

Now she relished the flirtations that came her way on a regular basis, for she was securely, and without question, Ryan's woman. She seldom challenged her position, only when the security she thrived on was threatened. The not so gentle, sometimes demeaning reminders Ryan gave her were sweet reassurance. Ryan had no shame about reprimanding her in public, especially on the issue of jealousy. Ryan maintained her autonomy strictly, and tolerated no breaches of it. It was with this in mind that Sanji replied contently with her soft Jamaican accent, "It was great. We had a really good rehearsal."

Ryan took her seat, nodded at the bartender and relaxed. She watched Sanji shed the lynx coat, revealing the pale blue leotard top and mauve skirt. There was a shimmering glow about her when she came from the dance troupe workouts.

Ryan's internal flames were ignited and kept burning on high by this seal-colored beauty. Sanji had a way of making Ryan want her, and after taking her, Ryan would be thirsting for more. From the bushy hair caught in a silver headband to the blue eyeshadow, expertly applied to the giant black eyes, Sanji was an artist at making herself desirable.

Ryan took it all in, surveying the line of the long, sleek neck and downward on the path to the firm rounded breasts. She couldn't go on; her need was too great. She licked her lips with longing, reached out and stroked Sanji's sharp cheekbone. Her hand followed the contour of Sanji's face to the chin; she grasped Sanji's jaw with authority and guided the full lips toward hers with approval. At first, the kiss was slow and loving, but quickly rose to a crescendo of passion.

The dance Rags and Leslie shared was over, and they were making their way back to the table. Leslie grabbed Rags' arm and dug her nails in hard when she witnessed the intruder at their table inflaming her new reason for living. "Is that her lover?" Rags nodded. Leslie laughed derisively. "I don't know why I thought someone like her would be single for a minute. Perhaps I had better go. I'm feeling amazingly sober just now."

Rags halted her retreat. "You can stay, they will be gone soon."

Leslie turned to Rags, her nostrils flaring. She didn't want to play in this game anymore. It was too complicated. These strangers just yanked her heart out of its socket and played keep away with it. She didn't want to grovel and cry for its return. Not knowing how to retrieve it or how to mend the damage angered her the most. How had she allowed herself to be so vulnerable?

She let go of Rags' arm and turned to where she had left her coat on her abandoned chair. She put it on with sharp, destructive motions and returned to the main bar to reclaim her purse.

As Rags had predicted, Ryan and her companion were gone. Rags sat, alone, lost in her thoughts, leaving a path open for Leslie to salvage a dignified departure. She picked up her purse and walked wearily into the frosty night.

3

Construction on the high rise in the next block continued, like it did everyday. Men perched perilously on metal beams hundreds of feet above certain death. Tiny figures labored in their subterranean mazes below. Giant cranes masterminded feats of slowmotion theatre in the sky. Leslie watched this activity with great interest. How was it that the world went on as before? Didn't these and others who went unalterably about their daily lives realize the world could never be the same anymore? She wanted to yell at them to stop and take notice of the cataclysmic events that had shaken her life the night before. Only the thick tinted glass of her eighteenth story office prevented her from doing so.

On her desk sat a cold cup of coffee that hadn't been touched, an unopened *Wall Street Journal*, a stack of unheeded mail, and a brief that demanded attention. In the doorway, watching this uncharacteristic scene, was her middle-aged secretary debating about intruding. Then, "Les?"

Wishing the real world would stop requiring her presence, Leslie reluctantly turned to acknowledge the inquiry. She stood behind her brown suede chair and pulled it to her stomach for protection without knowing why. She took the small solace its warmth offered and tried to relax. "Yes."

The secretary ventured closer and appraised the desk top. "Are you alright? You haven't touched your coffee."

Troubled, Leslie answered, "Charlotte, I wish I could say yes, but you know me too well to believe that."

Charlotte's brown eyes filled with compassion. "Sit down Les.

I'll get you another cup of coffee.''

Leslie pulled her chair away from her desk and collapsed into it. She knew the coffee would be served with a healthy dose of tender loving care and warm advice. Charlotte's loyalty was the cornerstone of her life, and just now she felt the need for something familiar and predictable.

She watched Charlotte close the sculptured oak door of her office and allowed herself to be coaxed into accepting the fresh coffee. Charlotte sat in a restored antique chair opposite her.

Leslie's office blended contemporary and antique motifs in a way that felt homey, yet professional. Numerous ferns vied for the diminished light of the northern window. Law books dominated the eastern wall, and the rest of the pale orchid wall was sprinkled with photographs of mountain wildflowers. Throughout, bringing the various woods and textures together, was a soft, dove grey carpet that matched her eyes. Charlotte seemed as integral a part of the office as the books and plants. Leslie couldn't imagine her office without the smiling, indulgent face of the law firm's indispensable legal secretary. She knew she had been installed in Charlotte's heart as the favorite of the three law partners. Delores was too moody and demanding. Susan Benson openly resisted Charlotte's maternal attention. Charlotte had once told Leslie that she seemed so fragile and alone and needed mothering. Leslie simply found it easier to be fawned and fussed over by Charlotte than resist. Out of this grew a deep affection and friendship between them.

Leslie had given up trying to convince people that she could take care of herself emotionally and socially. Only one or two people believed her; the rest spent needless energy protecting her from the world at large. On this morning, she wondered if maybe she was as helpless as others believed her to be.

"What's wrong, Les?''

Leslie stared into her cup, then forced herself to drink some of the hot brew before attempting an answer. "I never thought I would see the day when my best effort was getting to work in the morning. Now, I have no clue why I'm here.''

Charlotte's face reflected her dismay and pain. Her voice sounded grave. "I've never seen you so upset. What happened?''

"A woman,'' Leslie replied with equal gravity.

Charlotte sighed hesitantly. She speculated to herself that this was a sample of what love looked like on her employer. "Sounds serious. Did this woman hurt you, or is she just very special?"

"Both." Leslie lit a cigarette and gazed into its rising smoke. Ryan's eyes entered her consciousness through a secret passageway. The vision elicited a shock of arousal. An unmistakable moisture made itself known, and a smile formed on her face before she could mask it. She calculated a quick cough to break the moment and recover from the unbidden passion. A creeping ache supplanted the passion when she considered the young woman Ryan left with the night before.

"She is special, very special, *and* she has a lover." This was more distressing to her than she realized. It was mystifying.

"You sound pretty upset about it, Les." Charlotte hated to see trouble of any sort weigh upon the gilded head. The borderline despair radiating from the large, almond-shaped eyes was just the look she and others labored to avoid. Love shouldn't come in bitter flavors for one so lovely.

Leslie lay her head on her fist and gazed at her friend. She could see Charlotte understood, but somehow she didn't feel significantly better. "If this has anything to do with love, I don't want it, Char."

"From the looks of you, I'd say you don't have much choice. For now anyway." After a brief thought, she added, "This isn't a case of love from afar is it?"

"I wish. How neat and tidy it would be if I were dealing with a schoolgirl crush. No, I met her, and I fell for her immediately." She was disgusted with herself for allowing even a small margin for error in her behavior the previous evening. "What a laugh. I even thought that she felt something for me as well." She permitted herself a luxurious show of temper and stubbed her cigarette out fitfully in the ashtray.

Charlotte took note of the action. "How is it you know that she has a lover?"

Leslie sat up and gesticulated her answer. "That was easy, she showed up! Ryan just took off with her without giving me another thought!"

"Rejected?" Charlotte tried to keep the irony out of her voice. She couldn't help thinking about all the women who experienced a similar fate at the hands of Leslie's merciless detachment.

Rejection, in concert with longing. Leslie hadn't contemplated the possibility before now, but she knew Charlotte was right. It galled her more than she could speak of. Her resentment began to boil under the surface.

Charlotte quickly surmised the origin of the trouble. "Del wouldn't introduce you to someone who wasn't single, so is it safe to assume you met this woman at Cary's?"

Leslie hadn't raised her voice to anyone since she left home fifteen years ago. She found she didn't care what effect she had, only that it was a small release of the turmoil and felt good. "Yes, damn it. I met her at Cary's."

She watched the salt and pepper head shake furiously. "Leslie! I'm sorry. I just wanted to know."

The apology didn't soothe Leslie. "Don't you dare say 'I told you so'." She couldn't bear the humiliation she felt. Charlotte was as open about her disapproval of these visits to Cary's as the law partners were.

Leslie's display of anger worried Charlotte. She relaxed her approach. "I won't. What did you say this woman's name was?"

"Ryan." Leslie savored the sound of it on her voice. A small chill raced up her spine, softening her mood.

Charlotte proceeded cautiously; the masculine sounding name troubled her. "What does she do?"

"She's a pilot." This too gave Leslie a thrill.

The profession had potential in Charlotte's mind, so she tried to remain open. "Well, that's nice. Maybe you shouldn't be so hard on yourself, Les. She could have just swept her lover off to avoid a scene."

With a ragged sigh, Leslie leaned back in her chair. She closed her eyes for a moment, trying to still her tumultuous emotions. Charlotte's speculation encouraged her. "Do you think so?"

"Honey, there isn't any way in the world you could be that far off base. If you think she felt something for you, she no doubt did. She would have to be made of stone not to at least be interested in you."

Leslie felt a spark of hope ignite. "I hope you're right. Still, I wonder what would have happened if she had been single."

Charlotte smiled at her inexperience. "You would probably still be bumping into walls like you are now, but maybe you would be happier about it."

Leslie tried to imagine it and was unsure. "I don't like this feeling of uncertainty. Am I in love, Char?"

An indulgent look formed on Charlotte's face. "Looks like it to me. So, when do I get to meet this person?"

Leslie laughed. "I have to find her first. She didn't exactly leave a trail of glass slippers for me to follow. I won't go looking for her in Cary's and be open for that kind of embarrassment. I'll have to think this through before I do anything."

This was the Leslie Charlotte knew. Calm and thoughtful, not irrational. Charlotte's curiosity wrestled free of her judgment. "Well, at least tell me what she looks like."

Leslie wondered how she could adequately describe to her friend what she had seen the night before. What words would paint the picture in her mind, do justice to the striking difference between Ryan and every other woman she had seen. Dreamily, she set about trying to depict the appearance and qualities that had set her heart afire and disoriented her so.

Throughout her discourse, she was innocent of the reaction that was formulating within her audience. Free of the blinders of love, Charlotte was seeing quite a different vision. Her mind was creating a leather clad vagabond, unworthy of Leslie's notice, much less her heart. Images of seedy darkness and unsavory activity made her cringe. Her parental instincts and prejudices penetrated her reasoning. In her best maternal manner, she interrupted Leslie to chastise her. "What's gotten into you, Les? You can't be serious," she moaned. "This is a nightmare. She sounds like a scruffy hellion to me."

Leslie felt her face reden. Charlotte's words wounded her. This sudden turnabout made her seethe. Where was the support she counted on? Shock blended with indignation to form a volatile substance that her considerable self-control could not manage. "I'm dead serious, Charlotte. I thought you respected me more than that!" She turned sharply about in her chair and fixed her hot gaze on a distant point on the skyline.

"Les, don't be angry. . ."

"Please leave me alone," Leslie interrupted cuttingly. Char-

31

lotte's deadly observation of Ryan crossed over the boundary of friendship. Leslie was frankly insulted and hurt. She puzzled over her irrational reaction. Charlotte was her friend, and she had only just met Ryan. Briefly at that. How could love form so quickly and penetrate so deeply? This new set of emotions would undergo some serious scrutiny in the days to follow. She had to understand and manage them — of that she was sure.

Charlotte made her retreat quietly, closing the door behind her. Delores looked up from where she was seated in the much lived-in reception area, enjoying her morning paper and tea. "You look like you've seen a ghost."

"I wish I had. At least I could have guessed what to do." Charlotte sought the comfort of her desk. She was shaking when she sat down.

Peering over her reading glasses, Delores rested her paper on her lap. "A client this early?"

"No, Les."

"Come again?" Delores took her glasses off, stood, and walked to Charlotte's desk.

"Del, have you ever seen her angry? I mean genuinely angry?"

"Les? Never."

"Well, I just did and it isn't nice."

Delores gave a curious look in the direction of Leslie's door, then back to the secretary. She took a pencil from the cup on the desk and toyed absently with it. "What is she mad about?"

"My mothering for one thing. A woman for another." Charlotte controlled her shaking and took in a great, deep breath.

"Your mothering is enough to drive anyone crazy, Char. Who's the woman?"

Charlotte ignored the affront and answered shortly, "Her name is Ryan." She jumped at the piercing crack of the pencil snapping in Delores' grasp.

"What?" Delores was stunned.

Charlotte met the startled expression of the senior partner with wonder. She repeated the name quietly. "Ryan."

"Damn. What else did she say about her?"

"She said that she was a pilot, though I find it hard to believe from the rest of the description I heard."

"She's a pilot, alright, among other things. Les couldn't have picked a worse person to meet." Then concerned, "What did Ryan do to her?"

"Turned her head so far she can't see straight."

"Oh, Jes-us." A chafing crept into Delores' voice. "But why is she mad?"

"It's just a hunch, but I would say the real reason is because Ryan has a lover."

Delores snorted. "That doesn't surprise me. Ryan doesn't know the meaning of the word single." She set the pencil pieces on the desk thoughtfully. "That, however, may be to our advantage. We can't let her get involved in this."

"How in the world do you propose to stop her?"

"She can't be in that deep yet."

"Oh? Have you ever seen her interested in anyone before?"

"No," Delores replied evenly.

"You're going to have your hands full with that one."

"That bad?"

Charlotte nodded slowly. "The description I got of this person is quite enough for me to want to see Les avoid her. What is it about this Ryan character that has you so worried?"

"Let's just say that my opinion of her isn't very high. I've seen her in action before and I've picked up some of the pieces she's left behind. Les would have to work to do worse. There has got to be someone out there who could make Les a hell of a lot happier." Delores rubbed her square chin while she formulated an idea. "My birthday is next week isn't it?"

"You know it is, although no one could tell it for as quiet as you've kept it." Charlotte was nonplussed by Delores' sudden shift in the conversation.

"It's not too late to change that. I'm going to throw a party this town won't soon forget, and Les is going to be the main course."

"Which means your guest list is going to include a lot of single women?" Charlotte warmed to the plan. She could tell already what Delores was up to.

"Yes, ma'am. Get Dana on the phone for me. I have some hustling to do." Delores thrust her hands into her pockets with a firm determination and retired to her office.

With the lust of a conspirator, Charlotte turned to her task.

4

Winter always depressed Rags. It made her think about dying. Spring would come early this year. She was thankful for the knowledge, the only one of her gifts she was glad to have. Someone once guessed her age to be eighteen, and eighteen springs had passed since then. By that reckoning she was thirty-six years old, but Rags didn't know for certain. She had learned to cover for missing information about her life. There was no knowledge of where she was born or who her parents were, only that she had awakened one morning in Denver City Jail, on assault charges. They called it amnesia, perhaps from a blow she suffered during the fight she had the night before with a young man. He was in the hospital, and she was being asked a lot of questions she couldn't answer.

For years after that, her life was characterized by an endless stream of psychiatrists and court officials trying to unravel the mystery of her identity. Her reluctance to cooperate with their efforts was born out of a genuine lack of concern for who she was. To her, it was best to take each day, one at a time, without regard to long term plans.

Through the persistent, unorthodox methods of her parole officer, David Martin, the puzzle was solved. It required several years of investigation and coercion to place Rags in a compromising enough position to submit to hypnotism, the only pathway to her past. The result made all his endeavors worthwhile. Rags took the revelations garnered from hypnosis sessions calmly, as though she had known all along.

Having a past was no consolation for her, in particular one

that stretched far beyond this lifetime, into others. She wanted a future, the chance at happiness, like normal human beings. She didn't like to contemplate how empty she was, and always had been.

An early spring would be welcome indeed, especially if it brought with it the demise of Ryan's relationship with Sanji. Rags had long ago given up trying to keep Sanji out of her thoughts even though the excitement Sanji aroused in her gave her a sideache.

"Can I get you anything else, Rags?"

"Coffee is fine for now. I might order when Ryan gets here." She looked at the youthful waiter and smiled.

He nodded and walked briskly to his station. Rags absently appraised his dignified mannerisms. She was grateful for the welcome change Gay men had made in their images. It was a relief to her to see that the vicious parodies of women had fallen into disfavor among them. Women were to be admired and respected, not satirized. David had always challenged this tenet which she upheld in theory only. "If you respect and admire women so much, why do you keep beating the crap out of them?" Rags never answered him.

It would be different with Sanji, if she would return even a small portion of the love Rags felt for her. For two years Rags had dreamed of sleeping with the brown goddess. In her dreams she made sweet, gentle love to Sanji, then would awaken in a cold sweat, in the throes of stormy, embracing orgasms. For two years her obsession kept her from taking anyone to bed.

Now she could feel the time approaching when she would get her chance. The answer to her dilemma had walked into her life the night before. She gazed into the candle on the table, absorbed in the possibilities.

It was with reluctance that she turned her eyes from the quiet flicker of flame trapped in the crystal prison to greet Ryan.

Rags looked at Ryan's slender face, barely changed in six years since the night she had rescued the younger woman from the gutter and certain 180 proof death. Now, as then, Ryan's intensely handsome features were steeped in a haunting poignancy.

"Have you ordered yet?" Ryan asked as she put her gloves in her motorcycle helmet on the vacant chair next to her. She sat opposite her friend and leaned on her forearms on the table. "Sanji is too tired to make it tonight."

She waited for the disappointment to fade from Rags' face.

Rags was becoming more sensitive about the subject, and Ryan was learning to step lightly around it. It was for this reason that she kept to herself the reason why Sanji was too tired to join them. It was not because of the dance workout she had that day, rather it was the workout she had the night before. Ryan had taken her hard and long into the night, making it difficult for either of them to function in their daytime endeavors. These things Ryan didn't talk about, and Rags didn't ask.

It was never a secret that Rags had more than a passing fancy for the dancer. She was in the company of a handful of admirers, some of whom were quite aggressive in their attempts to take Sanji away from Ryan. None of the others gave Ryan a moment of worry. She knew her dinner partner was her only serious rival for the Jamaican beauty.

If the day ever came that Rags stopped insisting that Sanji come to her willingly, Ryan would be helpless to prevent Rags from walking in and taking Sanji from her. Sanji, too, would be at Rags' mercy and go, compliantly or otherwise.

For the present, Sanji had been granted the freedom to choose, and out of love she chose Ryan. She didn't want to go, nor was Ryan anxious for her to leave. They had a shared addiction; each was the potent narcotic that flowed through the other's bloodstream. Separation would force an unwanted withdrawal that neither of them was prepared to accept.

Briefly, Ryan entertained the possibility of how it would be if she didn't like Rags. Her Friday evenings would be free to do other things besides meet at The Coffee Shoppe for dinner and go carousing at the bars. She was unclear about what she would do, but the idea of having a choice intrigued her. If she didn't feel a deep loyalty to and kinship with the stalwart dyke, she would have been tempted long ago to liberate herself from the oppressive yoke of Rags' power. The relationship had endured for so long, Ryan wondered if she still knew how to get free.

"I haven't ordered anything yet. Do you want steak?" Rags asked.

"Sure," Ryan replied without thinking.

Rags signed for the waiter, "The usual," and relaxed in her chair. A mischievious grin spread over her face. "So, did you like Leslie?"

"Ummhmm." Ryan nodded quietly, trying to soften her interest.

"She likes you too. A lot."

Ryan felt the tingling, swollen feeling in her brain that signaled Rags' presence; probing mercilessly, extracting her true feelings for the attorney. Without moving, Ryan locked on Rags' wise hazel eyes. She hated the violation of her inner recesses and fought against it.

The waiter placed the salads and beers before them, looked from Ryan to Rags and a shiver went up his spine. All the personnel at the restaurant had come to know that look. They had learned from one very bitter experience the consequences of breaking the concentration that interlocked this battle of wills. He turned quickly to his station and his other customers in the front of the establishment.

In the war of wills, Ryan was the beleaguered confederacy. She won minor skirmishes and an occasional battle through the years, but it was only recently that she had found a way to shield her most precious thoughts from Rags. She was unable to prevent entrance, but now Rags could only discern the less important reactions Ryan had experienced the night before. Secreted away, in a place inviolate, were the more meaningful and critical responses to Leslie.

Rags withdrew from the contact, sufficiently pleased with Ryan's response. The meal was taken in silence, but all would be forgotten when the path from The Coffee Shoppe lead to Cary's.

The roar of Ryan's motorcycle echoed back at her from the walls of the English Tudor house she had called home for most of her life. A thin frost coated the brick driveway; the chill heightened her senses and kept her awake enough to navigate the slick drive. She pulled to a stop in the breezeway behind the house and turned off the engine. The sudden silence was surreal by comparison. The contrast emphasized the ringing in her brain and the burning in her groin. She smiled to herself and blessed her Irish heritage that allowed her to consume large amounts of beer and filled her with an unquenchable lust for women.

It was her hearty Irish stock that gave her the physical power to handle the motorcycle that was so much greater in size than she was. That her slender physique concealed great stores of strength from the casual observer was a source of pride. She shifted the weight of the large machine onto its kickstand and dismounted it with a grace that was all her own. Ryan mastered time and space and moved through it like an eagle through the thin air in the dizzying heights. The physical and material world held no difficulties for her, placed no obstacles before her.

Emotions troubled her. She didn't know what to do with them, and so she ran away from them. This night epitomized that flight. She had been thinking about Leslie and what Rags had said about her all night. She felt something when she met Leslie and was unsure what to do with the feelings.

Sexual desire she knew what to do with. She wasn't used to wanting a woman and not having her. This dilemma occupied her mind as she stood in the glaring light of the back porch. She found the key to disengage the alarm, then to open the door.

Inside, she set her helmet and gloves on the dining table and turned the light in the kitchen on. Having Leslie would have to wait, but labored breathing and pulsing adrenalin wouldn't.

Her footsteps sounded hollow on the textured Italian tile of the kitchen and hushed on the Oriental rug of the hallway. She stopped briefly in the bathroom to relieve herself then crossed over to the guestroom.

The door was open and the light from the kitchen shone on the familiar curves that heightened her desire.

For the last several years, anyone who lived with Ryan had known she was a guest, never a mate. Ryan hadn't allowed anyone to fill that painfully empty space. Sanji had graced this room longer than any of her predecessors, a feat in itself. She slept peacefully in the bed, covered with satin sheets and comforters. Her back was to Ryan, but even in sleep she could exhibit a sensual innocence that made Ryan wild with wanting her.

39

Ryan unzipped her jacket and slid her hands between her upper arms and ribs to warm them. She leaned against the door-jam for a moment to take it all in, casting her shadow across Sanji's hips.

The shadow shrunk as she stepped into the room. She went down on one knee to the bed and lifted the bed clothes in a slow tender movement. This revealed five foot eight inches of tight brown skin that packaged supple muscles and was outlined in grace. Ryan surveyed the scene, from the wrinkles on the soles of the feet to the loose shock of hair atop the head. It set her afire.

Carefully, she reached over Sanji, grasped an arm and brought it around so the wrist lay in the small of the back. The long, feminine fingers curved toward her. She pulled a pair of handcuffs from her pocket and began warming them. Her breathing continued to get heavier as she applied a slight pressure to Sanji's right shoulder. Sanji sighed and rolled over on her stomach. Ryan waited patiently for the expected movement. It came. Sanji shifted her weight in her sleep and freed her other arm.

After squeezing the thawed bracelets open she fastened them about Sanji's lovely wrists. She savored the familiar tumbler sound they made as they contracted against the unsuspecting wrists.

She unzipped the breast pocket of her jacket and produced a pack of cigarettes, a solid gold lighter, and a small key. She held the cigarette pack to her mouth and drew one out with her teeth. Her other hand occupied itself with the key, locking the cuffs in position. Years of practice made this an automatic motion. The key was returned to the pocket, and Ryan lit her cigarette with a deep inhale. The cigarettes and lighter were placed on the nightstand, next to the ashtray. She leaned closer to Sanji and exhaled the smoke into Sanji's hair.

Sanji coughed slightly and began to stir and stretch. Her heart quickened, sending electric impulses up and down the length of her flowing body. Her clitoris hardened when she felt Ryan's presence. Her sleepy rhythmic breathing fast became deep, staggered gasps when she tried to move her arms and found herself helpless.

A flood of stimuli overtook her. The liquor on Ryan's breath, the pungent smoke, the cutting edge of the handcuffs. They all combined in a swirling mass of lubrication in her crotch. Compounding this heady feeling was the certain knowledge of what was to follow. Her complete surrender to this woman who mastered her with such ease. Ryan's erratic breathing made the hair on the back of her neck rise in anticipation.

She rolled away from Ryan, presenting her front to her lover, boldly challenging and tempting fate. Ryan brought to life a special thrill that Sanji thirsted for. Never before had someone wanted her so badly or used her so thoroughly. Being helpless before this Irish tyrant released her inhibitions and allowed her to experience a freedom she hadn't thought possible for a human to know. Ryan took over total control from here. Sanji was free of all responsibility for her actions, emotions, desires and needs. Ryan would take care of everything, and take everything.

Ryan would forcibly rob her of her soul and demand every ounce of her orgasmic energy, then tenderly and lovingly give it back to her and make her whole once more.

She took the cigarette Ryan offered her in her mouth and inhaled deeply of it, holding the smoke within.

The cigarette was stubbed out in the ashtray, and Ryan reached for Sanji's hair, clasping a handful of it in her hand, and pulled Sanji toward her. "Give that smoke back to me, bitch." She covered the voluptuous mouth with her own thin lips and received the symbolic offering, inhaling the smoke directly from Sanji's lungs. Exhaling the smoke through her nose, she smiled widely.

The sleep haze cleared from Sanji's eyes, and Ryan gazed perilously into them. Unlike some, she preferred that her subject be fully aware of what was going on, and to anticipate each move, frightening or exciting. Sanji was never banned from direct contact with the eyes of her conquerer.

Sanji quivered, her spine tightened, the muscles of her buttocks flexed. Her tensile passion cried out through every nerve. She wanted Ryan to take her utterly and mercilessly.

"There isn't time to take you downstairs. I want you too badly."

That did it. An involuntary moan escaped from the depths of Sanji's being, and she entered an altered state where everything began to move in slow motion. Her eyes fixed on Ryan's hand, following it to a breast pocket of the jacket Ryan always wore.

With Sanji's hair firmly in her grasp, her free hand retrieved a small bottle from the pocket. She cradled it in her palm and twisted off the top, which fell to the floor. Using the last two fingers to close a nostril, she inhaled the fumes from the bottle in one continuous motion. Her heart rate became rapid as the vessels dilated, a small ache formed at the top of her head. The sensation intensified her awareness, brought everything closer. She shared it with Sanji, knowing the poppers would send her over the edge and solidify her willingness to accept the pain she was about to inflict.

Ryan tightened her hold on Sanji's hair, yanked her head to the edge of the bed, and kissed her with a violence that could only be tolerated in an altered state. There was no need to build to this level of pain; Sanji was accustomed to far worse and for great lengths of time. Her training with Ryan had been continuous and progressively more violent. It was mild compared to what Ryan used to require with other women, because Sanji gave Ryan what she needed through pure, raw sexuality.

Ryan released her hold as viciously as she had obtained it, thrusting Sanji back on her hands, making the handcuffs cut harder. Sanji gasped in pain; Ryan responded with more poppers, taking another hit herself, then placing the bottle next to the ashtray. Wasting no time, she made for Sanji's passion place. She forced the legs apart and pushed her finger inside, rapidly enlarging the opening. Her other hand came up to reassure Sanji with a gentle stroke on the face. "I want you, baby." She added another finger to the canal, pushing the folds of the flesh apart, deepening the insertion. Her fingers glided easily into the burning lubrication. "I love it when you're this ready for me. You know how to treat your Master, don't you cunt?"

"Oh, oh I want to do better. Please Master, show me how to do better," came Sanji's throaty reply. She was moving her powerful hips in time to Ryan's ministrations.

"Then open up further, bitch."

Sanji's obedience was immediate. She braced her feet firmly on the mattress, shifted her weight to her shoulder blades and opened her knees further. She concentrated on relaxing the muscles of her vagina to allow the opening to widen.

Ryan took advantage of the shift to come up on the bed with

her partner to get more leverage and put more force into her work. The two fingers were joined by two more and the pace quickened. Without missing a beat she leaned over for the bottle again and bolstered its waning effects for both of them. After placing the bottle back on the table she turned her full attention to what she was doing.

Her knuckles were meeting with resistance from the bony structure about them, and she resolved to eliminate that resistance. Ceasing the rhythmic movements, she moved her thumb to the inside of her palm and willed her hand bones to come closer together. Her hand slid into a fist and disappeared from sight into Sanji's womb, forcing another moan from her. The unbelievable sensation of the inferno her hand was imprisoned in elicited a rare moan from Ryan as well. "Oh god, you're incredible."

Such praise was hard to come by, and Sanji replied with a gripping of her internal muscles. One more trip to the bottle and the couple left normal feelings behind, jointly entering a nether world where few dared to tread.

The feeling of fistfucking was so intense, Ryan lost herself momentarily. Sanji's screams brought her back into control and the shrieking subsided. Still she continued to pound away at Sanji's insides with a vengeance; powerfully stroking in and out.

Slowly, she bent her head closer to Sanji's aching cunt, drawn by the heady smell and the sucking and sliding sounds her first was creating in the drenched forest she dominated.

A thrill raced through her. The thrill from knowing that if she had lost control and not heeded Sanji's pleas, she would have killed the sex goddess. There was a palpable wall at the outer reaches of her control, and she knew only the darkness of death lay beyond it. The challenge of maintaining, yet, at the same time, bringing Sanji to the end of her limits was all consuming for her. As her mouth got closer to the ravaged cunt, the wall loomed larger.

Her free hand applied pressure to Sanji's abdominal area, stilling her rocking response to the vicious thrusting. This was Sanji's cue to prepare for an orgasm. It allowed her to concentrate fully on her tensions, contracting her muscles in a single-minded focus of lust.

43

Ryan separated the skin that obscured the hardened button and watched her wrist appear and disappear inside the ebony cave. Gently she tickled the clit with her tongue, tasting it and sensing its hardness, its receptive state. Then suddenly, violently, she assaulted it with her mouth, increased the speed of her fist and in one, intense shout she demanded, "Come!"

Sanji's whole being obeyed without hesitation. Her athletic body acquiesced with all the energy of her youth, all the vehemence her being could muster. Her heart rushed, her buttocks muscles pulsed, her vagina contracted and fought against the intruder, her bladder threatened to violate her, and her clitoris softened.

Ryan encouraged her to a prolonged response by twisting her charcoal nipples and gently stroking the soft button with her tongue.

Ryan's breath was hot and staggered; the action brought about a wracking orgasm for her as well. The echoes of Sanji's raving reached her consciousness, and she relaxed; satisfied, satiated.

Slowly, luxuriously, she withdrew her hand from Sanji's paradise. The much visited receptacle rarely got the chance to heal between uses. Her hand was covered with blood, which she ignored. She fetched the key to release the tortured wrists from their bonds, and lay beside her partner; punctuating her comforting massage with kisses. She kept them light and tender to avoid the trap of Sanji's seduction. Neither of them were recovered enough to keep out of reach of passion's snare.

"You were great, great. The best." She took Sanji in her arms and consoled her with feather kisses on the face. She resisted the temptation to trace the lithe back and seek the buttocks. If she pulled Sanji any nearer, they would not sleep.

Sanji was in heaven. Ryan's reassurances, praise, and tenderness was what she worked for. The approval, the satisfied look on the pale face, meant more to her than her own orgasm. She would give it all up in a moment to hear Ryan say, just once, "I love you." The words never came; Ryan just passed out.

5

There was a lull in the activity of the law office. The filmy snow that collected during the weekend turned to zero visibility fog, which chased the three attorneys to the warmth of their lobby. The lobby/reception area was comfortably decorated with couches and coffee tables. The fluorescent lighting had been disconnected and replaced with softer lamp light. This was what they generally referred to as their breaktime, and they were extending it for as long as they could get away with.

Susan Benson, their ace tax lawyer, took the cup Charlotte offered her. "What a pit day. Even the airport is closed and I was expecting my friend from Philly." Everyone laughed. Susan's friend from Philly was her fictional sidekick; conveniently arriving and vanishing whenever she found herself in a sticky situation with a woman. Susan bubbled with lighthearted appeal, but her popularity got her in deeper than she always knew how to handle.

A knock came at the front door, drawing the attention of everyone. In the doorway stood a skinny boy with an arrangement of two dozen salmon colored roses that dwarfed him. His head poked out from under the arrangement. "Got a delivery here for Leslie Serle," he announced with an air of importance.

All present gasped in unison, each for her own reasons. Susan rose briskly and rescued the flowers. She set them on the secretary's desk and stood back to admire them. The delivery boy cleared his throat and waited for his gratuity.

"For god's sake, Char. Pay the kid," Susan teased.

Charlotte pulled her gaze from the floral apparition and took some money from her desk drawer to pay him. The amount was sufficient to make his trip worthwhile; he skipped happily out of the office.

Leslie was standing in a trance, hand over her mouth, eyeing each flower in disbelief.

"Read the card, Les," Susan prodded, handing the envelope to her.

She took the card out of its sheath and read it, ignoring Susan, who read it with her. Susan looked disappointed when all it said was, "Call Me, Ryan," and a phone number.

"A guy huh?"

Delores and Charlotte looked at Susan with surprise.

"Who's Ryan, Les?" Susan needled.

A very special *woman*, Susan," Leslie replied in kind.

Susan didn't try to hide her confusion, but was congratulatory just the same. The beaming expression on Leslie's face told her all she wanted to know. "Somebody cracked the nut, eh? Well, that's just great. When do we get to meet her?"

"Soon I hope," Leslie answered as she scooped up the flowers and floated into her office; closing the door for privacy.

Susan turned her nonplussed expression on Delores and Charlotte and said, "A woman? R-Y-A-N?"

"No, a woman, T-R-O-U-B-L-E," Delores clarified.

"You know her?"

"Unfortunately. From the looks of things, she's moving in for the kill too." Delores stood and escorted Susan into her office for an explanation.

"Peterson's Flight Service," answered the pleasing, mature male voice.

"Is Ryan there, please?"

"Just a minute."

In the background Leslie could hear, "Hey, O'Donnell!" "Hey, Peterson." "Phone. Female." Pause.

"Hello."

Leslie felt a stir in her heart. "Ryan?"

"Leslie! You got my message, I was hoping you would call."

"I got your message indeed. They're lovely. How did you know that salmon was my favorite color for roses?"

Ryan ran her fingers through her hair, absently taking a seat at the cluttered metal desk Phil had used for the past thirty years. He withdrew to the far side of the warehouselike room, joining the other pilots who were being held captive by the fog. It was virtually impossible to enjoy a private conversation in the building. Sound carried like a gunshot in a snow laden valley.

"Lucky guess, I'd say."

"Rags didn't have anything to do with it?"

"I swear. I just thought that color would look good with your eyes." Ryan's head lifted with a jerk in response to the cough she heard from the lounge area, alerting her that hers was the only voice in the room. "Just a second, Leslie." She moved the receiver away from her mouth in a slow deliberate action and let it rest on her shoulder. She turned slightly in the swivel chair toward the sound. "Cut it out you guys." After the symphony of hoots and whistles died down someone finally turned on the radio. Ryan accepted the teasing with aplomb and smiled, shaking her head. She returned to her conversation. "I'm sorry to keep you waiting; I had to get my daily dose of harassment out of the way."

"So I heard. Do they hassle you like that all the time?"

"Yeah, but it's all in fun. So, where were we?"

"You were about to tell me how you knew where to find me."

"That was simple. There aren't that many female attorneys in this city, fewer still are gay, one of whom is my attorney. I called her and she told me where you were," Ryan recounted.

"That makes sense," Leslie chuckled, feeling less vulnerable. "Who, pray tell, is your attorney?"

"Barbara McFarland."

"I owe her a lunch for making it so easy. I was wondering how I was going to get in touch with you."

"Yeah?" Ryan was pleased.

"Yes."

"Well, that makes this whole messy day worthwhile."

"How so?"

"We can't fly in this junk, so Phil roped me into catching up on these detestable quarterly reports. I had chalked this entire day up for a total loss, but talking to you has raised my spirits considerably."

"Now that you mention it, I believe that talking with you has done the same for me."

"Can't ask for more than that. Let's say we make it official and meet for dinner tonight?"

"I'd like that," Leslie replied candidly.

"Great, how about The Coffee Shoppe over by the University? I'm a creature of habit, and I like good food."

"Sounds good. What time?"

"Seven. But I can't pick you up. I'm not using a car these days."

"I don't mind meeting you there. Seven it is."

Ryan hung up the phone like it was made of crystal and stared into space for a long moment, savoring the feelings she got from hearing Leslie's voice. Feelings she had forgotten existed.

"I never thought I would see that look on your face again. She must be special." Phil Peterson had been Ryan's mentor for almost a quarter of a century, and most recently had settled into a paternal role, a legacy he accepted willingly. If Ryan was the son Mr. O'Donnell could never have, she was the daughter Phil never had. He had taken Ryan under his wing when she was just seven years old, headstrong and determined to learn how to fly. Phil jumped at the chance to have someone follow in his footsteps, having failed to interest his two sons in the profession. Ryan had proved an able student with an insatiable thirst for knowledge. She was precocious and talented from day one.

Phil's solicitous attention gave her no trouble and she, like everyone else, knew that one day she would inherit the rest of the business.

"Very special, Phil. It almost hurts to feel this good about someone again."

"I would love to see you this up all the time. Still, I curse your father for not teaching you about responsibilities to people. Does Sanji know about this woman?" Phil moved closer and lay his hand on Ryan's shoulder, a gesture he used often to show Ryan he was trying to teach her a concept, give her something she needed to survive.

Ryan raised her head; challenge in her eyes, jaws clenched. Phil's pale blue eyes pierced through the silence between them. His greying temples and leathery skin reinforced the authority he wielded so gently, yet firmly. Stressful seconds passed, Ryan yielded her ground; the resistance transformed into self-reproach. She disengaged her eyes from Phil's and looked down at her lap. She shook her head in reply.

Phil hated dishing out reality like castor oil. He told himself that someone had to teach Ryan to be accountable for her actions. A sadness came over him when he considered how much pain Ryan was immersed in. Since her father passed away, he had not seen her shed a tear for her loss. Except for an attempted suicide, she had never approached her grief. He could see clearly that Ryan was on a collision course with tragedy, and he was powerless to stop it, so strong was her will to suppress the pain. Everything he tried to head off the destruction fell short of its mark. He let go of Ryan's shoulder and walked out into the fog, hoping the mist would disguise the tears on her face.

—◦◆❊❊◆◦—

Fog made it difficult for Rags to concentrate. It blended with the ethereal atmosphere and disassembled the boundaries between the spirit world and the physical world — Rags would sometimes forget which one she was in. David's voice brought her around to the real world.

"I want to talk to you about this guardianship." David had learned over the years to be blunt and to the point with Rags. When she was in his office for her parole reports, she very often drifted off somewhere — to a place he couldn't follow. Abruptness was the only way he'd found to bring her back.

She shook her head slightly and rubbed her forehead. She focused on the ruddy, animated face of her parole officer, David Martin, and struggled to answer him. "I said I was thinking about it, David."

David went on. He had her attention — for the moment. "You can't afford that luxury. I had lunch with the City Attorney last week, and he dropped a little footnote on me before he left. He said that if one more charge is brought against you, he's going to make it stick. You can't get a parking ticket plea bargained in town anymore, buddy.

"My boss said if you so much as sneeze in the wrong direction, he's going over my head to send you back up. The only way I can guarantee your freedom is if you agree to let me be your guardian."

Rags hated talking about the reality of her tenuous position within the justice system. "I'll take my chances. It just doesn't appeal to me."

David raised his voice, which he normally only did with his other parolees. He had to be tough to assure respect, but reason worked better with Rags, and he knew it. "Chances! Rags, get your head straight, woman. Besides Ryan, you've found fifteen clan members, and you've done what Anara wanted with all of them." As soon as he had said it, he wished he hadn't. This was not the way to deal with her. Rags was defensive about her lack of success with Ryan, and it showed in the bitterness in her voice.

"I'm not done with Ryan yet." She bored into his perturbed brown eyes and read his thoughts. "You don't think I'm going to beat her. Do you?" She was angry now.

"No, and frankly I don't care." The conversation was not going the way David had hoped. Because Rags could see the truth of things, he couldn't manipulate her to do things his way. His main concern was for her freedom. This, they both knew. "I'm worried about clan member number seventeen. What if she isn't too frightened of you to file charges?" He relaxed. His question hit the mark, and Rags was temporarily off the scent. "My hands are tied."

"What if she doesn't exist?" Rags wasn't beyond being obstinate. "It has been two years since I've found one."

David softened his approach even more. This was critical to him. "Rags, let me put you under. Let's try again to find out if there are any more."

Rags sighed heavily. She was nervous now. "No. No more hypnotism. It takes me weeks to recover from going back there — it isn't worth it. Can I go now?"

"Yes." David waved her away; disgusted with himself for ruining another chance to save Rags from herself.

The departed fog left in its wake a clean chill and cloudless sky. Ryan was perched comfortably on her motorcycle, untouched by the cold, parked in the street in front of The Coffee Shoppe. Bathed in the peach glow of the vapor streetlamp, she preoccupied herself with cleaning her fingernails over and over again with a switchblade.

The Coffee Shoppe was frequented by many of the gays that live nearby and the college students from the University that had recently discovered its warm atmosphere and reasonably priced cuisine. Activity around the restaurant remained constant most of the day; people coming and going. Most of them were accustomed to Ryan's scandalous presence. Occasionally, someone would stop to stare or comment, usually when Ryan was with Rags, which magnified the effect. Ryan paid no attention to what others thought of her. Only two people were able to force her into awareness of herself or her behavior. Phil called attention to the unkind acts she perpetrated on others, but made no mention of the way she dressed. Indeed, the camel flying scarf dangling from her neck was a gift from him. Rags awakened her rage and rebellion and taught her to use it sexually. She listened to no one else.

Her agitation mounted, whetting her palate for a drink. She looked at her watch: 6:56. She stared into the night beyond, tapping the blade against her palm. Her wandering dispelled with the sound of her name.

"Ryan." The soft greeting made Ryan's heart palpitate. She blinked and turned to the sound instinctively. Next to her stood Leslie, in a chocolate brown velvet cape that draped haltingly about her feminine form. The hood framed her delicate features in a way that caught Ryan's breath and held it for an instant.

Leslie appraised Ryan for a moment, wearing no hat, only a leather jacket that met at the waist with black Levis. She had marvelled that Ryan wasn't shivering. "Aren't you cold? It's freezing out here."

"Forgive me." Ryan stood quickly and swung her leg over the

51

seat of her motorcycle. "My manners are a bit rusty. I should have met you inside. Too nervous I guess." She became aware of the knife. Using her thigh for leverage, she retired the blade and slipped it into her jacket. She bent over to retrieve her helmet and riding gloves from the curb and noticed Leslie's narrow, leather boots and followed the line up to the hem of the cape and beyond. The effect was powerful; Leslie's beauty impressed her, more so even than Sanji's. She was sure that Sanji had shaken her soul to the depths, but in Leslie, Sanji had met her match.

"Nervous?" Leslie wondered.

"Very. Not being able to fly does that to me." Ryan wasn't sure she wanted to let Leslie know what part her role was in causing the energy disorder.

"I see." Leslie stepped from side to side trying to generate heat. Her nerves had been having a field day with her as well. Meeting Ryan had been both frightening and compelling. The sight of the knife made her want to leave, but the sound of Ryan's voice made her want to stay. "Isn't that illegal?" she asked rhetorically, motioning to the now concealed weapon.

Ryan laughed mischievously. "Yes, counselor, it is. Let's get you inside and warm. Shall we?" Ryan could sense Leslie's discomfort and hoped she wouldn't leave.

Leslie contemplated Ryan's nonchalant disregard for her person and decided that it was part of what attracted her to Ryan in the first place. With some resolve, she answered, "Yes, please." With that, they entered the restaurant.

Inside, Leslie stopped shivering from the cold, but was still aware of a slight tremor coursing through her. As they stood, waiting to be seated, she felt her heart flutter from Ryan's nearness. She found that even the clean, indescribable scent that clung to her date excited her.

The approach of the maitre d' broke the moment. "Ryan! Why didn't you call? I could have had everything ready." He took Ryan's hand in a firm shake and clapped her shoulder affectionately. He boldly appraised her dinner guest who was removing the hood of her cape. The exposed gold of her hair made Teri suck in a hiss. "Not too shabby, my friend." His eyes widened with approval and he flashed a sparkling grin at Leslie. "Right this way. Best table in the house." Then he floated pompously toward the main dining room.

Ryan looked skyward and waited until Teri was out of ear-shot to follow. "Teri's an actor. Don't let him embarrass you."

"I won't, thank you." The humor of the scene brought Leslie's defenses tumbling down, and a grateful smile escaped from her being. She followed Teri through the front part of the restaurant, drawing an occasional stare from some of the patrons. She didn't know if it was her, or Ryan, or their unlikely pairing that attracted attention, only that she felt a sense of exultation that lightened her step.

After weaving through a series of little tables, reminiscent of a sidewalk cafe, they reached the main dining area. The walls were of a warm red brick with rough mortar accent. The booths were separated by dark wood-stained latticework. Leslie noticed that each booth was decorated differently, but each had a Toulouse-Lautrec print hanging on the wall above the table.

Their booth was adorned by "Woman Fixing Her Stocking." Leslie had an odd feeling of recognition when she looked at it. The picture was surrounded by a wide cream border and gold frame. The color scheme was repeated in the plush upholstery and the striped tablecloth. Ivy monopolized the latticework and in places invaded the brick. Track lighting nourished the foliage and offered a subdued invitation to the diner. Teri waved his hand in the air with a grand gesture befitting his title. "Your table."

Ryan reached for the back of Leslie's cape. While waiting for her to untie the bow at the throat, she squeezed her shoulders softly. A tiny gasp escaped from deep within Leslie and her knees threatened to become jelly, unable to support her. As the weight of the cape transferred to Ryan's willing hands, Leslie regained her equilibrium and she turned to reward Ryan with a smile. The light in the restaurant was stronger than it had been at Cary's, and she was able to see the sharp lines of the hands that were now covertly caressing the velvet of her cape. The paradoxical move served to further convince her that she was standing next to someone who could awaken new life for her.

Teri stood by, with the menus he had garnered along the way. He watched with undisguised fascination as Ryan placed the cape on the antique gold coat hook at the end of the booth. In all the years he had known Ryan, he had never witnessed such a display of attention. This would be a night to remember. Once the diners were seated, Teri handed them their menus. To Ryan he gave the simple wine list. It was just a formality with him; he knew exactly what Ryan wanted. He vanished, and as quickly returned with a bottle of Bernkastler Dokter and the wine glasses.

Leslie's shocking beauty made it difficult for both himself and Ryan to concentrate on the ritual of opening, tasting, approving and pouring the wine. She was dressed in a stunning grey silk suit coat and skirt, accented by a peach blouse that framed one of the loveliest necks he had seen. Gold chains rested on her bodice and fetched the light as she breathed.

This was clearly a night to make the waiter scarce and the wine plentiful. His services performed, Teri walked back to the kitchen to get Jack to take the table. The waiter he chose was the one most familiar with Ryan's tastes. It didn't pay to annoy one of the owners, especially when she was courting a beautiful woman.

"This room is very comfortable," Leslie observed.

Ryan leaned back in her seat with a contented sigh; a broad grin tracing a line in her face. "I'm glad you like it. I hope you don't mind that I ordered a white wine. I don't care for much else."

"It's delicious, and I don't mind at all." Leslie looked at the label of the bottle and memorized it. A question formed in her mind. When Teri was pouring the wine, she had glanced at the wine list; this one was not on it. It would have to wait, along with others she was itching to ask. She was gathering evidence to prove her hunch about the enigma seated opposite her.

Ryan's manners were not rusty, as she had claimed. They were charming and natural. The suggestion of a light meal of crepes was agreeable to Leslie. She couldn't trust her nerves yet and didn't want her first meal with Ryan to sour in her stomach.

The salad was served and the evening was under way. Ryan's questions unveiled Leslie's past like sheets turned back for sleep. She found it relaxing to share her background, despite the growing realization that it didn't fit her image anymore than she suspected Ryan's did.

A native of Denver, she had been raised on the north side, in a heavily Catholic neighborhood, by rather plain parents. Her father was a bus driver and her mother a nurse. She related that she was "somewhere in the middle" of nine siblings. She had remained aloof and somewhat a loner throughout her traditional parochial education. She then left home the first chance she got and worked her way through law school by modeling for local department stores. She had never developed bonds within the framework of her tightknit family, due in part to her loner tendencies and a troubling sense of differentness. The widening gap between her and her family grew to an unbreachable chasm when the Serles learned she was a Lesbian. Several years had passed since she had seen any of them, and there was little hope of purging her outcast status.

"Did you tell your parents you're a Lesbian?"

Ryan stopped in mid-bite; no one had ever asked her that before. She considered how to tell her as she finished what was in her mouth. "Well," she reached for her wine glass to assist her, "my father raised me as his son, so the fact that I liked women didn't strike him as odd. He encouraged it."

"What did your mother say about that?"

"She wasn't around to stop him. She died in childbirth."

The frank reply shook Leslie, as would many of Ryan's replies in the months to come. Leslie learned next that Ryan was the single issue of that marriage, which made it easier to see why she bore the burden of being the son.

She kept her prying guarded. Ryan's emotional limits were difficult to read. "What do you feel about that?"

Ryan talked to her wine glass instead of her interrogator. She wanted Leslie to know the answers, but she couldn't look her in the eye. "The pain I suffered from my mother's loss came from watching it chip away at my father. He never recovered from it."

Sympathy was swelling Leslie's throat, but she continued to draw Ryan's past out of her. "Did he ever hate you for living and not her?"

"If my face had mirrored her image instead of his, he might have. I was lucky."

It was a simple matter for her to visualize the sire's face. It couldn't be far from the look that held her heart captive. "You don't seem bitter about being raised that way.''

Ryan's head came up slowly. She regarded the classic beauty carefully. It was hard for her to relate to the brutally relentless questions coming from such glossy, sensuous lips. Their small, delicate curve beckoned to be kissed. She blinked back her desire and answered, ''I'm not at all bitter about it. I loved my father. He did what he thought was best, and I managed to make do with the outcome. You're probably more unhappy about what your parents did than you let on.'' She tried to sidestep the issue.

''I'd say you're right about that. Tell me to back off if I start pushing too hard, but you have only referred to your father in the past tense.'' She watched the uncompromising face, with its fine bone structure, register briefly the extent of the sorrow that was housed there.

Ryan swallowed heavily and forced her reply, ''He's dead.''

They both looked away. Leslie was unaccustomed to experiencing another's feelings. Ryan's registered themselves in hitherto unused vessels of her heart and it hurt. She hadn't bargained for the depth of their intimacy, and she was awed by it. With a large sigh she approached it tenderly. ''I'm sorry, Ryan. It would seem we are both bleeding wounds in the parent department. I appreciate you sharing that with me.''

Ryan looked up. Their eyes met in a concordant embrace. For the first time in her life, she felt safe. She wanted to rest forever in the grey softness of Leslie's eyes. They looked like miniature doves; peaceful and calm. The wanting of it made her ache.

A few bites of crepe remained on her plate. She pushed it aside and reached in her jacket for her cigarettes and lighter. Dinner didn't seem important anymore.

Leslie followed suit. She accepted Ryan's offer of a light and watched as Ryan lit her own. ''May I see your lighter for a minute?''

Ryan cocked her head curiously and handed the lighter to her guest. Their hands touched briefly in an electric flash, arousing them both.

Leslie cradled it in her hands, sensing the body warmth that remained from Ryan's touch. Her sensitive fingertips could distinguish the powerful vibrations stored in the gold object; an accumulation of years of contact with the slender hands. Bold, scrolled initials were engraved on the side. RO. "What does the O stand for?"

"O'Donnell."

She nodded to herself. "I remember hearing that on the phone this morning. You're Irish. I don't know why I didn't figure it out sooner."

"Why is that?"

"Ryan, you have the faintest of accents. I could tell you weren't a native of Colorado, but I couldn't tell where you were from. Were you born in Ireland?"

"Yes."

"You can't have been there long."

"We moved to the States when I was three. Between my father and the housekeeper he brought over, I got enough exposure to develop an accent." She was smiling now, grateful for the change of direction the conversation had taken.

"Well, like everything else about you, it's charming."

Ryan shook her head and chuckled to herself. It never failed to amuse her how much importance people placed on what they called charm. She was doing what came naturally, just as Leslie was naturally beautiful.

To satisfy her curiosity further, Leslie inverted the lighter. Closer inspection showed her what she was looking for. Stamped on the bottom was 24k. "I knew it."

Ryan exhaled smoke through her question. "Knew what?"

"I thought I saw it when we met on Thursday, but I wasn't sure. There is a real thoroughbred under all that leather, more than just an Irish heritage would account for. I smell 'Old Money' mixed in with your cologne. You hide it well, Ryan O'Donnell, if that's your intention."

Before answering, she flicked her ashes into the ashtray and poured more wine in both glasses. "Most people never get it. What gave me away?"

Leslie regarded her steadily over the rim of the wine glass. "You are trying to hide it then?"

"Not particularly, just not flaunt it. It's not my style."

"I began to suspect it right away. Your face is anything but ordinary, and you literally ooze confidence. Tonight, we were brought straightway to the best table, without a reservation. This wine is *not* on the wine list. I know special attention when I see it. Most places wouldn't even let you in the door dressed the way you are, much less serve you. What I can't figure out is how they knew.''

"You're good. I'll bet you make one hell of an attorney — you're observant and thorough. Rags would appreciate that. She says that I don't pay enough attention to what is going on around me.''

"It is 'Old Money' then. I was right.''

"You're right, but that isn't why they're so eager to please here.''

Leslie's eyes grew large with confusion. "Go on.''

"A few years ago, I met Roger and Denton, the guys that run this place, in a bar. We were getting along great and having a good time, so they told me about their dream for a restaurant. I liked their idea for the casual atmosphere, the good food, the patio out back. It just sounded right. They only had a couple thousand dollars saved and were trying to get a loan, so I decided to finance it.'' She swept her hand in a motion that said, 'here it is.'

"I love it. I just love it,'' Leslie giggled. "Who would have thought you owned this place. You certainly don't look like any of the business women I know.''

Ryan enjoyed Leslie's amusement. "You're right there. I avoid business at every turn. That is what accountants, bankers and attorneys are for.''

"I'll drink to that.'' She polished off her glass, feeling the effects of the wine and not caring. This was the best fun and the greatest challenge she had had in years. Keeping up with Ryan could prove to be a full time occupation and she relished the idea of trying. She could tell her tongue was getting looser and was feeling less responsible for what she was saying. "Is Rags for real?'' she blurted.

"She is,'' Ryan replied defensively, knitting her brow with annoyance.

"Oh, Les,'' she chastised herself. "Pardon me, that came out wrong. I was just so spooked by her reading my mind.''

Ryan relaxed. Finding out that someone was listening in on your private thoughts was not an easy thing to deal with.

"That. . . bothers most people. Yes, it is for real. Rags generally uses a great deal of discretion. She has the utmost respect for people when it comes to privacy." She didn't add that Rags didn't extend that courtesy to her. Ryan was learning to block the invasion of her privacy on certain occasions, but more often than not, her mind was fair game.

"She was very respectful and kind. I warmed to her right away. It wasn't until I left the bar that I began to question if it was her ability or my alcohol level."

"You'll get used to her if you can stand honesty at all. She doesn't play around."

"I've noticed that. Neither do you for that matter."

"That is one of the drawbacks of spending time with Rags. She always makes you feel like time is marching down your throat."

Leslie turned introspective for a moment, like she was rehearsing something inside her mind. Finally, "That certainly was a neat maneuver she pulled the other night, whisking me out to the dance floor when your friend showed up." The bitterness bled through her voice against her will.

Ryan winced. She knew it would come up sooner or later. It troubled her that Leslie seemed upset. "Rags is highly protective, of me, of Sanji and now, of you. She did what she saw as the best thing."

"Sanji," Leslie said flatly. "Does she live with you?"

"Yes."

"Do you sleep with her?"

"I have sex with her."

"Do you love her?"

"No."

Leslie had been prepared for everything but the brevity of the answers to her inquest. She had steeled herself for excuses, dodges, any number of ploys, but she hadn't counted on the abrupt confidence with which Ryan tackled the subject of the inconvenient relationship.

The idea of someone living with a person and having sex with her, yet not caring in the least for her romantically, was foreign to Leslie. "I'm not sure I understand."

"Sanji is a good woman and is quiet company. She is by far

the hottest woman I've ever touched, but we still have separate bedrooms. I care about her, but I don't love her.''

Ryan ran her hand through her hair and stretched the tension out of her upper torso. She looked at her watch and remembered the backlog of work she had waiting for her the next morning. She stilled Leslie's objection, ''Listen, I don't think you have anything to worry about on that score. I have to go. It's going to be a long one tomorrow. May I walk you to your car?''

Leslie dropped it. Ryan had given her a red light; loud and clear. ''I'd be offended if you didn't.''

On the way out of the restaurant, Ryan stopped Jack. ''Nice piece of work. I'll call Denton tomorrow.'' Jack beamed silently, knowing that she meant she would put in a word for him to get the headwaiter position that was to come available soon. He also knew that in so doing, she would insure he'd get it.

Leslie fell gracefully into step with Ryan's sturdy pace as they traversed the flagstone sidewalk enroute to her car. The streetlamps cast an eerie glow along the way. The uncanny silence of the night accentuated Leslie's rapid heartbeat pounding in her ears. She forced herself to pay attention to where she was, instead of where she wanted to be; in bed with Ryan. ''It's right here.'' She pointed to her Mercedes with reluctance. Its presence signaled the end of the most stimulating night of her life. Stepping off the curb to unlock the door, her heel opened a paper thin patch of ice. The squeeking crackle ripped the tapestry of quiet and jostled her back to reality. She bent over to unlock her door and was strangled momentarily by the power of her own passion. Unaccustomed to such intensity, she fumbled with her keys. She had to will herself to complete the task. Finally, she gained access to her car. She felt compelled to drive away as fast as was humanly possible. Before she could make her move, Ryan, who was standing disconcertingly close, reached out and firmly grasped her upper arm. Her heart rolled over, her will exhausted itself.

Ryan turned her around authoritatively and pulled her near. Their breaths condensed in the cold air and rose in unison.

''Good night, Leslie.'' Ryan's voice had turned dark and mysterious, punctuating the stillness.

Leslie's mouth opened involuntarily in a small round O. She was hypnotized by Ryan's narrowed gaze. The shadows of the night couldn't disguise the deep movement of Ryan's rib cage as it filled and emptied against hers. Ryan's free hand encircled her back, applying steady pressure between the shoulder blades. Leslie's urge to flee dissolved when she felt the touch of Ryan's lips caressing hers with a self possessed power, unknown to her before. In that moment, she got her first taste of abandonment, a taste that would be etched indelibly on her palate.

Every nerve was nourished by Ryan's desire, every pathway cleansed by the insistence that translated through that one kiss. When Ryan pulled away, they both knew that this would not be the last kiss they would share.

Ryan summoned the full extent of her willpower to release her hold on the golden beauty, knowing if she tarried, she never would. "I'll call you." The restraint caught in her voice.

Leslie hesitated for a moment, wanting to ask when. She thought better of it, sensing that Ryan wasn't the sort one could expect to answer that question. She turned, got in the car and closed the door with a firm resolution to rescue herself from herself. She started the engine, turned to look over her shoulder to see Ryan one more time, but she was gone. She looked up to her rear view mirror, expecting to see Ryan's lithe form from the back. Instead, a dark figure, a woman with untamed hair, darted across her line of vision.

The hair on the back of her neck tingled, a vague feeling of recognition pressed on her consciousness. She chose to ignore it, deciding she had had too much to drink.

6

Ryan didn't call Leslie. Instead, she sealed herself in a whiskey bottle, like a miniature ship. Meeting Leslie had a profound effect on her that caused a visceral reaction which haunted her and drove her to inebriant flight. She didn't question her lack of emotional courage or her confusion. It was important only that she run from what was too dangerous to feel.

When she left Leslie at the restaurant, she found herself at the bar, rather than at home sleeping as she had planned. The following morning Phil grounded her, as he did each subsequent morning when she insisted on showing up for work in a debilitated state.

"What hit you?" Phil asked good naturedly.

Ryan held her head for a minute before replying, "Nothing." She picked up a flight plan from the counter. She looked apathetic and relieved when Phil took it gently from her and laid it back down. He scrutinized her bloodshot eyes, summing up her condition.

"Have you been drinking whiskey again?"

She nodded her head painfully.

"Stick to beer, it doesn't undo you like this. I thought you took Leslie out last night?" His concern was warm and nonjudgmental.

"I did."

"And?"

"I don't want to talk about it, Phil." Even with her eyes half open, in a hungover fog, she could flash a warning that the stoutest of hearts would heed.

Phil backed off and tried another approach. "Go home and sleep it off, Ryan. You won't accomplish anything here."

"I can't." Ryan pulled her fingers through her hair and closed her eyes against her discomfort. She hadn't bargained for a guilty conscience about taking someone other than Sanji out. She couldn't face Sanji. It troubled her that Sanji might mean more to her than she lead herself to believe. Her relationship with the Jamacian was well defined and nonthreatening. Leslie was anything but.

Sanji thrived on Ryan's demons; Leslie would force her to confront them. Leslie's excursion into her heart left an indelible imprint of truth that wouldn't wash away. Now, the solid pattern of her life had been disrupted, and her fast paced rhythms assailed. Leslie's serene beauty had rocked her foundation, and she felt herself sinking into a quagmire of churning emotions that she saw no way out of.

"Sanji is a good woman. Maybe you ought to stick it out with her. She loves you, Ryan, and that isn't a bad problem to have," Phil prompted.

Ryan regarded her mentor quietly. His advice, though worthy of consideration, was too close to the truth. She turned to the area of the pilot's lounge, stretched out on one of the leather couches and fell asleep.

Each day that week saw Ryan recovering from the previous night in the relative comfort of the leather couch, under the watchful, worried eyes of Phil, her fellow pilots and the ground crew. They would coax her to eat as soon as she was able and cautiously suggested non-alcoholic diversions. Their concern fell on deaf ears. The moment her body would cooperate, she vanished without a word.

Each night presented a new challenge. The torment of love penetrated her drunken haze earlier, pressuring her to double her alcoholic intake to battle it back.

By Friday, she was consuming alarming amounts of liquor at the bar in her redoubled efforts to seek relief from the jagged ripping in her heart. She was torn. Sanji was comfortable, but she didn't love her. Leslie was damned uncomfortable, and she refused to accept that she was falling in love with the sophisticated attorney.

To further obfuscate her perceptions, she monopolized the juke box with hard, blaring rock music and joined in rowdy conversations with numerous drinking buddies. Interspersed between the laughter and joking would be occasional references to Sanji's absence. Ryan's behavior resembled that of a love gone sour, a place they had all been at one time or another.

They were quick to take advantage of what they thought they saw. "Hey, Ryan, I'll take her," or "Send her my way, I'll take care of her." But Ryan would dodge the inquiries and suggestive remarks deftly. She had no intention of serving Sanji up like a sacrificial offering to the circling pack of wolves. If anything, the badgering aroused her desire to protect her young partner.

Then she would consider Rags and leave the thoughts behind. There was nothing to protect Sanji from as long as Rags wanted her. In the field of contenders none stood a chance against the squarely built heathen.

Ryan wanted to follow Phil's advice and stick with what was safe, what she knew, and forget about Leslie.

But Leslie wouldn't forget about her. She had avoided the temptation to call Ryan all week, thinking Ryan wasn't to be pushed. She was stubborn herself, and had no intention of letting the one woman who could stir her heart slip through her fingers. Undaunted by Ryan's neglect, she decided to take the offensive and come to the bar in search of the elusive pilot.

It was a warm evening and the seasonal Chinook winds tossed her hair as she made her way from the parking lot to the door of Cary's Bar. She purposely chose a casual corduroy suit to help her appear calm and unconcerned. The balmy weather prompted her to leave her coat in her car, so she knew perspiration on her palms betrayed her anxiety, not her body temperature.

She noticed Ryan's motorcycle parked in front of the bar, which was both encouraging and frightening. She hated wanting to see Ryan badly enough to act so irrationally. With each step she took, she cursed herself and her pounding heart. She rehearsed the possibility of Sanji being in the bar with Ryan, the two of them entwined in a passionate embrace. Panic caught in her throat when she considered Ryan not wanting to see her at all.

She summoned her courage, telling herself that not knowing was worse than knowing, and marched toward the bar; headlong into Rags.

"Where's the fire, lady?"

"Oh, my!" Leslie started, dropped her small handbag.

Rags bent to pick it up and handed it back to her. "We've got to stop meeting like this."

Leslie smiled and gave in to the relaxed feeling Rags' presence generated in her. "Thank you." She looked from the motorcycle back to Rags. "Can we talk for a minute?"

Rags was restless and edgy and had been trying to walk it off before going back into the bar to deal with Ryan's inebriation. She was grateful for the distraction Leslie's problems would offer. "Of course." Rags invited her into the privacy offered by the shadows near the front door.

Leslie hesitated a moment, absorbing the visual effect Rags elicited. Sleeves rolled partway up the forearm exposed rocklike muscles. The left wrist was covered by a wide black watchband that accentuated the veins of the broad brutal hands. One easily forgot that Rags was not tall; her presence was unavoidably evident. She dressed with a subtle masculinity, intentionally obscuring any hint of her gender. Leslie caught a glimpse of the broad back and the promiment black gloves hanging from the left back pocket of Rags' jeans. With her eye for detail, Leslie could see that they were part of the whole. One needn't spend much time around Rags to realize that nothing existed about or around her without a purpose. Briefly, she wondered what use and/or meaning the gloves had.

Rags positioned herself so she could monitor the comings and goings of the patrons; unobserved. Within the shadows of her vantage point, it was too dark to pick out the details of Leslie's face, so she relied on her considerable insight to sense the uneasy feelings radiating from her company. "What's wrong?"

"You must know that I've seen Ryan again."

"She told me."

"She said she would call, and hasn't. I'm a nervous wreck from waiting for her to. Part of me is angry because I think it's rude for her not to have. I found myself being jealous of Sanji, which is totally foreign to me. Finally, I got worried about her. As you can see, I have managed to create enough reasons to come looking for her." Leslie knew she was getting away from herself; her

66

confidence was on shaky ground.

Rags leaned against the wall and folded her arms across her bust, gauging Leslie's emotions and, at the same time, watching women enter the bar. She found her greatest comfort dwelling in the collective consciousness of those around her. The ethereal realms, unknown to most, beckoned to her, offering her a medium of existence that was far less troublesome than the physical world. She could easily divide her attention, simultaneously scouting for negative or destructive vibrations, and listen to Leslie without her being the wiser. This talent made it possible for her to forecast behaviors. She developed a tandem talent for interceding tactfully between potential combatants and heading off numerous fights before they began. Her skill did not, however, extend inward. She was never aware in advance when she herself would come to blows with someone.

She sympathized with Leslie's position. "I don't think Ryan was being rude for not calling you. She usually doesn't say she's going to do something and then not do it. If you knew her better, you wouldn't be angry with her, or jealous. But worried? Yes. I'm concerned myself."

Out of the corner of her eye, Rags spotted the one person she had hoped would pick another night to come to the bar. Standing on the well lit front porch was a woman with midnight black skin, about a half foot taller than Rags' five foot six inches, and approximately twenty-five pounds heavier. The rancor on her face cleared a path before her wherever she went.

Rags had to concentrate fully to penetrate the strange combination of drugs in the woman's system to judge her intentions. Nothing concrete would present itself, which was often the case for people in seriously altered states.

The shift in attention brought Leslie's head around to see what was occupying Rags' interest. The woman had stopped to wait for a friend, allowing Leslie a clear look at her. The sight made her spine tighten.

"Who's that?" she asked acidly.

"It ain't Peter Pan, I can tell you that. We call her Crazy Jess. She works in the same warehouse district I do. And. . . she hates Ryan's guts."

Leslie waited for the stranger to enter the bar before going on.

"Is that why you're concerned about Ryan?"

"One of many reasons. The worst enemy Ryan has right now is Ryan — and the bottle."

"I don't understand." Leslie hadn't thought of Ryan as a heavy drinker.

"Ryan's in there," Rags pointed toward the bar, "drunk out of her mind. This makes the fifth night in a row."

"This early in the evening?" Leslie was amazed.

"This early, and it keeps getting earlier, and she keeps drinking more and more."

Leslie hated to ask for fear of the answer, but she forged on, despite herself. "Why?"

Rags knew Leslie wasn't the direct cause of the trouble. Rather it was Ryan's reaction to her. There was no way to answer her gently. "Self annihilation."

Leslie tried to control her mounting horror. "It's going to take a while to do that just by drinking."

"Not with Ryan it won't. Alcohol has an odd effect on her involuntary muscle functions. Six years ago, I found her in the gutter out front of the bar here, and she had stopped breathing."

Leslie gasped audibly, "Are you kidding?"

"No, I wish I were. Apparently she knows this about herself and she was trying to commit suicide that night."

"Suicide! Ryan?" It seemed so unlike the woman she thought Ryan was.

"She took the death of her father pretty hard, Leslie. It took a lot of time and hard work to get her interested in living again. Life doesn't hold much fascination for her, so it doesn't take much to make her think about bailing out."

Leslie felt an urgent helplessness. "Can't you stop her?"

"From drinking. Yeah. I can go in there and scare the hell out of her and she'll quit drinking if I tell her to. Then what? Figure it out — she drives a motorcycle, she's a pilot, she carries a knife and owns several guns. Name your poison. Nobody can make her want to live."

Leslie refused to consider Ryan succeeding; it was too painful. "Can I help?"

Rags stood erect and ushered Leslie into the bar. "I have no idea."

Inside, Crazy Jess had spotted Ryan at the bar ordering a drink. She stood by the pool table a moment to let her eyes adjust to the diminished light. Scanning the bar, she realized that now was one of the rare times when Ryan was alone, and she decided to make her move. The drugs in her system did not hamper her balance or her determination. She covered the distance between herself and Ryan with no difficulty.

Ryan's back was to her, giving her the full advantage of the element of surprise. With all her might, she engaged Ryan's shoulder. Unhindered by the bulky leather jacket, she pulled her around to face her fate. The shot glass Ryan was about to empty careened to the floor. The sudden action aroused the attention of most of the crowd in the front part of the bar, but no one came to Ryan's aid. Crazy Jess was as mean as she looked and intimidated people easily.

Crazy Jess grasped her enemy with both hands and slammed her against the bar counter. The edge of the bar dug into Ryan's back. She could feel the pain through the liquor, but showed no sign of it. When she was flying or if she was drunk enough, Ryan was fearless when faced by physical danger. Her eyes challenged Jess with a fierce pride that angered Jess even more. "Whoa CJ. Take it easy, man," she taunted.

"All right, motherfucker, say your prayers. I've had it with you." Crazy Jess' eyes reddened and narrowed. Those closest backed away. Unlike other fights over women, this one wasn't likely to end in a semi-harmless brawl. "Slavery was abolished a long time ago, you honky shitface." With that she slammed Ryan against the bar again. "I'm going to take Sanji away from you so you can't hurt her anymore."

Ryan winced from the pain and her head rolled slightly. She shook away the fog to focus on Jess. "Over my dead body, you mangy asshole." The feeling was returning to her arms, and she became aware her feet weren't touching the ground; denying her the leverage she needed to extricate herself from Jess' lockhold.

"That can be arranged, bitch!" Jess threatened.

Before Ryan could plan her next move, Jess let go of her shoulder and pulled back to strike her. Ryan braced herself for the blow, but it didn't come. She gathered her wits and looked to see why.

Standing to the right of Crazy Jess was Rags, blocking the black fist with her hand. A staredown ensued between Rags and Jess, arch enemies for many years. Jess' grasp lessened slightly, and Ryan could tell she was going to back down again as she had done numerous times before when a confrontation reached this stage with Rags. Ryan watched the muscles of Rags' forearm tighten and flex. Her jaws locked powerfully, and her chest rose and fell threateningly. The advantage in the faceoff shifted to Rags, and Ryan eased to the ground. When her feet touched the floor, she freed her other shoulder from Jess' massive hand. The poised fist relaxed and Jess turned her gaze to Ryan.

"One of these days I'm going to catch you without your watch-dog, honky, and you won't live to tell about it."

"That's enough, CJ," Rags snarled.

Crazy Jess turned her back haughtily to Rags and walked away from the scene to the rear of the bar, preserving what she could of her injured pride.

Leslie watched Ryan's rescue with a detached concern, uncertain how to respond and immobilized by the undercurrent of fear of those around her. She was forced to witness a side of Ryan that she could scarcely believe existed. A seed of doubt germinated in her mind.

Ryan appraised the damage and decided it was minimal. "Thanks."

"Anytime." Rags straightened Ryan's collar solicitously.

Ryan clasped her friend's arm urgently. "What's she doing here?" Leslie was walking toward them.

"She cares about you, Ryan, whether you like it or not. Although for the life of me, seeing you now, I don't know why."

Ryan was puzzled by Rags' irritation. "I need a drink." She turned and took the bottle the bartender was holding and a glass and filled it for herself. A moment later the glass was empty. She turned to find Leslie standing next to her. Ryan weaved unsteadily before her.

The feelings of concern and worry that built inside Leslie when she spoke with Rags quickly turned to disgust and anger when she saw Ryan's condition. "Haven't you had enough? I can drive you home." Her voice was low and furious.

Rags prepared for Ryan's reaction.

Ryan's eyes widened in disbelief, then narrowed with resentment. "It's none of your fucking business, Leslie." She pronounced each syllable with a cruelty that stung Leslie like a whip.

Rags divined the backhand slap before Ryan's muscles could produce it and acted immediately, wrenching Ryan's arm down and behind her back. Her intercession was coupled with the gravest of warnings. "If you ever lay a hand on her in anger, you'll never see the inside of a plane again. Do you get my meaning?"

The blood crowded in Ryan's head, her anger and frustration built to a crescendo. She replied hotly through her clenched teeth, "Yes," and burst through them to the door, drawing stares the length of the bar.

Leslie ran after her, followed by Rags who stopped to pick up the forgotten helmet. They were too late. Ryan pulled away, leaving Leslie standing impotently on the curb. She listened as the roar of the motorcycle echoed Ryan's anger, broken by punishing pauses as the gears shifted. She stared out into the darkness, shaking, until the sound lessened and finally was indistinguishable from the other sounds of the night.

Suddenly, a drink became the most important thing to her. She turned to go back in the bar and saw, to her dismay, Rags talking to the woman she knew was Sanji. Sanji was cradling Ryan's helmet in her arms and nodding her head in reply to Rags.

"I want you to check her pulse and breathing from time to time if she's unconscious when you get there. Do you know what to do if she isn't doing well?" Sanji replied that she did. "Good, now if she's awake, steer clear of her. If she does anything that scares you in the least, I want you to call me at home. I'll come right away."

"She'll get mad at me for coming into her room." Sanji was disquieted.

"You just tell her that I told you to do it." Rags put a comforting arm around Sanji's shoulders and told her to go.

Sanji passed Leslie on the way. They eyed each other suspiciously, but said nothing.

Rags watched and read the thoughts of both. Leslie's ill feelings toward Sanji, she expected. Sanji's thoughts yielded more knowledge about Leslie than she cared to see.

After Sanji drove away, Rags approached Leslie. "You look like you could use a drink."

Seated at Rags' favorite table, they stared into their drinks and composed themselves before talking.

"Leslie, you cannot talk to Ryan like that."

"She has quite a temper. I can see I have a lot to learn about her."

"In a way I'm glad she showed some temper. It means she hasn't given up yet."

Leslie reproached herself for letting her pride rule her actions and began to worry anew about the woman she was growing to love. "Will she make it home alright?"

"Yeah. Ryan has a sixth sense about machines. She makes them get her where she wants to go, no matter what condition she's in."

Leslie accepted what reassurance she could and thought about the evening's events. She began to wish she had found Ryan in Sanji's arms instead of Jess' claws. "May I ask you a question?"

"Shoot."

"Why didn't someone boot Crazy Jess out of here?"

"She's harmless," Rags laughed.

"I'd hate to see who you consider dangerous then."

"You already have. I have to go. I'm really sorry you had to see this tonight. You don't deserve it." Rags didn't wait for a reply before leaving.

Leslie was left at the table to nurse her drink and sort out her feelings about the reversal her life had taken since meeting Ryan.

Sanji drove up to the security station in the pale green Volvo Ryan had given her when they first started living together. This ritual always made her nervous. She knew the guard was slower to open the iron gates for her than for other people.

She patiently suffered the scrutiny and the leering looks she sometimes got from a few of the guards. The guards were careful to keep their prejudices from developing into open confrontations — they valued their jobs. The exclusive community they protected leant prestige to their position. Ryan, and several other residents of the neighborhood, had no tolerance for even the slightest show of insubordination. The guards made Sanji uncomfortable in subtle ways that couldn't be detected by anyone but her. Security was tight, but in her heart, Sanji knew that even Rags got better treatment when she drove up in her ancient Apache pickup truck.

She smiled to herself as the gate opened, trying to imagine the intimidated looks the guards probably got on their faces when Rags appeared. She admired Rags and the power she seemed to have over people.

Power was something Sanji understood well — she understood that she didn't have any. Living with Ryan taught her that even women could have power if they had enough money, but no amount of money could change the color of her skin or people's hearts.

Surrender was something she clearly understood as well. She surrendered herself to Ryan willingly, but Ryan's capitulation to Rags was brought about by force.

In many ways Sanji was wise beyond her years. She knew that she was at the bottom of a pecking order. Power didn't live without surrender, and the more power someone had, the more she had to surrender. She chose her status out of love and her slavery to her own passions. She learned early on that Ryan was more imprisoned than she would ever be.

Rags dominated every aspect of the Irishwoman's life. Rags had great power, but even she had to answer to someone with more. Anara.

As Sanji drove through the quiet twisting streets, winding her way home, Anara's magnificent face formed in her mind. The disturbing white eyes were her most prominent feature. They burned if she stared into her mental image of them too long. Anara had come to her in a dream saying nothing, just existing with her frightening beauty.

She remembered telling Ryan about the dream. Ryan knew her by name, for she dreamt of her sometimes too. This was the

73

ultimate power — power from beyond life.

The spirit world was a fearful place to Sanji. She came from a strongly superstitious background, and it troubled her that Ryan seemed unworried by the shimmering specter stalking their dreams. Sanji didn't know how she discovered the relationship between Rags and Anara, only that she knew.

Sanji always thought about Anara when she was afraid. She was afraid now, as she pulled into the drive and saw the motorcycle parked defiantly in the breezeway between the back terrace and the carriage house.

She parked in front of the carriage house that sheltered an abandoned Rolls. The car and the entire second floor of the main house stood together as mute symbols of the passing of Ryan's father, collecting the dust of Ryan's neglect.

A fog was beginning to gather in the atmosphere, trapping the acrid smell of smog. It stung her nostrils when she opened the car door. She picked up Ryan's helmet lovingly, and thought about the long, thrilling rides up the dizzying curves of The Switchbacks with Ryan. They would wind around the mountain roads and return recklessly down the Interstate past Dead Man's Curve. Their wild journey would bring them home in an exaggerated state of arousal that would vent itself in violent lovemaking sessions, followed by deep sleep. The memories stirred the place between her legs.

As Sanji walked to the back door, a neighborhood cat strolled up to her and demanded attention. Sanji leaned over to scratch its chin, and for an instant wanted to trade places with it. Then she turned to the back door. It was open. Her heart leapt.

She forced herself to go inside, praying that Ryan was the only person she would find. She found the light switches that would illuminate the first floor and stairway to the second floor. She peered up the stairwell, but the door at the top was closed as it always was. She inspected the basement and the first floor and decided there was no prowler, only her active imagination.

She made her way to Ryan's bedroom and there, face down on the antique four-poster bed, was Ryan's fully clothed form. One arm dangled off the side, inches away from a half empty whiskey bottle.

Sanji forced herself across the threshold and beyond to the bed.

Gingerly, she felt for Ryan's pulse. It was strong and normal, as was the breathing. She sighed heavily with relief and smoothed her hand over the raven head. It hurt down to her toes to see Ryan in such a condition.

Realizing that she still had the helmet in hand, she grabbed the whiskey bottle and walked out to the dining room. She set the helmet on the table, where Ryan would expect to find it, and put the liquor away. The cat that had followed her inside rubbed against her leg. "No way little kitty. Ryan would have a fit if she found you in here," she whispered. She locked the door behind the ejected feline and turned the alarm on. "Ryan must really be loaded," she thought to herself. "She never does that."

She fixed some coffee and, with leaden resolve, went into her room to find a book and a chair. She settled down for the long vigil she hoped would end in a simple hangover. She silently cursed Leslie. "You did this to her, you whore. May you rot in Hell."

7

A bird gave a solo performance outside Leslie's window, plaintively urging spring to quicken under its feet. February was traditionally Leslie's worst month, and this year promised to follow suit. The upset of the previous night brought on the last day of her period with an unaccustomed severity.

Pampering herself, she sat on her couch, cuddled in a pastel angora afghan, and sipped on some hot red raspberry leaf tea. She made her legs stretch out to lessen the effects of the cramps and tried to lose herself in *The New Yorker*. The late morning sun blazed through the skylight above her. The sky was robin's egg blue and looked soft next to her white ceiling.

The magazine couldn't compete with her mental wanderings. She leaned back indulgently into the mass of pillows that propped her up and let her eyes restfully scan her living room. Her converted condominium was a product of the gentrification that transformed more and more of Capitol Hill. The hardwood floors, red brick fireplace, twelve foot ceilings, polished wood windows and oak moldings created a warmth that suited her. The simple lines of her modern furniture pleased her eyes; the abundant foliage plants relaxed and nourished her soul. She had long since overrun the walls with watercolors collected from women artists in town.

The scent from the fresh body splash she used after her bath summoned a laziness that almost put her to sleep. Semiconsciousness brought up Ryan's image; uninvited. She didn't want to think about Ryan dying. How would she even know? Who would think to call her if something did happen? "Sweet

Diana, please watch over her," she prayed.

The chime of her telephone answered her prayer. She reached over the back of her couch to the table that held the phone and a large Boston fern. "Hello."

"Leslie, this is Rags."

Her heart skipped a beat. She imagined the worst. "Is everything alright?" she asked urgently. The forgotten magazine slid off her lap to the floor as she sat up straighter, hoping to hear better.

"Everything is fine. I hope you don't mind me calling. I got your number from information."

"Not at all. That's why it's there. I'm relieved that you called. You must have read my mind from a distance. I was just thinking about Ryan, trying to figure out how I would know if anything was wrong."

"Ryan doesn't know how lucky she is to have someone like you to worry about her."

"I suspect that Ryan requires a great deal of worry from a lot of people." Leslie lay back in the cushions again, reassured by Rags' powerful tenor voice.

"I would like you to meet Ryan and me at The Coffee Shoppe for brunch. I think she owes you an apology."

Leslie twisted the telephone cord around her finger, searching for an answer to the unexpected invitation. "Do you always patch up Ryan's problems for her?"

"When I can," Rags replied frankly. "If you stick around long enough, Leslie, you'll learn that Ryan topples off pedestals with very little effort. She hasn't got much of a conscience, so it generally doesn't occur to her when she has hurt someone's feelings. Even then, it doesn't always matter to her."

"I appreciate your thoughtfulness, Rags."

"Seeing you two get together is what I'm after. This wound needs to be sewn up now, before it festers."

Leslie purred for a moment. It felt good to hear someone who wasn't opposed to her having a relationship with Ryan. "Do you think we will ever get together? Ryan didn't seem too interested in it last night."

"If I have anything to say about it, you will. Ryan gets mean when she drinks whiskey, which isn't often. Come to brunch and

78

give her a chance to redeem herself."

"You *do* want us together." Leslie was surprised.

"I wish I could say my motives were unselfish, Leslie. I want you two together because I'm in love with Sanji."

Smiling to herself, Leslie answered, "I see. Well, I can't blame you for that. I hope you know what you're doing. Alright, brunch it is. What time?" She could taste the irony, like peanut butter, sticking to the roof of her mouth.

"In about an hour. I can't guarantee Ryan will be completely recovered, but she'll be civil."

A twinge of excitement invaded Leslie's nether regions as she hung up the phone. She found herself excited about seeing Ryan again, regardless of the circumstances. Her flow tugged urgently at her, and she left her warm nest to challenge her fate once more.

—◦❖◦—

Sanji awakened stiff and groggy. The arm of the chair she had slept in creased her side and nagged her to get up. She rose slowly and began to stretch her long, responsive muscles. The movement sent a flurry of dust motes through the air, calling attention to the lateness of the morning hour. The sun lit her room until noon, then disappeared behind a stand of spruces in the front yard.

She walked to the night stand and focused on the digital display of the clock — it was 11:33. "Oooh," she moaned. Shaking the last vestiges of sleep from her head, she listened for a sign that Ryan might be awake. She could only hear bluejays enjoying the unseasonable warmth outside.

She stood in Ryan's doorway and stared at the mussed bedspread with disappointment. She had grown more at ease about entering the forbidden room after checking on Ryan several times during the night. She walked in to pick up the mess of abandoned clothing and a damp towel.

This, too, was foreign to her. Ryan was normally impeccably neat. What little mess there ever was, was left for the housekeeper.

The bedroom was dominated by heavy brocades on the win-

79

dow, chairs and bed. She picked up the soiled laundry and walked into the master bath to deposit it in the chute. The cold, impersonal tile of the bath contrasted heavily with the warm, chili pepper reds of the bedroom. She felt the symbolic resemblance to Ryan. To her, Ryan was the cold impersonal tyrant, unresponsive to the pain she felt at times like these.

The bath still held the steam from a shower taken less than a half an hour before. Sanji picked up a bottle of Grey Flannel from the sink counter. She wanted to throw it in frustration. Instead, she caressed it affectionately. A tear mixed with the condensation on the label. She knew that Ryan left without waking her, not to avoid disturbing her, but because she didn't care. Ryan wouldn't thank her for the sleepless night, indeed even acknowledge it. Life would go on as before. She set the cologne back in its place and wandered sadly back into the bedroom.

The reds and brocades of Ryan's love were denied her. Those tender emotions were saved for youth.

On the wall above the dark lacquered dresser, mounted like trophies, were a dozen or so glossy photographs of young girls. Ryan's love spilled over the edges of her tightly controlled emotions into the lap of an occasional teenager that caught her fancy. They were not banned entrance to Ryan's private sanctuary, and Sanji resented their status.

Of all Ryan's eccentricities, this one alone bothered her. She tried to tell herself it was because they were so young, but she knew that wasn't the reason. She studied the portraits, and something familiar struck her about a look they all seemed to have. She knew that there, embodied in the set of pictures, was the type of woman that could lay claim to Ryan's heart. A wave of sickness threatened to cut short her revelation. The thought hammered away in her mind, and she realized who the youths resembled. "That bitch," she hissed under her breath.

She had seen Ryan kiss the new woman earlier in the week, then had seen her again with Rags and she was certain, now more than ever, that she had acquired a rival. The months and years of unrequited love were suddenly unbearable. "This is not going to happen. I won't let it," she thought to herself.

She looked down at her wrinkled clothes and decided that there was no time to change, that she had to act before she lost her nerve.

She knew Ryan well enough to guess she could be found recovering at The Coffee Shoppe. Her emotions carried her there with the swiftness of a gale-force tailwind.

In front of the restaurant, parked like conspirators, were Ryan's motorcycle and Rags' black Apache pickup. She drove half a block further before she found a parking space. She turned off the car and felt her temper heighten and her skin tingle. All reason was replaced by unreason. Her actions took on the force of a woman possessed.

Without knowing why, she checked the patio first. She came around to the far side of the restaurant where the patio was. It was lined by a brick half wall that was planted with privet hedge and had a canvas awning that sheltered half of the diners. The entrance to the street was trellised by unadorned limbs of climbing roses.

She spotted Ryan instantly, sitting with her back to her, talking to the hated rival. Rags was nowhere to be seen.

Her rage overpowered her. Her animal instincts moved through her unrestricted. She ran up behind the unsuspecting Ryan, and with the strength gained from the adrenalin ravaging her system, she pulled the chair out from under Ryan.

Unseated, prone, Ryan was temporarily defenseless. In that split second Sanji had the physical and logistical advantage. She used that advantage to vent her anger. With a savagery unknown to her before, Sanji began kicking Ryan in the ribs, trying to eradicate the years of injustice and jealousy with each blow.

The profit she gained by surprise quickly shifted to Ryan. Unaware of the peril she placed herself in by standing over a wounded animal, Sanji didn't think to protect her feet.

Ryan reached out with her considerable strength, caught Sanji by the ankle, and jerked. Even Sanji's native sense of balance and limber body couldn't save her. She fell to the pavement.

The other diners around them were responding in various degrees of upset, alerting those inside to the trouble on the porch.

Rags, who had retired to the indoors to allow Ryan some privacy, was aware at once of the trouble on the patio. Her reflexes, polished by years of fighting experience, helped her cut a path through the gathering crowd. Her crisp agility, despite her square frame, allowed her to reach Ryan in the instant before a crashing blow could make contact with Sanji's head. Rags pulled Ryan, who had crawled over the toppled chair to ambush Sanji, to her feet and shook her to her senses. Leslie followed suit and repaired Sanji to a safer distance.

Rags had Ryan in a hammerlock and was talking quietly in her ear. Ryan was listening with a vacant expression on her face. Her muscles began to relax gradually and the immediate danger passed.

The crowd began to return to their tables with Denton's reassurances that all was well. Leslie overheard Denton explaining to one of the more vocal customers that he couldn't kick Ryan out because she was the owner, and apologizing to another couple.

Sanji realized that she was in Leslie's grasp and wrestled her way loose, exposing herself to the elements. Alone and vulnerable, she became aware of what she had just done. Her eyes widened and moved from side to side like a cornered dog. She flinched when Rags let go of Ryan. She wanted to dash out into the street, run until her lungs burst, anything, but be where she was. Terror immobilized her, sweat stung her eyes. She began wringing her hands. Her peril magnified itself in Ryan's eyes.

Ryan's hands held her ribs as they caught at her progress, but her eyes were relentless, holding Sanji spellbound. Ryan took three measured steps toward her with unmasked menace. "You bought it now, dancer." Her warning was punctuated by an afflicted gasp for air. "Get your ass home. . .now. And stay there." The wrath in Ryan's voice unnerved everyone close enough to hear.

Sanji replied humbly in a voice only Ryan could hear, "Yes, Master." Then she propelled herself out of the restaurant like a stone released from a slingshot.

Sanji's exit broke the tension. People resumed eating, and the waiters resumed serving. The scene normalized. Ryan righted her chair and sat down, followed by Rags. Leslie remained standing.

"Are you hurt?" Leslie asked. She was thoroughly embarrassed and uncomfortable. The outburst had frightened and angered her.

Ryan reached for the Bloody Mary she had been drinking like medicine and finished it before replying sardonically, "I can take care of myself."

"I, personally, was concerned about your ribs. I can do without the sarcasm."

"They're fine," Ryan lied. She had had broken ribs before, and she knew that at least one of them was now.

Rags confined her response, knowing that Ryan was not revealing the extent of her injuries, nor was Leslie revealing her upset. Rags was more concerned with Ryan's injured pride. An insult of this proportion could be just the thing to push her over the edge.

"Fine," Leslie answered. "Now, if you don't mind, I'll take my leave."

"Suit yourself."

Leslie's indignation intensified with Ryan's barbed reply. She turned to Rags. "Thank you for the invitation. I wouldn't want it to be said that I was as rude as some people." The flush in her face deepened. She turned and left, her heels ringing out on the pavement.

Rags leaned toward Ryan, worried by the pain etched across her friend's brow. "How many are broken?"

"At least one, maybe two." Ryan caught Denton's attention. The almost aging man came to her table. "Are you alright?"

"I will be, when you get me another drink and a phone." Ryan tried to smile.

"This isn't good for business, you know." Denton lodged his complaint as gently as possible.

Ryan was in no mood to be bothered with his concern. "The phone, Denton," she commanded irritably.

Denton longed silently for the day when he and his partner could afford to buy her out and turned to fill her request.

"Why did you lie to Leslie about your ribs?"

"I don't want her pity, Rags. I don't need it." Ryan lit a cigarette and tried to relax. "Women." She looked Rags squarely in the eyes. "I hope you know what went on here, because I sure as hell don't."

"You don't know jealous rage when you see it?" Rags asked, amazed.

"Jealous? Sanji?"

"Yes, my friend. I don't know how, but Sanji has figured out that she's losing you to Leslie, and she isn't about to take it sitting down."

A waiter brought fresh drinks for both of them and plugged

the telephone in. He set it on the table before Ryan and disappeared. Ryan eyed Rags suspiciously as she called her doctor at his home. She made arrangements to meet him at his clinic for X-rays and hung up.

It galled her that even Sanji could see what she wished weren't true. It had to be true, for Rags was never wrong about love. Sanji was losing her to Leslie. She could see it now for the first time. Apologizing to Leslie hadn't been difficult; she had actually wanted to. She was sorry that she hadn't spent more time with her.

"Why did Leslie leave?"

"You embarrassed the hell out of her for one thing. She isn't used to this sort of thing. Her life is pretty sheltered compared to yours. You've met your match, O'Donnell. That's one prideful woman."

"Hey! I didn't ask for that crazy broad to come in here and cause a scene." Ryan stirred her drink fitfully.

"Yes, you did. Ryan, you can't carry on with one woman and expect the other to stay in the dark about it. They have their ways of finding out. They also have their ways of letting you know they don't like it." Rags continued to probe Ryan's mind for foreknowledge of what lay in store for Sanji. "If you and Leslie ever get past all that pride, it will be a small miracle."

Even through her pain, Ryan managed to keep her intentions from Rags. "I'll see you later, at the bar." She stood, took three stiff swallows of her drink and left.

Rags scowled at her drink. She knew Sanji had to be punished for insubordination. There was no doubt in her mind that Ryan would follow through with that. If only Ryan had opened herself to let Rags see the extent of her anger, it would be possible to know how hard Sanji was going to pay for what she'd done. She hoped Ryan would slip in her mental concentration when they were drinking later at the bar.

Delores stood in the midst of her guests, satisfied with the collection of propsective suitors for Leslie. She wasn't glad to be turning forty. Grey was filtering through her dark brown hair. She kept it short, which made it all the more obvious. Her natural athleticism helped her to keep her body fit and basically appealing. Still, it was becoming more difficult to manage her lover and her roving eye. She shook off her thoughts and turned her attention to the task at hand.

Now the party, which moments ago threatened to turn somber and maudlin, would get a little more lively. She relaxed, slid her hands into the pockets of her tuxedo, and began to mingle. "Somewhere in this crowd, is the person who will take Les' mind off Ryan," she thought paternally. Eavesdropping on fragments of conversations, comments about Leslie's stunning black dress and alluring figure, assured her that her plans would meet with success.

"Leslie, let me show you around. I don't think you've seen the house since we finished redecorating." Dana's voice was silvery, inviting.

Leslie regarded Dana for a quick moment. It always shocked her that Dana was so beautiful. The off color remarks she heard about Delores robbing the cradle could easily be justified if one didn't know that there were only eleven years between their ages. Dana looked twenty years Delores' junior. The world would mourn when the youth faded from her lusty blue eyes.

She followed her graceful hostess on a lighthearted tour of the western style home.

"Del always says that Haley's Comet comes around more often than you do," Dana giggled.

"It's hard to think about coming this far up into the mountains to see someone I'm with five days a week," Leslie smiled.

"Don't be silly. Star and Brigid only live ten miles further up and on the same road we do," Dana persisted.

"Can't argue with that kind of logic," Leslie conceded. To change the subject she halted midway down the hall to the bedroom area. "Isn't this a Gorman?" The artwork that rarely went without notice by guests dominated the wall before them.

Dana couldn't resist the invitation to boast about her favorite piece. "Yes, it is. You collect art don't you?"

"My love is for local women artists. No one of renown yet."

"Del bought this for me on my last birthday. She likes him

too, especially the way he paints women."

The sensuality of the painting reflected Dana's so clearly that Leslie wondered if it had been planned. The fragile touch of Dana's hand on her arm brought her admiration around to the real work of art held by the home.

Leslie felt her knees weaken as a sense of the fragrance Dana wore lulled her reflexes. Inside herself, she could feel the power of Dana's seductive charm. It didn't surprise her that Delores indulged this girlike vision.

Leslie couldn't look into the blue traps that sought her gaze. Instead, she followed the line of the auburn tresses as they disappeared behind the rounded shoulders, blending with the hazy peach fabric of Dana's dress. The tour of the house became a study in form. A discussion about painted art was fast turning into a lesson in living art. Leslie's eyes were irresistibly drawn to the bodice line that terminated in the delicious, freckled cleavage. The flimsy cloth outlined Dana's firm rounded breasts. She watched the nipples harden. Her hand came to her mouth, muffling her desire. "Ohh."

The music and the safety of the living room pierced her consciousness, and she shook her head, trying to extract herself from Dana's seizure. Words failed to form in her mind. Blind instinct made her turn, determined, to walk toward the music and laughter. She could sense Dana's eyes boring into the back of her head, quickening her pace.

Safe in the arms of the first person to ask her to dance, she remembered why she had only been to visit Delores and Dana once before. Her third dancing partner let her go after a too closely danced ballad. She headed for the bar and some liquid fortitude. She heard her name spoken in a high-pitched voice. "Les!"

Leslie smiled her recognition. "Star. Join me, I need a break."

"The vultures at it again?"

"I'm afraid so. I didn't think you ever bothered with these parties."

"I don't usually. You know me. I'll avoid dressing up at all costs. But, I felt I owed it to Del for surviving this long."

"Amen to that." Leslie saluted her friend with her drink. Star's robust style and healthy shine relaxed her. She adjusted quickly to the obvious change the blue pantsuit and red blouse made.

Missing were the jeans and flannel shirts Star was normally seen in on the twenty-five acre farm she shared with Brigid. "Where is Brig?"

"She's flying around here somewhere. She loves parties. I think I hold her back that way."

"Not to worry, my friend. She wouldn't trade your love for all the parties in the world." Leslie enjoyed Star's bold laughter. It was affirmation of the happiness that seemed to be the hallmark of her relationship with Brigid.

Around midnight, Delores cornered Brigid in the kitchen. "Brig, I don't know what to do anymore. I'm not having any luck with Leslie at all."

"I didn't know you were interested in her," Brigid replied calmly. The six-foot redhead remained sober. Her missing leg was a testament to what drinking and driving had done for her on her twenty-first birthday. She hadn't tasted a drink for ten years, but never commented on the indulgence of others. Her clear grey eyes penetrated the smoky kitchen atmosphere, searching for Delores' meaning.

"I'm not, but Ryan is."

Brigid shifted on her metal crutches, adding more weight to the counter she was leaning on. Her solid cheekbones flushed sightly, the vein in her temple pulsed nervously. "Is the feeling mutual?"

"I wasn't sure until tonight, but I think it is."

"So why aren't you having any luck tonight?"

"I was hoping she would find someone else to take her mind off Ryan."

Brigid put her crutches together and extracted her right hand from the metal circle on her arm. She placed her hand heavily on Delores' shoulder. "You're about as subtle as a freight train, Del."

Delores looked up into Brigid's eyes and swayed slightly. "Dumb huh?"

"I'd say so. Does Dana know?"

87

"Oh no," Delores replied emphatically.

"Advice?"

"Yeah."

"Leave it alone. I'll talk to Les and see what gives."

Del nodded her head in defeated consent.

Brigid returned her hand to the crutch and unselfconsciously carried herself out of the kitchen in search of Leslie.

The light from the hall was enough to illuminate Leslie's golden head, shaking in the darkness of the den. She was outlined slightly by the glow seeping through the large window behind her. Below, the view etched out a likeness of Denver's glittering skyline. Leslie wiped the tears from her eyes and focused on Brigid's distinctive form darkening the doorway.

"Amazing view. I've always envied Del for finding this property." Brigid glided into the den and joined Leslie on the couch that faced the window. She placed her crutches against the seat and settled Leslie in the crook of her arm.

Leslie accepted the artist's hand gladly as it stroked her hair like a lost pup. She nestled into the softness of Brigid's bulky white turtleneck sweater and gazed absently at the firm lines of the right leg, covered with tan wool slacks. She thought back to the time when Brigid tried and rejected a prosthesis as unreal. As always, her own problems took on a new perspective. Her problems were small by comparison to what Brigid dealt with every day. She listened to Brigid's patient heartbeat and relaxed.

Brigid lifted the delicate chin and gazed compassionately into the swollen eyes. "Better?"

With a relieved smile Leslie answered, "Yes, much. Thank you."

"Del told me about you and Ryan."

Leslie blinked her eyes several times in surprise and cocked her head. "Told you what?"

"She seems to think you two are interested in each other."

"So?" Leslie sat up defensively.

"You don't see it, do you?" Brigid was amazed at Leslie's innocence.

"See what?"

"Del wasn't going to make a big deal about her birthday. I was surprised when she decided to have this party. She did it for you." Brigid continued in answer to Leslie's quizzical expression. "More than half the women here tonight are single, and they all have the hots for either you, or Dana, or both. It was Del's wild dream that somebody would get lucky and leave with you tonight and that you would forget all about Ryan."

"Why?" Leslie's confusion mounted.

"Del has no great love for Ryan; not many people do these days. She just wants to rescue you from what she considers a fate worse than death."

"Failing that, she calls in the cavalry." Leslie gestured vehemently, indicating Brigid.

"Please don't get hateful with me, Les. I'm one of Ryan's biggest fans, and I like you too well." Brigid's alto reprimand cut Leslie's rancor short.

"Forgive me. It's been a long day." She slumped back into the couch, reached to the table for her ignored drink and finished it off, followed by a cigarette lit with shaky hands. She stilled them and recaptured the receptive mood with a heavy sigh. "You know Ryan? I've never heard you speak of her before."

"You can thank Star for that. She doesn't think any more of her than Del does. I've known Ryan since elementary school."

Leslie regarded her redheaded friend with a new interest. "You went to a school for the gifted, didn't you?"

Brigid gave a small laugh. "So did Ryan. She studied aeronautics, physics, math and astronomy. She has a marvelous sense of the physical world and what makes it tick."

"I envy you Brig. It seems like so many people know her, or of her, and I'm practically in the dark about her."

"I think you're in love."

"I think you're right. But, how can I be? I only met her two weeks ago."

"Ryan is very appealing, and you are past being ready."

Leslie toyed with the dinner ring on her finger for a moment, then stood to look at the city glow. She knew it was more than being ready. Never before had she wanted to be with someone as much as she did with Ryan. "I don't understand it, Brig. She has so much going for her. Why don't Del and Star like her?"

With some reluctance, Brigid pulled herself up from the comfort of the couch and joined Leslie at the window. "They don't understand her. Ryan is a lot like a wild horse that was broken badly. She's stubborn, unpredictable and mean.''

"That's not very endearing.''

"Ah, but she's brilliant, talented. . .''

"Charming.''

"Sinfully so. She needs gentling, Les. Some steady handling could work wonders with her. You could be just the person to do that.'' Brigid caught a sparkle in the otherwise cool eyes.

Leslie felt encouraged. "Really?''

"Yes. What Ryan needs more than anything is patience and understanding.''

"And not condescension.''

"No. Never!''

"I found that out already.''

"Did she hit you?'' Brigid cringed at the thought of it.

"No. I'm not sure, but I think she was going to. Rags stopped her. Why?'' Leslie was more curious than ever.

"You got off easy then. The quickest way in the world to get Ryan to come out fighting is to question her judgment.''

"I guess we both suffer from cases of over-inflated prides.''

"Do I need to tell you that you'll be the one who has to swallow?''

"No. I can see that she won't bend.'' Leslie considered the whirlwind events of the past two weeks. "Brig, do you realize that she has been in two fights in the last twenty-four hours?''

Brigid chuckled softly. "I'd be surprised if she hadn't.''

Leslie bent to put her cigarette out in the ashtray on the table near her. "Are you kidding?''

"Hardly. They don't call us the fighting Irish for nothing.''

"You. You're not a fighter.''

"Oh, right. I forget. I'm supposed to be the laid back ceramicist who escaped to the peace of her mountain farm with her feminist lover and never makes any waves.'' Brigid's voice wasn't bitter, just informative. She shifted her weight on her crutches; she was starting to tire.

"That is the image you portray.''

"There isn't any way I could grow up with Ryan and *not* learn to fight. Granted, my reputation isn't as notorious as Ryan's, but I get in my share of them.''

"But you don't even go to the bars." Leslie was taken aback.

"I don't go to Cary's. When Star and I aren't getting along, I call up Ryan and we go raise hell in some of the less reputable bars in town. Crutches aren't any protection against a good fight. And Ryan, she doesn't even have to look for fights. They find her."

"I thought I knew you."

"You know the part of me that Star is comfortable with. She can't stand for people to know that we argue, or that I like Ryan. She thinks it would ruin the image she is trying to uphold."

"That's fascinating. I'm amazed." Leslie smiled. "Still, it feels good to have someone sincere on my side. I thought Rags was, but it turns out that she's after Sanji."

Brigid's expression soured. "That's to be expected. The women who aren't after you or Dana are after Sanji. Rags." Brigid felt a bitter taste in her mouth. "There is someone you should definitely stay away from. She is major trouble."

"Is she?" Leslie wondered.

"Absolutely. Steer clear of her. You look tired. I know I am. I've been up since four A.M."

"I'm exhausted."

"You could do with a farm fix. Why not come up next weekend? We can talk more."

"I would love to."

"Good. Now let's get out of here. All these drunken dykes are depressing me."

8

Rags crawled out of her sleep to answer the phone. She reached beyond the covers and grabbed the receiver from the stand next to her bed. "Hullo." She rubbed her eyes and focused on the clock. 12:30. It was dark.

A thick male voice vibrated in her ear. "Rags, you better come down here."

Rags could hear loud music and voices in the background. "Come down where? Who is this?" Sleep still dulled her senses.

"It's Barry at The Shed."

"What's wrong?"

"Ryan's causing all kinds of problems, trying to start fights and throwing things. I've asked her to leave twice, but she won't budge."

"Just throw her out. Wait! The Shed? I sent her home two hours ago."

"I wish. Can you come and get her out of here?"

"Yeah. Crap. I'll be right there."

—◦✦❀✦◦—

Barry hung up the phone and went back to washing glasses behind the bar. A burly, bearded patron leaned over to complain, "I can't believe that skinny girl is raising so much hell. Why doesn't somebody throw her out on her ass?"

"Because," Barry paused in his chore, "that skinny little girl owns this place. I don't know about you, bud, but I need my job.''

"A girl owns a men's bar?''

"You must be new around here, fella. I don't care who pays the bills. She usually doesn't come around, but when she does, nobody bothers her.''

The disgruntled patron took his drink and walked away, shaking his head.

When Barry looked up next, Ryan was gone. "Oh, shit.'' He turned to call Rags again, but there was no answer.

Ryan didn't know herself how she got home, but arrive she did. Sanji was still awake. Ryan was glad she wouldn't have to hassle with locks or alarms. She just walked in the back door and closed it carefully behind her. She did so to show Sanji, standing in the living room, that she was still able to control her actions. The smell of fear permeated the room, blending with the piquant odor of liquor on Ryan's breath.

Sanji tried to get drunk earlier in the day, hoping to shore up her courage for when Ryan returned home. Afternoon and evening passed — Ryan didn't show. Sanji spent the rest of the night sober and frightened. She vacillated between worrying about what Ryan would do when she got home and concern that she might not make it home.

About ten, she had gotten the idea that Ryan could be distracted sexually. She showered, fixed her hair in a knot atop her head and donned the dress Ryan showed the most favor toward. Thus she remained, paralyzed, for hours.

The stony gaze she fell under mimicked sobriety and encouraged her plan. Ryan pointed to the floor before her. Sanji measured the distance between her terrified stance and Ryan's firmly rooted feet. Ryan's supremacy attracted her like flame that draws insects to their peril.

Ryan knew what Sanji was up to, dressed in white, revealing her long legs with each step she took. Alternately the sleek legs would expose themselves through the slit that originated just below her crotch. The breasts were covered simply with triangles

94

of fabric that tied behind the neck, leaving the back fully naked.

A soft sheen of perspiration shimmered on her warm brown skin. The light made it sparkle and brought an insistent burn to Ryan's groin. Ryan focused on the dusky eyes and let the magic flash through her bloodstream. She allowed the sex goddess to grow more secure that her enchantment was taking hold.

The well-used scenario began to play itself out. As a hundred times before, they retraced Sanji's steps through the living room to the door adjacent to the front entrance. The door to the basement.

Ryan opened the door and turned on the light. She looked down the stairs and steeled herself for the descent. She was beginning to feel her involuntary muscle control weaken. Summoning the full extent of her will, she grasped the handrail for support and took each step with deliberate care.

Two steps from the bottom was a landing edged by a wall. A wall whose presence she welcomed. Bracing her back against it, she looked up at Sanji and smiled. Her expression was inviting on the outside.

Sanji didn't hesitate to take her cue to descend to the pleasure palace, knowing her every move would be voyeurized and devoured by the despot at the foot of the stairs. Her full length gown trailed along the steps behind her. Silver, strapless heels challenged her grace and made her breasts sway with each step. She watched Ryan lick her lips hungrily, mentally devouring her dark triangle, clearly visible to her from where she stood. Sanji would always pray for the last steps to come, knowing that her own desperate need would threaten to betray her and make her falter.

She managed to reach the landing, her will completely consumed and possessed by Ryan. A willing victim, she surrendered the last vestiges of her spirit, placing her full trust in Ryan's hands.

Ryan reached for the base of Sanji's neck and guided the beauty down the last two stairs of their journey. The basement was cool and quiet, the sound of Sanji's heels announced their arrival on the tile. Sanji in tow, Ryan turned on the light above the pool table. In advance, she decided to forego any number of games they could indulge in and get directly to the climax.

In the middle of the basement was an unpainted steel pole.

Several feet up its length, hanging from a hook was a pair of unlined wristbands. It was here that Ryan halted. She untied the knot on Sanji's neck and casually watched the fabric slide down and expose her breasts.

With automatic efficiency, Ryan took the wristbands from the pole and fastened them to the black wrists. In one fluid motion she clasped them together and returned them to their perch on the pole. This maneuver brought Sanji flush against the frigid steel and left her feet just barely touching the floor.

The contrast of the cold steel against Sanji's smouldering flesh concentrated the agony of her need in her vagina.

Ryan manipulated the shining sable globes, separated them to wedge the two-inch shaft in the tight cleavage, compressing the breastbone against its unforgiving strength. Sanji moaned softly as the pain transmitted pleasure to her brain. Ryan used her boot to nudge her victim's feet apart and away, robbing her of what little balance and leverage she still had.

Before inspecting her work, Ryan walked across the barren room to the small bathroom and relieved her urgent bladder. In Ryan's brief absence, Sanji relaxed the muscles in her neck and let her head fall against her strained back. She took inventory of the silence and the sterility of the basement. Ryan's eccentric use of white tile on the floor and walls manifested the need to keep distractions to a minimum. The furniture was limited to a pool table, rarely used for pool; a bed; a chair; and a set of antique gun cabinets. She closed her eyes and shivered a moment at the thought of the contents of one of the cabinets — not guns.

Somewhat refreshed and restored, Ryan returned to her subject. She stood in front of Sanji and surveyed the helpless scene, the firm bosoms protruding vulnerably, caressing their steel prison; the long arms straining against the full body weight; the imperiled feet.

Ryan's body began to rebel; she swayed slightly. She caught herself and willed its obedience, despite the alarming volume of alcohol in her system. Her hands performed as they were bid, and she lit a cigarette, then reached for Sanji's nipple.

The sound of Ryan's loud exhale was the first sound Sanji heard from her. She tensed, knowing the touch would follow.

With the cigarette cradled carelessly between her first and

second fingers, Ryan twisted the hardened nipple cruelly, eliciting a heavy sigh from Sanji. The filter of the cigarette rubbed along the tortured skin in the process. Ryan bent to it and inhaled from the cigarette, simultaneously sucking the nipple into her anxious mouth.

Sanji wailed softly. Though one of the shortest sex games they played, it remained her favorite.

While gluttonously attacking the tit with her mouth, Ryan's hand unerringly located the moist clitoris and began massaging it. The object of their game was for Sanji to come before the cigarette, lodged in the crook of Ryan's fingers and spilling smoke up the gauzy dress, could burn her hand.

The orgasm consumed Sanji's body and rampaged her system. The force of her contractions knocked the ashes off the glowing coal that had burned within a quarter inch of its goal.

Ryan dropped the cigarette to the tile and stubbed it out with her boot. She didn't stop to soothe and relieve her partner. She walked away from the scene; cool and detached.

She walked over to the one cabinet that had no guns in it and opened its carved door. She wasted no time deciding which implement to use; that decision had been made hours ago at the restaurant.

Determined, her hand encircled the worn bullwhip. She savored the feel of it, noting how she had missed using it. The effects of Rags' directive against its use on Sanji were overpowered by Ryan's ungoverned rage.

Sanji's sobs ceased and her breathing became more regular, allowing her once again to be aware of her surroundings. The position of the cabinet, relative to her captive stance, was by design. Denying her foreknowledge of what instruments of pain/pleasure Ryan might contemplate using heightened sexual tension.

Confusion set into Sanji's mind. By now she should have been released from her bondage and led to the bed for a night of lovemaking. Her wrists began to ache, no longer protected by the altered state of arousal. Cramps began to form in her neck. She moved her head from side to side to chase away the stiffness. She found comfort lodging her head between the pole and her right arm. The sweat that covered her was beginning to cool.

Ryan's footsteps, closing in from the rear, gave her gooseflesh. Her sweet womanly odor soured with fear. She bolted inside her skin when Ryan coughed deeply. For tense seconds her own breath failed her as she listened to the rasping struggle Ryan was suffering.

Ryan held her ribs tightly. The piercing pain served to clear her mind for the task at hand. Once recovered, she walked up to her enslaved partner to speak her only words of the night.

In clear deliberate tones she addressed her victim. "You didn't honestly think you were going to get away with this, did you?" She watched Sanji's eyes widen fearfully. Ryan looked directly at Sanji to force her to anticipate what lay ahead. Purposefully, she held the whip out of the line of vision. Not caring if Sanji answered, she revealed the intensity of her evil intentions with her eyes. "I made you come because I want what I'm going to do next to *hurt*. You will regret what you did today for the rest of your life."

Before the echo of her warning could disappear into the night chill, Ryan stepped away from her target, the distance gauged easily from years of practice. The sound of the leather falling to the floor broke the silence, followed closely by the pitched wail as the snake severed the air. Ryan planted her feet squarely, balancing herself to absorb the thrill that overcame her as the whip reversed directions and made contàct with Sanji's unsuspecting back.

The whip rewarded Ryan for the life she had given it with the narcotic of pure sound. The wha-ack heralded the intense, high frequency of Sanji's blood-curdling scream. Ryan abandoned her hold on reality and reveled in the sensations. She floated outside of herself and watched her body deliver the blows. Gone were the restraints she normally placed on her inner demons. This was not to be a carefully executed sexual discipline. This was premeditated, unabridged punishment, delivered without mercy. For a moment, Ryan stoped caring if Sanji lived to regret it.

Mercy came, unbidden, in the form of Ryan's rebellious body. The exertion of wielding the whip exhausted her recesses of energy. Ryan didn't know when Sanji stopped screaming or how many blows lay open the limp form. She didn't care.

A sickening dizziness overcame her, and she blinked against

the swaying floor. Drawn like a magnet to the chair, she staggered to it, sat down and joined Sanji in the realm of unconsciousness.

—◦◆◊{◊◆◦—

Rags sped down the winding lanes to Ryan's home. More worried than angry, she knew something was wrong. Pulling into the drive and seeing the lights of the house still glowing at such a late hour did little to ease her concern.

Barely securing a full stop in her truck, she jumped out, yanking the keys out of the ignition. When she reached the back porch, her key for the alarm was poised. She halted in mid-action, seeing the red light was not on. Her concern doubled when she tried the door and it yielded to her touch. She closed the door behind her and looked about for signs of trouble. "Ryan?" Her heart sank when she sensed the pain emanating from the area of the basement. She made a beeline through the dining room and living room and braced herself at the top of the stairs. Hurling herself down the steps two at a time, she used the handrail to brake her descent.

She stood on the landing for a brief moment, her face a frozen landscape of horror. Only her eyes moved, taking in the scene. Following the line of destruction from Sanji's limp head, down the desecrated, ruined back, then down the soft white dress, steaked with blood that had not yet dried. A drop of blood clipped her vision, falling silently in the small pool on the tile. To the left, the reddened tip of the venomous weapon drew her attention to the perpetrator of the bloody vengeance whose aftermath she was witnessing.

Sorrow rose to her throat. "Oh god," she breathed. She took the last two stairs individually, with grief laden steps.

Cursing audibly, she expertly freed Sanji. "Why? Why Anara? Will your thirst for blood never be sated?" Cradling Sanji's limp form in her strong arms, she listened for the answer. It came, disrupting her thoughts. "What is needed, is done."

The voice seared in her brain, devoid of emotion. Rags had learned to keep her exchanges with this voice from beyond to a relative few, minimizing the pain they caused her. The response came as no surprise to her. Anara would have her way, and Rags would do as she was bid in her service.

The intensity of her emotions, the sadness she felt for the ravaged beauty she held so dearly, alerted Rags that she was becoming far too human. She ignored the danger signals.

She laid Sanji gently on the bed and whispered to her, "Stay unconscious, my love. You don't want to know this pain." She inspected the back. What little skin was left was puffy and welted. She knew she couldn't take proper care of devastation this extensive; she needed help. She wrapped Sanji in the blankets from the bed to guard against shock and smoothed some loose hair away from the unresponsive face with a tender gesture. "I love you."

In the next moment Rags felt the psychic monitor she placed on Ryan sever and float away like a feather caught by a breeze. "No!"

Instantly, she crossed the room and pulled Ryan from the chair. The handle of the bullwhip fell to the floor. She stretched Ryan on the floor next to it and began to force air into her lungs. "Breathe, damn you!"

Resentment mounted inside Rags as she labored to save Ryan. She knew she couldn't leave her to die, no matter how tempting it was. Yet, her thoughts were for Sanji's welfare. Torn between her best friend and the woman she loved, for the first time she experienced what it was to feel helpless.

After what seemed like an eternity, Ryan reclaimed her fragile hold on life and began to breathe on her own. Rags sat back on her heels and sighed. "You're gonna pay for this in *this* lifetime, bitch. Don't think for a minute that I'll let you slip away that easily. Let's walk."

She hoisted Ryan to her feet and began pacing the length of the basement.

When she was no longer sure she cared what happened to Ryan, she heard a faint moan come from the depths of Ryan's being. Then a louder one, followed by a jerk. Rags stopped and lifted Ryan's chin. "Stay with me." She guided Ryan to the pool table and let go. Ryan's reflexes worked and she caught herself on the table, breaking her fall.

Ryan opened her eyes. She squinted immediately, trying to focus on Rags' boots. Her gaze followed up the faded jeans and the wrinkled shirt and, reluctantly, the rugged face.

"How many?" Rags held up three fingers.

"Three." Ryan's tongue stuck to the roof of her mouth, hampering her reply.

"Do you know where you are?"

Ryan looked at the table that held her up and winced from the light. Her survey continued around the white room, halting at the bed and the figure that lay there. A vague sense of what she had done floated into her consciousness. "Yeah."

Rags felt for a pulse, found a strong one. "You'll live." The crisis had passed, Rags knew from the last time Ryan had done this. "You need to eat."

Ryan nodded her head compliantly.

Rags closed in and grabbed Ryan's shirt collar. "You know you're in deep shit here. If you ever want to fly again, you'll do as I say." Her voice was husky and deadly.

Ryan remained expressionless, but attentive.

"Eat. Sleep it off and dry *out*. Call Phil so he won't worry. I *am* taking Sanji from you." She let Ryan go, knowing her point was driven home. She turned to gather Sanji and the blankets in her arms. "I have to get her to a healer. I'll be back later for some of her things and the Volvo."

Ryan watched Rags disappear up the stairway, feeling nothing.

9

Staring at the cheese and apple slices on the plate before her, Ryan massaged her neck, trying to relieve the tension. The peace of sleep was not possible. Liquor languished in her bloodstream, slowing her physically. The cathartic effect of returning to life brought a mental alertness to her.

Filled with a sense of purpose, she partook of the sparse meal before her as though it were her first. Refreshed, stronger, she pushed the chair away from the breakfast bar that lined the wall between the refrigerator and the entrance of the dining room.

The kitchen was small and convenient, unlike the vastness of the rest of the house. The fact that there was any food in the house at all was a tribute to Sanji's healthy appetite and the housekeeper's indefatigable attempts to care for Ryan.

Ryan put the plate and knife in the sink. Truth forced an enormous sigh. "What are you running from, Ryan?" she asked herself. "What out there could be more frightening than what you've become?" She knew the time had come to turn and fight her demons.

Just a few steps from where she stood, beckoning to her out of the past, was the stairway to her father's vacant apartment. Ryan ran her fingers through her hair, summoned her courage, and ascended the stairs in the dark.

At the top, she paused on the landing before the heavy, masculine door. It opened easily in the face of her determination. The smell of pipe tobacco lingered on the dusty walls and furniture, assaulting her memory. To lessen the visual impact, she made her way to a small table lamp. She turned the lamp on, and straightened to take it all in. The rich wooden paneling soaked up the rays greedily, softening the shadows. The bookshelves bulged with fine leatherbound volumes on history and art, her father's favorite interests. Massive furniture crowded the study, making dents in the thick woven carpet. In the corner, by the fireplace, the cherrywood desk she had used for her studies despaired in its disuse.

She walked over to it, barely managing the flood of memories it brought to her. The days of devouring every bit of aviation history and technique from books her father would bring home, sometimes from England, Germany or France, filled her heart.

She shook her head and took a cigarette from her jacket pocket. She found an ashtray and sat in the overstuffed chair before the fireplace, stirring a puff of dust that settled on her black jeans. She lit her cigarette and forced herself to look at the portrait that hung above the mantle.

Peering through the shadows, her father's grieving green eyes regarded her. His crisp black hair, lightened at the temples, drew out the translucent skin. She recognized the family sorrow, seeing it etched daily in her bathroom mirror.

A beam of sunlight brightened the room. Ryan sat, unmoved; lost. The portrait resumed its one-dimensional silence. She blinked, unaware of low long she had been staring into her father's oil eyes. Depressed, lonely, she stood and addressed him. "If you couldn't teach me how to live without you, the least you could have done was to show me how to die gracefully."

With a great need for consolation, she left the apartment, turning out the lamp and closing the door quietly behind her. Once in her room, she lay on her bed to search for the mercy of sleep.

She slept straight through Sunday. She roused Monday morning. A glance at the clock on the stand reminded her of Rags' admonition. She picked up the phone, put it on her abdomen and called her friend. "Phil, I'm too wrecked to fly today."

"God, what's wrong?" Phil was worried.

"Man, it's just too much booze. I'll be fine by tomorrow."

Ryan hoped fervently that she would be. She hung up the phone and closed her eyes against the emptiness in her heart. Leslie's face burned an image on the back of her eyelids. "Are you going to let her in or not?" Her heart and hand replied in unison. She opened her eyes and dialed information. "What's the number for Western Union?"

"Have a telegram for Leslie Serle."

Charlotte looked up from her typewriter, surprised. "I'll take it. She has a client just now."

The handsome youth smiled and let Charlotte sign for it. He handed it over and walked out, hurrying to his next delivery. Charlotte laid the envelope on the desk and patted it as if to feel if hidden inside was a dangerous animal.

Telegrams made her uneasy, a holdover from the war that robbed her of her husband. She accomplished little in the time before Leslie emerged from her office with the client. Once the client was seen safely out the door, Charlotte held up the envelope with trepidation.

"This came for you."

"Why so worried?" Leslie took the envelope and opened it.

"Telegrams make me nervous."

Leslie flashed a sympathetic look in Charlotte's direction and read the cable.

"Peace? I want to see you. Be home all day. Please come by. Ryan." At the bottom appeared a phone number and address.

"Well?"

Leslie smiled broadly at her friend.

"Good news?"

"The best. I finally got invited to Ryan's home. Hopefully, she'll be alone."

"I'm happy for you." Charlotte tried to share Leslie's enthusiasm.

Leslie was too excited to notice the insincerity in Charlotte's voice.

As soon as Leslie had gone back to her office, Charlotte

knocked on Delores' door.

"Come in."

Charlotte opened the door partway and poked her head in. "Can I talk to you a minute?"

"Sure, come in." Delores waved the secretary to sit down.

"Leslie just got invited to Ryan's home." Charlotte didn't bother to sit, instead stood, wringing her hands.

Delores stopped writing, looked over her reading glasses at Charlotte. "Not good. We're going to have to escalate things a little." Delores bent her head a little to write a name on a note pad. Handing the page to Charlotte, "I want you to get me the court record for this person as soon as possible."

Ryan finished drying her hair and dressed in fresh clothes. Sleeping through the day had made her stiff and headachy. She wanted desperately to have a drink, but refrained, mindful of Rags and what would happen if she disobeyed her. The shower helped wake her up, but did little to settle her stomach. The thought of eating made her head pound all the harder.

The days were beginning to lengthen, the house was still light. Venturing out of the womblike darkness of her bedroom she made her way to the living room and sat in one of the pale upholstered chairs near the front window. Her eyes sought the cathedral ceiling, lined with dark beams with two massive chandeliers hanging from them. She rubbed her temples in easy, circular motions.

The telephone demanded her attention. She sighed and got up to answer it. "Hello," she said flatly.

"Miss O'Donnell?"

"Un hun," she replied, annoyed.

"Ma'am, this is Mark at the guard station. There is a Miss Leslie Serle here to see you. Shall I let her in?"

Ryan's heart skipped a beat. "Yes, please! Mark?"

"Ma'am?"

"Will you give her directions for me? Miss Serle has not been here before."

"I'll be glad to. Anything else?"

"That will be fine, thank you."

Ryan hung the phone up and made a victorious fist to herself. "Alright."

She didn't bother to soften her happiness. Leslie's arrival made her headache flee temporarily, allowing a clear sparkle to shine in her eyes.

Leslie stood in the doorway answering Ryan's joy with a satisfied smile. "I could devote my life to making those eyes sparkle like that."

"I won't stop you. Do come in." Ryan stepped back into the circular foyer to allow Leslie to enter.

Leslie walked in and passed Ryan, not waiting to have her coat removed. Instead, she made straight for the painting above the fireplace. She stared in unabashed fascination for a moment then turned to Ryan. "Degas! Danseuses a la Barre, isn't it?"

Ryan walked up to Leslie and took the fur from her and laid it on the couch. "You know your art, but it's just a replica. If I'd been sober the day of the auction my agent could have talked me into going the extra fifty thousand or so over his million dollar limit that it would have taken to get it last year. I don't know what got into me. Not ruthless enough, I guess." A tint of sadness colored her statement.

Leslie's eyes widened visibly, then she shook her head in amazement. "You are outrageous! You actually sound upset you didn't win the bid."

Ryan took her eyes from the painting and looked at her guest standing before her, alive and animated with wonder. She could scarcely believe that Leslie had actually come to see her. She was finding herself aroused by Leslie's youthful enthusiasm. "I was, for a while. Something my father always used to say about patronizing the artist, and not the work." Ryan felt herself moved by the springy bounce in Leslie's blonde hair, and the crispness of the grey eyes that seemed confused just now.

"What do you mean?"

Ryan found it difficult to stop looking at Leslie's incredible figure, outlined by a blue linen suit and rose crepe blouse, long enough to form an answer. "He always thought it incredibly narcissistic to spend that much money on one piece of art." She stopped to lick her lips, distracted by the stirring between her legs.

"He liked to help out an artist or two while they were living and in need, not make some dealer rich. I just haven't gotten around to following his advice."

"Well, I can think of a couple. . . what are you doing?"

"I'm going to make love to you," Ryan replied evenly as she unbuttoned Leslie's blouse.

Leslie's breath quickened and faltered as she watched Ryan, standing with such nonchalance, reach out and pull open the front of her blouse and gaze hungrily at her breasts. She closed her eyes. Her sex quickened with electric shocks darting through her system. She knew her nipples were hardening; she opened her eyes to see the effect register on Ryan's face. She was not disappointed. She wanted to swoon.

"Where's Sanji?" she managed to whisper.

"Moved out."

The absence of feeling in Ryan's reply reassured her that they were indeed alone. The kind of alone she had yearned for since the night at the restaurant when they had first kissed. The memory of that kiss reinforced her passion.

Ryan passed the back of her fingers over Leslie's nipple with a gentle deliberateness. Leslie let out a fierce moan.

"Come on." Ryan slipped an arm around Leslie's contoured waist and guided her down the hall to the bedroom.

She offered no resistance to Ryan's invitation. Ryan's style intrigued her. There had been no real preliminaries. She had simply opened her blouse, touched her ever so slightly and was escorting her down the long hall that she assumed led to love.

She tried to watch Ryan instead of where they were walking. To her surprise Ryan's gaze was fixed on her bouncing breasts. Leslie looked down and glimpsed her firm, pointed tits playing hide and seek through the opening in her top. The visual effect overpowered her. She wanted to stop there, in the hall, and make wild, abandoned love.

Ryan pressed on, tightening her grip on her weakening prey, demanding without words that Leslie control herself.

She complied, sensing that Ryan knew what she was about and exactly what she wanted. Ryan's uncompromising certainty aroused her curiosity — she held on. She wanted to know what was going to happen now that she could see Ryan was not to be swayed by momentary passions, rather could direct her actions through her arousal.

At the doorway to the bedroom, Ryan stopped and reached in front of Leslie to turn on the light. The rich reds and textures assaulted Leslie's senses; so unprepared for the way the room looked compared to what she had imagined. Yet, somehow she had expected the drapes to be pulled and the room dark. She looked down to the creamy carpet devouring the spikes of her heels, slowing her progress. The warm lamplight bathed the room; the bed looked as firm and unforgiving as Ryan.

"This is your room?" Leslie whispered with a tinge of awe.

Ryan eased around to Leslie's back and kissed her softly on the neck. Leslie relaxed to her touch, making it simpler for Ryan to remove the suitjacket. Ryan folded it and laid it on top of the dresser behind her, then returned to attend to Leslie's neck. She traced a line up the shoulder to the ear and answered with a warm whisper, "Like it?"

"Oh, Ryan." Leslie turned to face her. "I do, but I like its occupant better. I have wanted this for so long." The strain of her desire was wearing on her brow. The closeness of Ryan's body was driving her mad.

Ryan reached up and curled a lock of Leslie's hair playfully around her finger. Leslie was so distracted by Ryan's tormenting detachment, she didn't notice that Ryan's other hand had unbottoned and unzipped her skirt. When it slid to the floor, Ryan smiled. "Then we'll just have to do something about that."

Leslie sighed frantically. The mischief in Ryan's voice was making it difficult for her to maintain a hold on what little sanity she had left. She retained enough awareness to feel Ryan's thumbs hook in the elastic of her slip, the tug of the waistband straining against her buttocks, the featherlight sensation as the slip fell in a wreath atop her skirt.

"Take them off," Ryan demanded with gentle authority.

Without coaxing, Leslie stepped out of the circle of clothes, slipped out of her high heels and removed her pantyhose, the last barrier to her burning crotch. She bent to gather her clothes and fold them in a neat pile. When she rose, Ryan took them from her and placed them on the dresser.

"I prefer garterbelts and stockings," Ryan instructed, with a deep warmth that preserved Leslie's dignity.

Leslie watched Ryan stop to light a cigarette, grateful for the delicate way she handled herself.

Tactful still, "Put your shoes back on."

Leslie knew that the last statement was not a request; it sounded distinctly like an order, couched in restrained courtesy. Instinctively, she stepped back and donned her shoes. They felt odd without nylons. Now her feet felt as vulnerable as the rest of her. Her desire mounting, she wanted Ryan to capitalize on her weakening will.

Ryan made a small hand signal. Leslie pivoted to give Ryan the overview she wanted. She relied heavily on her experience as a model to pull the turn off with some finesse on the plush carpeting. Facing again in Ryan's direction, she saw, by the expression on Ryan's face, how truly vulnerable she really was. Beyond the obvious sensations of nakedness, clad purposely in just an open blouse and heels, she knew an inner vulnerability, brought on by the subtle interplays of giving and receiving. She was giving her will and Ryan was receiving it, skillfully, like it belonged to her all along.

Ryan inhaled audibly, "Outstanding," then blew the cigarette smoke out slowly, teasing Leslie. She offered the filtertip to Leslie's lips, narrowing her eyes as she extracted the final control over Leslie's sexuality.

Her eyes focused on the veiled menace in Ryan's green eyes, and she told herself from that moment on she wanted always to belong to Ryan in this way. Her heart treated her to a special thrill, an inner satisfaction of knowing that her figure met with approval. She was glad that Ryan made her wait, compelling her to savor the gradual building of sexual tension. Ryan abandoned the cigarette in an ashtray on the dresser and was coming toward her. She swayed and was caught in Ryan's confident grasp.

"I want you." Ryan squeezed Leslie cruelly in her arms. Her throaty statement melted into a wanton kiss.

Self-government was abolished in Leslie's soul as she found herself being seated on the bed. Ryan's fingers tangled in her hair, palms covering her ears, pressure was applied, her head was guided downward.

Leslie was no longer able to look at Ryan's face. Instead, before her was a churning crotch, tightly bound in black denim. Ryan's fingers gripped hard and forced her lips into it. Leslie felt something snap inside her, loosing an animal from within. Savagely, she attacked the grinding cunt with her teeth. Ryan's heady fragrance intoxicated her, encouraging her to do her utmost to satisfy this merciless need. The barbarous, gutteral moans reaching her ears from Ryan's depths disconnected Leslie from the pain of the brutal beating her mouth was suffering. Without noticing, she was assisting Ryan's movements with her hands on the black hips. Her own noises blended with Ryan's and built in a crescendo, climaxing in a piercing scream as Ryan let go her ferocious orgasm.

Not pausing to recover, Ryan brought Leslie to her feet, picked her up and placed her on the bed. She crawled on top of her, making her bear the full weight of her body and kissed her and caressed her wildly. Unable to speak, she went on mashing the delicate mouth until her breathing became less labored.

Ryan seldom allowed anyone to make love to her. She usually took whatever orgasms she got from sheer excitement, but they were never as intense, the release never on a par with what she was feeling now. She shifted her weight to her elbow and slid part way off her lover. Leslie was glistening with perspiration and the heat of passion, her eyes were glazed, Ryan's clear. "Where have you been all my life?" Ryan asked sincerely.

A sexy smile penetrated the lust haze on Leslie's features. She knew that she had just been paid the highest compliment possible.

Ryan closed Leslie's eyelids with kisses. She ran her tongue down the bridge of the nose, stopped to kiss the lips gently. She rolled further off to the side and began to follow the inviting trail that wound down the neck, over the breastbone to the crossroads between the breasts. Leslie hissed her approval as Ryan administered first the right one, then the left.

She reached down to the back of the soft white knees and brought them up, the feet followed. The spikes of the shoes dug into the spread they lay on. Ryan shifted more and urged Leslie to edge further up the bed. She took her place between Leslie's bent knees and massaged her hips. Leslie began to relax and cooperate as Ryan bent her head toward the willing blonde cunt.

111

Leslie could feel Ryan's hot breath on her wet lips, sending chills up her spine, but she was totally unprepared when Ryan hoisted her thighs on her strong shoulders and straightened under their weight. Ryan came up on her knees, cradled Leslie's hips and dived into the anxious love palace.

Leslie gasped in surprise. She was inverted helplessly. Ryan's thighs were planted powerfully behind her shoulders. Leslie's knees were above Ryan's head. She strained her neck to see what the spectacle looked like. She had no way of preparing herself for the unearthly look on Ryan's face, lost in her task. Leslie squeezed her thighs together, let her head relax and joined her lover in the other land of sexual abandonment. She let Ryan's talented tongue send her over the edge, push her beyond the boundaries she maintained carefully in her waking, adult life. She knew that she wouldn't be able to linger there long; the pressing urgency of her sexual organs brought her to a pinpoint focus. Her own incoherent raving made her come back to her senses. The blood rushing away from her abdomen fell doubly hard to her heart and head. She was very near begging for mercy from the intensity of her orgasm. At the very instant she felt she could no longer bear the painful bliss, Ryan lay her gently and lovingly down. Ryan joined Leslie on the bed and gathered her up into waiting arms and spoke soft, comforting entreaties in her ear.

She pulled the spread from the side of the bed and covered Leslie's happy body with it and propped a pillow under her head. She put her head on her hand and rested on her elbow.

With her left hand she reached into her shirt pocket and freed the pack of cigarettes, shook one up and grabbed it between her teeth, then drew it out. She put the pack on Leslie's stomach and dug her lighter out of her pant pocket. Before she lit it, she brushed a damp strand of hair out of Leslie's eyes. She lit the cigarette and inhaled with a hiss and offered the filtertip to Leslie, who took it hungrily. Ryan let the smoke escape through her nose as she watched Leslie close her eyes; satisfied. "You okay?"

"Never better. Where have *you* been all *my* life? Leslie wondered happily. She rested her head next to Ryan's chest and listened to a heavy sigh escape its confines. "What's wrong?"

Ryan took another deep drag. "I'm falling in love with you, Leslie."

A warmth swelled over Leslie, making her short of breath. "What's wrong with that?"

After extinguishing the cigarette in the ashtray next to the bed, Ryan lifted Leslie's chin up to look into her soft grey eyes. "Nothing. I'm just not used to things going right in my life, and I don't want this to end."

"It won't if I can help it." Leslie touched Ryan's face gently. "I'm already in love with you."

"Come here." Ryan closed the conversation with a luxurious kiss. They drifted into the dreamy sleep of lovers.

—◦✦❦✦◦—

Leslie woke with a start. "Rags!"

Her exclamation stirred Ryan. "What?" she inquired evenly.

"You filthy whore!" Rags crossed over to the bed threateningly.

Ryan stilled Leslie, who had risen slightly in protest. "Shh, she means me."

"You have absolutely no shame," Rags yelled.

"I had the best teacher," Ryan replied hotly. She sat up and found the cigarettes that had fallen between Leslie and her leg, casting an angry sideways glance at Rags.

Rags' wrath filled the room with a steely presence that wavered on the verge of taking on a life of its own. She curtailed it just ahead of the crisis point as she was wont to do. She checked her labored breathing and stabilized her system. "Sanji had better not ever hear of this. Even you can see the wisdom in that."

Ryan nodded her head in agreement. Leslie let out her breath in relief.

"Where are the keys?"

"On the dresser."

Rags turned her back on the couple and walked to the dresser, opened the carved alabaster box and found the spare set of Volvo keys. "When did you eat last?"

"This morning."

"Get your ass in the kitchen and eat something. I want to talk to you." Rags left them to find some of Sanji's personal things.

113

Ryan handed Leslie a cigarette and took one for herself, lit both of them then headed for the bathroom.

Leslie had surprised herself with how calm she was feeling. She looked in the direction of the light in the bathroom and threw the cover off. She opened the closet door in search of a robe. She put it on, savoring Ryan's lingering scent permeating it. She glanced at the photos on the wall then walked into the bath. "Does Rags always walk in unannounced like that?"

Ryan stopped in the middle of swallowing pain pills. "She has keys. She didn't expect to find anyone here." She finished taking the pills. "That looks better on you than it ever did me."

Leslie picked up the bottle of pain pills and read the label. Percodan. She looked at Ryan. "Just how bad are your ribs anyway?"

"Two of them are broken," Ryan answered.

"Why didn't you tell me?"

"Would you have made love with me if you'd known?"

"No."

Ryan gave her a "there's your answer" look and a quick kiss. "I have to eat something."

After Ryan left the room, Leslie looked down at her shoes and it occurred to her that she was glad Ryan hadn't told her. A rush shot through her. "Steady Les." She splashed water on her face — her stomach rumbled. She didn't finish the cigarette Ryan had given her. She wasn't accustomed to the flavor of it. Wanting one of her own, she walked out of the bedroom and down the hall to the living room to retrieve her purse.

In passing the first entrance to the kitchen, she saw Ryan at the sink, head bent over her work. When she reached the second entrance her eyes were drawn to Rags standing next to the stove, pulling the gloves out of her back pocket. Curiosity made her stop; alarm suspended her.

Ryan was absorbed in the chore of slicing cheese; the motion of Rags taking the black leather gloves from her back pocket had gone unnoticed. Rags slid her hand into the black sheath, her eyes fixed on Ryan, waiting for Ryan's attention to be diverted in her direction. Her fingers located their individual homes. Rags stretched out her hand and flexed her fingers, while tugging on the base of the glove.

Ryan saw the ominous black hand flexing out of the corner of her eye. The knife fell from her hand into the sink. Her knees buckled under her, driving into the cabinet door below the sink. She caught herself on the countertop, and turned toward Rags; eyes widened. "God. No."

Rags took a step closer, smoothed the leather over her fist, showing the knuckles more clearly. "I think it's about time you had a refresher course in obedience."

Ryan's new found survival instinct gave strength to her legs. She began to take slow, uncertain steps backwards, edging along the counter, transfixed on Rags' hands. Her mouth went completely dry.

Rags slid her other hand into its glove, countering each step Ryan took.

"No." Ryan found her voice again. With each step she took, her pleas became more frantic. The wall halted her progress. She was cornered; a frightened animal. She was unable to look into Rags' eyes, not wanting to know what she would find radiating from them. Once before she had and the memory of it choked her. Her vision tunneled in on the powerful fists. "No. Please no. Rags, I'll do anything, just don't." Her eyes filled with tears. She summoned all her strength to hold back the sobs, knowing it would only aggravate an already desperate situation if she allowed herself to be reduced to a weeping supplicant. She managed to take her eyes off the dangerous fists and find retreat in the ceiling. After the battle with her tears was won, she returned to a respectful posture.

The left hand was smoothing the right fist, summoning Ryan's consideration. When Rags was certain that Ryan was completely demoralized, she spoke. "I've had it with you, Ryan." The peril in her voice reverberated in Ryan's mind. "I *will* not take any more crap off you. I can't believe you went to The Shed. I sent you *home*." Rags' anger flared anew. Ryan's disobedience made her blood boil over.

Ryan took short shallow breaths — her fear trembled through her.

"Sanji's a fucking mess. You, by god, better stay away from her."

"I promise. Anything you want." Ryan's voice quivered

erratically.

"Stay away from me too — I can't stand to look at you. God, you make me sick," she spat.

Ryan nodded her head in agreement, unable to speak.

Rags pointed toward Leslie. "You can fucking forget about seeing her!"

Ryan's hand came to her mouth and her eyes opened wider. She looked at Leslie in despair. Leslie met Ryan's eyes in shock.

Rags saw their response and was satisfied that she had dealt a blow as destructive as any her fists ever could. She left Ryan plastered to the wall and walked by Leslie to finish the chore she came for.

Ryan watched Rags remove the gloves and return them to the back pocket. As an afterthought, Rags added, "If you need a piece of tail, go find Christine." She picked up the suitcase she packed and left.

Ryan closed her eyes, and her hand came down to brace herself against the wall. "Oh, shi-i-i-t."

Leslie took her hands off her cheeks and found she could move again. "What was that about?"

Ryan ignored her, felt tentatively for the countertop, gained its support and tried to calm down.

Compassion overrode Leslie's curiosity. She passed through the kitchen and assisted Ryan to a chair. Ryan folded an arm on the table and rested her head on it. The other cradled her aching ribs. Leslie quietly busied herself with fixing some food and making coffee. She poured a cup for herself and a glass of milk for Ryan. "Here. This will settle your stomach."

Ryan lifted her head, sighed and drank it down. "I need a cigarette."

Leslie rose and found their cigarettes. Ryan took both packs and the lighter from her. She shook her head at Ryan for the stubborness she displayed even in a crisis. She took the cigarette offered and held Ryan's hand, steadying it as it shook the lighter. "I've never been so frightened in all my life."

"That makes two of us." Ryan toyed with the buttered flat bread in front of her.

"I don't want to stop seeing you, Ryan."

Ryan put her hand on Leslie's knee. "Nor I, you."

116

"What are we going to do? You can't just accept an edict like that."

"Yes, I can and I will."

"Why?" Leslie's voice was edgy and near tears.

Ryan sighed. "This isn't going to make you feel very good, but I just traded you for an airplane."

Leslie was nonplussed.

Ryan looked at her hands, barely believing she escaped once more from her ultimate fear. "I'm still in one piece," she explained with wonder in her voice. "That means I can still fly."

"So?"

"Les-lie." She was growing impatient. "Something you had better understand up front is, that given a choice between a plane and a woman, the plane will win every time. Rags let me off easy. Probably because she saw the best way to hurt you."

Leslie was still trying to take it all in. "Hurt me?"

"Don't you see? It's perfect. I hurt the woman she loves and that hurt her. So, she hurts the woman I love and gets to me."

The logic made sense to Leslie; the reasoning escaped her. She couldn't comprehend why Ryan bargained their love for her vocation. "You'd stop seeing me so you could continue to fly?"

"Jesus Christ! This isn't a game we're playing here." Ryan pointed to the back door. "That woman is *dangerous*. She put me in the hospital for three months before. She'll do it again. She's that mad at me. I won't recover so nicely next time, she'll see to that. No, Leslie, I will see you when *she* says I can, and not before." Ryan was grateful to Leslie for not crying. She knew she couldn't bear it. "Go, Leslie. Just go."

Leslie could see that Ryan was on the verge of collapse, and it tore at her heart. She wanted to stay and comfort her. And be comforted. At last she had found love, declared it, and had it returned in kind. Now it was being ripped from her in the name of a revenge she didn't understand. She rose and went to the bedroom to dress. She let herself out and drove home to shed her tears.

10

"Les, will you come in my office for awhile?" It had taken two days to get the information Delores was looking for. She didn't want to waste any more time.

Refreshed from the eighteen holes of golf she just finished, her walk was springy and alive. The unseasonably warm weather encouraged her to drag out some white pants and a blue LaCoste. On her way into her office she stopped at the serving table and poured herself some tea. "Charlotte, will you see that we are not disturbed."

The secretary nodded her assurance.

Leslie followed Delores into her office and took a seat in front of the desk. Delores walked around to her side of the desk and set her tea down. Leslie's appearance made her worry. She was tastefully dressed, as always, but the crisp, vital air that clung to her like perfume was missing. The maroon pantsuit looked too somber and accentuated the scratchy looking eyes. Delores sat down. "Your eyes look pretty red."

Leslie dodged her. "It's just the smog."

Delores glanced casually over her shoulder, out the eastern window of her office. "You can see for miles out there."

Leslie continued to evade the issue; she wasn't used to confiding with Delores. "You wanted to see me?"

Delores dropped it, sympathetically, sorry that she wasn't closer to her partner. "I have something I want you to read." She handed her a sheet, folded at the top.

Leslie could tell it was a court record before she began to read it; the format was familiar. The charges ranged from assault to attempted murder, ten in all. All ten had been plea bargained to lesser charges. A prison sentence of one year had been served. The rest resulted in either probation or victim restitutions. There were four minor parole violations, and the subject was currently out on parole. Leslie looked up. "This person must have one hell of an attorney to still be on the streets."

Delores' serious demeanor deepened. "Yes, she does."

"She!" Leslie unfolded the top of the sheet and read aloud, "Regina Cooper. Who is that?"

"Read on, Les."

She looked down to see what additional information there was, "aka Rags." For long minutes she stared at the page, fighting back the tears. Ryan's tortured expression dominated her thoughts. Finding out first-hand what a demon Rags was gave her little solace for Ryan's safety. She wanted to comfort Ryan and couldn't. Even a phone call might endanger the life of the woman she had grown to love so completely. A tear escaped the confines of her burning eyes and fell audibly on the court record.

Delores handed her a tissue.

Leslie composed herself. "Why isn't she in prison?"

"David Martin, her parole officer. It amazes me how he keeps her out of lockup. Why he does it is beyond me."

Leslie put her elbow on the arm of the chair and propped her head on her knuckles. She contemplated Delores and shook her head slightly. "Why are you doing this, Del? First the party, now this?"

Delores had been toying with her glasses patiently. She animated her answer with them. "I'm trying to keep you from getting hurt, but from the looks of you, I may be too late."

"I know I should be grateful for your meddling, but right now, the way I feel, perhaps you are too late."

With a heavy sigh, Delores sat back in her chair. "Do you really think I'm meddling?"

"Yes, Del, I do." Leslie stood to leave. "May I keep this?"

"It's yours. Les?"

Leslie halted in the doorway. "Yes."

"Is Ryan in love with you?"

"For all the good it does, yes she is," Leslie replied cryptically, and walked out, closing the door on a frustrated colleague.

The blessings of early signs of spring were not as evident on Brigid's mountain farm. Frost was still a regular visitor, remaining late in the morning, nestled in the long shadows of February sun. Eight inches of old snow clung to the uncleared parts of the compact farm. Leslie arrived before sunset. Her Saturday had been spent sleeping late and running the errands that had accumulated in the past weeks.

She looked forward to her visits to the farm, tended so lovingly by her friends. This was her time to relax and forget about the troubles gathered by cosmopolitan living. Her tensions fled as she let herself in the unlocked front door. She put her bag down and let loose a luxurious sigh. An overweight, yellow dog greeted her, nuzzling her hand for attention. "Hi, Tish. Where is everyone?"

The dog lumbered out toward the kitchen and back door, past three cats snuggled in their individual overstuffed chairs. Each eyed Leslie sleepily as she walked by them, ignoring the noisy floorboards creaking under her hiking boots.

The kitchen smelled warm and spicy. She couldn't resist looking to the cookstove, lifting lids on pots and dipping a spoon into the soup. The hearty textures of lentils and rice tempted her. "Ummm."

She followed the dog's path to the backdoor where it waited patiently for her to open it. Outside she followed the sound of woodchopping to the corner of the barn. "Les!" Star laid down her ax and strode over to her guest. She greeted Leslie with a full hug that nearly lifted her off her feet. "It's good to see you."

"Thank you. Something smells good in the kitchen. Are you baking?"

"A vegetable casserole. One thing you can say about us is that we eat well around here," Star replied, patting her full hips with joy. "Brig is in her shop, putting drone bees to shame. I wish she would catch a good case of Spring fever. She works too hard, especially this last week."

"Let's go rescue her."

"Let's," Star gleamed.

Leslie followed Star down a path to the workshop, savoring the crisp air and the fading blue sky along the way. Soggy pine needles lined the stone pathway that branched from the house in one direction to the barn, the other to Brigid's ceramic shop. Leslie relished every opportunity she got to view the new creations Brigid turned out with unfailing regularity. The subtle roses, greys, and beiges interwove with each other in glazes that caught the eye and the imagination off guard.

Her work was becoming increasingly popular in California, where a friend marketed it with great skill. Only a favored few had received pieces as gifts in their homes in Colorado; otherwise they were not to be seen locally. Brigid preferred it that way, although she couldn't be persuaded to say why.

Her shop was not unlike a greenhouse in its openess, allowing her a full view of the mountains she loved. They found Brigid bent with concentration, her head rolling slightly from side to side, following her brush around the rim of a vase.

Star halted outside, catching Leslie's arm. "Doesn't she look incredible? I never get tired of watching her work." Leslie assented with a soft sigh, delighted by the blend of woman and craft, tucked away in the pine-scented mountains they all loved so dearly. Star opened the wooden door that wanted for oil in the hinges and alterted Brigid to their presence. "Want some more light, love?" Star reached for the kerosene lamp on the bench by the door.

Brigid looked up from her work. "No, I'm done here. Hi Les."

Leslie walked to Brigid's side and accepted the gentle caress around her hips. "That's lovely, Brig."

"Thanks, you're easy to please." Brigid had difficulty accepting priase for the work she did. It made her self-conscious in a way her missing leg could never do. She reached for her crutches and brought her frame to its full height and bent to kiss Leslie on the cheek. "I think you look better in those jeans and that flannel shirt. You look more relaxed and younger, if that's possible."

"You better watch out, Star. I might snatch this woman right out from under you."

"If anyone could, it would be you my friend," Star answered

half seriously.

"Hungry?" Brigid inquired.

"Starved."

"Let's find out what this gorgeous hunk of an Earth Mother has cooking on the stove." Brigid reached playfully for Star and gathered her up in a ravenous kiss. "Get moving woman," she teased.

Star giggled with contentment and led the way back to the house.

After dinner the trio curled up in front of the crackling fire to drink herb tea. Leslie took the seat closest to the fire, removed her boots and wiggled her toes indulgently in the glow of the flames. Star put some soft flute music on the stereo and settled in her favorite chair, opposite Leslie, leaving the chair in the middle for Brigid.

Brigid curled up like one of her cats, sinking into the overstuffed cushions eyeing the butter mints on the table next to her. She lit a homemade cigarette instead and waited for everyone to get settled. She watched Star get up to tend the fire, enjoying the way the firelight added cheer to the coarse waves of blonde streaked hair and gave definition to Star's well-carved face. Star once again folded herself into the receptive, low built chair that seemed to be all arms.

Brigid smiled at Star, the special smile she gave when she was admiring Star's healthy roundness. Star offered the comfort Brigid liked to get lost in. "You know that comment you made earlier about Leslie snatching me away from you? That couldn't happen you know."

"I know, love, I wouldn't let her try." Star smiled warmly at Leslie, who answered with a lazy half smile.

"She wouldn't try; she's in love with Ryan." Brigid waited calmly for the import of her statement to register with Star.

Star gave a sharp laugh. "You're joking." Her high-pitched voice echoed in her own ears. Time stood still for a moment when she realized they weren't laughing. She looked from her lover's face to her friend's; both were serious. Disgust filled her. In Star's estimation, being in love with Ryan was on a par with falling in a dung heap. Desperately, she searched Brigid's composed face for a sign that she was the brunt of a bad joke. No such sign appeared. Again she looked at Leslie. There, she found defensive resolve. Her voice was replete with hatred. "The Irish Executioner? Be realistic."

Leslie's face went ashen.

Brigid sat squarely in her chair and leaned toward Star, addressing her with authority. "That is the last time you will call her that. While that label fits Rags quite aptly, it does not apply to Ryan."

It fits them both perfectly and you know it. Do we have to hash this out in front of a guest?"

"Les isn't a guest. She is a close and dear friend. Are you that worried about your image?" Brigid was ready to drop the conversation and spare everyone if necessary, but the chord had been struck. Star wouldn't miss an opportunity to slander Ryan, even at her own expense.

A knot formed in Leslie's stomach, crowding her meal. She watched the veiled hostility between the couple with dismay. The ignominious title Star used for Ryan cut like a knife. She struggled with it, but couldn't make it fit her. She had no trouble, however, seeing how it suited Rags. She wished she didn't want to know more. "Star, what are you talking about?"

"Do you know what she does to women? She ruins them. Les, I couldn't bear to see you end up the way some of her ex's have."

Brigid sat back to watch Leslie deal with all she was about to hear. The horse was out of the gate now. There was no stopping Star on one of her diatribes until some of her fervor was spent.

"Ruins them. That is a pretty broad statement to make. How does she ruin women?"

"She beats them, with whips and things," Star provided with her purest disgust.

Leslie turned her widened eyes searchingly on Brigid. "Are we talking about the same person?"

"You are."

"How is it that you know this? Name your sources, Star. This isn't funny."

"Damn right it isn't funny. It's sickening. She's been doing it for years. I first found out about it from a friend who was studying herbal remedies from a healer in town. My friend was working at the healer's home when they brought one of their victims in to get attention."

"They?" Leslie asked.

"Rags and Ryan," Star stated like Leslie should have known. "Rags does it too, but much worse."

Leslie wondered silently to herself if Ryan wasn't a victim too. What she witnessed in Ryan's kitchen began to make some sense. "Who was this 'victim'?"

"Her name was Beth. My friend assisted with the examination. Oh, Les, it would have made you sick. The poor woman had welts all over her back and the insides of her thighs." Star pointed to the various parts of the body to emphasize her description. "Her wrists were gouged from handcuffs, her jaw was broken and her insides were a wreck."

After a confirming nod from Brigid, Leslie went on. "When was this?"

"About five years ago. They call it sex, I call it senseless, brutal rape."

"How do you know it was sexual?"

"I got to know Beth after she stopped living with Ryan. She told me about it. She was actually proud of being used that way! She wanted to go back, but Ryan wouldn't have her. I never saw her again, but I heard she ran off with a motorcycle gang. Les, I swear, if I believed in a Devil, I'd know it lived in Ryan's soul."

"That's enough!" Brigid's fist slammed the table next to her, rocking the lamp and upsetting the bowl of mints. The action brought instant silence to the room.

Star was shocked, bewildered and somewhat afraid. In the seven years she lived with Brigid, she had never seen her openly express anger. She had no idea how hard Brigid worked to keep her temper under the surface and live peacefully. She didn't understand why Brigid would find Ryan on occasion to go out to the bars and raise hell, then return home bruised, but quieter and calmer. Violence was anathema to Star. She sat still and swallowed.

Brigid went on, "You may not believe in the Devil, but I do. *And*, by damned, I will not have you talk about Ryan like that anymore. Now get a civil tongue in your mouth and act like a reasonable woman. Do you hear me?" Brigid didn't need to yell. Her voice was disturbingly low and even.

"Yes." Star was too disconcerted to continue.

Leslie was immersed in herself, struggling with what Star had told her about Ryan. She didn't want to believe it. Brigid's outburst meant nothing to her; she was becoming numbed to displays of temper. She didn't know that Brigid and Star's fights were usually more subtle and quiet, that things often went unsaid. She assumed that they fought like this occasionally and gave it no thought. She interrupted their staredown. "Brig, is Ryan still doing these things?"

She pulled herself free of Star's angry, troubled eyes to answer, "She's pretty hard on Sanji, but I don't know how hard."

Leslie shook her head, confused. "I just didn't see that with her."

Star couldn't let that statement go unchallenged. "You've slept with her?"

For the first time, Brigid wanted to hit Star. She was appalled by Star's insensitive prying.

Leslie went back on the defensive. "Yes, of course. Do you think I would fall in love with a woman and not sleep with her the first chance I got?"

"In her basement!" Star had the look of someone who stares at a dead body with morbid fascination.

"I didn't realize that house had a basement. If it matters, we were in her bedroom."

Star's prurient curiosity continued to build. "She didn't hit you?"

"Of course not," Leslie replied indignantly.

Brigid ignored the way the conversation was deteriorating. Her thoughts congealed around Leslie's innocent revelation. She thought back to the last adult Ryan had taken in her bedroom.

Leslie continued, "Star, I don't know what it is you have against Ryan, other than her sex practices offend your political sensibilities. She has shown herself to be warm, sensitive and very exciting."

"It's Rags she's angry with," Brigid purposely hastened the issue.

"Rags? What has she done to you?"

She put my best friend in the hospital for two months. She almost killed her." The naked bitterness in Star's voice soured

126

the atmosphere. She got up to tend the fire and deal with her hatred. Leslie reached over and smoothed Star's hair compassionately. "I'm sorry, I didn't realize. I don't blame you for being mad at Rags. I am too right now. Can't you be willing to give Ryan a chance? For me."

Star was touched by Leslie's sincerity. She agreed to try. She turned to sit in her chair, but was headed off by a crutch, softly drawing her attention toward its owner. Brigid placed a small footstool in front of her chair and urged Star to sit near her. Star relented, glad for some peace. She took her place, turned slightly toward Leslie and rested her arm on Brigid's leg. Brigid massaged her shoulders with firm dexterous hands. She relaxed and accepted a gentle kiss on her cheek.

Leslie envied the familiarity and domesticity of the scene. She longed to be held by Ryan in a similar fashion. She gazed wistfully into the fire. "Her home is so fascinating. All that rich color, everywhere. Yet," she turned to look at her friends again, "she always dresses in black. Why does she do that?"

"You won't have to sort very far through your art education to find the answer to that," Brigid supplied.

A golden eyebrow lifted curiously.

"What did Renior say about black?"

Leslie smiled to herself, "The 'queen of colors,' I should have known. She certainly doesn't look the type to be interested in art. Did you know she actually bid on an original Degas?"

Brigid relaxed, pleased to be talking about the real Ryan, the person she wanted Star to understand.

"She didn't win it because her father had always told her to patronize the artist, not . . ."

"Not the work," Brigid finished.

"He said it that often?"

"I'm surprised Ryan ever listened, especially since Patrick O'Donnell was a great art collector."

"He was?"

"Yes, my dear, and if you ever came out of that fog you live in you would have remembered seeing his and Ryan's names on several plaques at the museum. About half the O'Donnell collection is on loan to the museum here, and the rest of it is spread across the country."

"I never noticed." Leslie shook her head. "So why was he so adamant about Ryan not collecting?"

"Every piece Patrick picked up, he'd do so with Ryan in mind. He knew she would inherit them all, so he thought she should do other things with her money."

"She said she hadn't gotten around to taking his advice. What does she do with her money?"

"That isn't entirely true. She patronized this artist."

Star turned a quizzical gaze on her lover.

"You didn't think I could afford this farm, did you?"

Star asserted frankly, "I guess I never thought about it. You come from a wealthy family, and you make good money from your work."

"I got cut off years ago because I wasn't willing to play straight to keep my money. Ryan bought this farm and gave it to me. I have since paid her back, but only because I insisted on it. If I hadn't been so lucky with my art, she wouldn't have let me."

"Why didn't you tell me that before?" Star questioned edgily.

"I didn't think it was important."

Star conceded to herself that it probably wasn't since Brigid had paid Ryan back. The idea of being in debt to Ryan wasn't appealing.

"What else does she do with her money?" Leslie wasn't satisfied.

Brigid hesitated. She didn't like what Ryan did with some of her money, and revealing the information might lead to trouble if she wasn't careful. She proceeded cautiously, "She owns The Coffee Shoppe, although Roger and Denton are buying her out of it. She owns a third of the flight service she works with, and . . . she collects Gay bars." She knew as soon as she said it that Leslie had figured it out.

"Cary's is one of them, isn't it?"

Star's eyes grew large, and her nostrils flared. "Is it?" she demanded.

Brigid shifted uneasily in her chair. "Yes."

"How could you? You've known all along that she . . . wait! I heard two people owned that bar. Who else owns it with her, Brigid?" Star eyed her lover suspiciously.

Brigid began to wish she had learned to lie to someone who

asked her a direct question. She answered with a resigned sigh, "Rags."

"How long have you known this?" Star was getting angrier by the minute.

"Since Ryan bought into it five years ago. Where do you think Rags got the money to pay Jody's hospital bills? Jody didn't have insurance, so the court ordered Rags to pay them."

Star felt betrayed. Her pride was hurt deeply. She hated the tears that welled in her eyes, but she couldn't stop them. "That's just great Brig. What perfect revenge. You know how I feel about them, and that I wouldn't dream of going to Cary's knowing they owned it. So you let me go there and make a fool of myself. You knew damn well that would make it look like I had been compromising my beliefs."

"Or not upholding your image properly?" Brigid resented being accused of doing it on purpose. "I never saw that any real harm was coming from your association with that bar. It's clean and men don't go there. It's always been available for your benefit dances, rent free. Worse people could own that bar — someone who was into exploiting the community." Brigid was becoming frustrated by her lover's judgmental attitude.

"There is no way I'm going back there, and I'll see to it that none of my friends do either."

Brigid feared this would be Star's reaction. "Star, I know what you're thinking. A boycott isn't going to accomplish anything constructive. It will just divide an already splintered community."

"I doubt that."

"Nor is it your place to even the score for Jody." Brigid's voice turned low.

"Or any of the other people Rags has beaten to within an inch of their lives?"

"That's right. No one died and left you in charge."

"Will you try to stop me?"

"I won't be around to. If you go through with this and force me to choose sides, you'll lose more than you think. Ever since you found out about them and have been carrying on your one-woman vendetta against them, I've put up with it because I love you. So far you haven't done anything that I would worry about." Brigid tried to control her emotions. She wanted Star to under-

129

stand. "I regret now, not spending more time with Ryan when we first met. If you knew her better, you wouldn't be acting like this. She wasn't like this before her father died. She was different, much different. Now she has a chance to get well." Brigid gave a loving look toward Leslie. "I'm not going to get in the way of that and pit myself against Ryan when she needs friends the most. I would give everything I have, including you, to see her be happy again. She would do it for me, it's the least I could do for her. Don't do this, Star. You'll be sorry."

Star answered with a stony silence. She rose, ignored the fire wanting for attention and retired to the bedroom.

"Is she going to be alright? You were pretty rough on her."

"I hope so. I suspect she has some hard thinking to do." Brigid felt a chill in the room from Star's absence. She reached for her crutches and lifted herself out of the comfort of her chair to add another log to the fire. "Why are you mad at Rags?"

Leslie stretched the tension out of her muscles, relieved to be free of defending herself against Star. Brigid was a kindred spirit. Her unfailing quest for independence displayed itself with every act, from one as simple as restoring the fire, to declaring her loyalty for a friend. "Because she told Ryan not to see me."

Brigid had been stirring spent wood in the fireplace, pensively questioning her judgment with her lover. Her head came up suddenly. "Why did she do that? That's a bit extreme, even for Rags."

"Considering the circumstances, I think not. Ryan said we got off easy."

"What circumstances?"

"Do you remember last week when I told you that Ryan had been in two fights?"

"Yes," Brigid answered, fearing the worst.

"One of them was with Sanji," Leslie revealed.

"And you saw it?" Brigid was amazed.

"Along with everyone else at The Coffee Shoppe."

"Ryan fought with Sanji in public?"

"It was more the reverse. Sanji attacked Ryan."

Brigid suddenly needed to sit down. She set the poker in its rack and returned to her chair where she was joined by a large orange cat. "You're kidding?"

130

"No. She broke two of Ryan's ribs before Ryan could stop her. Thinking back on it, I'm glad Rags was there to stop Ryan from getting back at Sanji." Leslie took a cigarette from her purse. The memory of the scene made her nervous.

"Then what?"

"Ryan sent Sanji home, and I left shortly after that."

"You can bet Ryan made Sanji pay for *that*."

"She must have done something. Sanji is with Rags now."

"Huh," Brigid snorted. "I'm not surprised. If I know Ryan, she didn't waste any time seeing you then."

"Apparently not, which would have been fine if Rags hadn't caught us in bed together."

"That's disgusting."

"I wasn't too pleased about her walking in on us either, but I didn't get much chance to ponder it. Have you ever seen Rags *wear* those gloves she keeps in her back pocket?"

Brigid slumped into her chair and shook her head sadly. "No, but I've seen my best friend become a shell of the person she once was because of those damn gloves. Ryan would be in the hospital now if Rags had hit her, so it sounds like you did get off easy."

"Ryan said that Rags put her in the hospital before."

"Ryan was just one of many. Del told me she showed you Rags' court record. I hope you know why I told you to stay away from her. That attempted murder charge was Star's friend Jody. Rags is one of the most frightening people you could ever come across."

"You'll get no argument from me on that score. Ryan is scared to death of her."

"I hope you are too, by now." Brigid searched Leslie's eyes for conformation.

Leslie rested her head on the back of her chair and spoke to the ceiling, "I am. I simply can not figure out why Ryan lets this go on, or why Rags isn't in prison."

"Ryan hasn't got any choice, or I'm sure she wouldn't let it go on. Rags has Ryan completely under her control. Del already told you why Rags isn't in prison."

"David Martin."

"Yes ma'am."

"How did Rags get control over Ryan in the first place?"

131

"Pure, brute force. Ryan has one major weakness and Rags capitalizes on it."

"Flying?"

"That's right. Ryan is absolutely obsessed with flying, and Rags knows it. If Ryan gets out of line, she risks losing her ability to fly."

"You know that I would rather be finding these things out from Ryan, don't you?"

"I know, Les. This is not how I would have wanted things to work out for you two."

"Me either. You obviously wanted me to find something out about Ryan or you wouldn't have gotten Star started on her." Leslie looked directly at her friend, challenge in her eyes.

"I want you to understand why people don't like Ryan. What you do in bed with her is your business. I'm not worried about that."

"Why?"

"Les, Ryan is in love with you," Brigid informed her.

"She is? She is, or so she says."

"Believe it. I know her."

Leslie relaxed and curled into her chair with the cat that had joined her. It warmed her heart to have what she was beginning to doubt confirmed. "I wish I didn't have to drag information out of her."

Brigid smiled sympathetically. "She is an intensely private person. She won't volunteer much about herself."

"Still, she has answered some very personal questions that I've put to her."

"If she thinks enough of you to take you in her bedroom, she won't hold back anything from you. That room is like a sanctuary to her. Very few people have been in that room."

"From the looks of all those pictures on her wall, somebody has." Leslie stroked the cat on her lap absently and wondered how Brigid would justify them.

"You're right, somebody has," Brigid answered abruptly.

Leslie could sense that she wasn't going to get what she wanted from Brigid.

"Who's Christine?"

Brigid looked skyward and thanked her saints that she didn't

132

know. "I don't know."

Leslie dropped it and asked the most important question she had on her mind: "Am I going to get to see Ryan again?"

"I don't know that either."

11

In the weeks that followed, Leslie made only sporadic appearances at her office. Her legal partners and secretary grew more concerned daily. Even the jovial Susan began to show signs of irritability during her absences. Susan started taking extended lunch hours, scouring the bars and parks in the downtown area. Her search continued for two weeks until she found Leslie in the Art Museum.

Sitting on a marble bench, lost in an obscure Impressionistic piece, Leslie looked strained and sad. Susan joined her quietly on the bench and scrutinized the painting. Her curiosity was aroused — she wondered why Leslie had chosen that particular work to escape in. She got up to read the tiny block letters pressed under the glass plate to the right of it. The dedication informed her the painting was on loan from Ryan O'Donnell in memory of Patrick O'Donnell.

She returned to her seat and handed a tissue to her swollen-eyed friend. She spoke quietly. "Ryan must be some kind of woman. Del hates her and you love her."

Leslie turned her puffy eyes toward Susan. It was difficult to talk. "She doesn't inspire indifference, in anyone."

Susan was deeply moved by Leslie's intense heartache. "So why aren't you with her?"

Leslie gazed at the painting again. "Someone very formidable and frightening has come between us, and that is about all I can tell you, Susan. Damn, it hurts."

Susan drew her own conclusions based on what Delores had told her about the situation. Leslie's pain was more real to Susan than Delores' distaste. Everyone had fought so hard to protect their young partner, that none had prepared for what to do with failure. Susan put her arm around Leslie and drew her near. Leslie wept openly. Susan soothed and comforted her to the best of her ability, then went on to assure her that she could take as much time off as she needed. They left the Museum allies.

Susan covered Leslie's broken appointments, neglected paperwork and court appearances with a dedicated cheer. When time permitted she would plead with Delores to relent and accept the relationship between the unlikely couple, support Leslie in her time of need and bring peace to the office once more. Delores clung stubbornly to her belief that loving Ryan was a fate worse than death. Susan was undaunted and continued to divide her time to give Leslie the space she needed to cope with her protracted separation from Ryan.

Much of that time Leslie spent on lonely walks along the Platte River, oblivious to the energetic joggers and cyclists passing her. Puffy white clouds gathered into storms and shed rain instead of snow. She walked on; lost. Twice she found herself parked outside the fence surrounding Peterson's Flight service, hoping to see Ryan. When Ryan did ride by without seeing her, she felt her heart collapse. She lost the courage and nerve it took to follow her home, rooted in the memory of Ryan's agonized face. Instead, she would drive herself home to an uneaten dinner and fitful sleep.

If Leslie's work suffered, Ryan's improved. She threw herself into it with a passion she hadn't felt since her youth. She spent as much time in the air as was permitted, opting for the longer executive shuttle flights to Cheyenne, Wyoming, and south to Pueblo. A new strength flowed through her veins. Her hands were steadier, and her mind more alert. She regained the edge she had lost from her excessive drinking, restoring her self-confidence and the confidence of her fellow pilots. Her main battle rested in covering the pain in her ribs. She let it leech out the pain in her heart. Her nights were spent in a drugged sleep.

Phil followed her around like a lost pup, unsure of his good fortune and unaware of the condition of Ryan's ribs. She knew that she couldn't fly impaired by pain relievers, so she flew without them. Phil was only worried that he might look away, then look back to find her in a bottle.

As days of sobriety turned into weeks, Phil began to relax a little and enjoy Ryan's company as he had done when she was younger and innocent of the world's pain. He remained firm on his stance that her nerves weren't what they used to be and kept her away from the fleet helicopters. "I'm not paying those Viet Nam Vets top dollar for nothing, you know," he scolded. After three weeks of friendly bantering, Ryan accepted her fate with as much grace as she could muster. Her nerves were raw and she knew why.

The warm March winds blew life into the fire that was consuming her reason. She took off work late on a Wednesday morning in search of the cool elixer that would equalize her passions.

—·◦◆◖◗◆◦·—

Parked outside the high school near her home, Ryan removed her helmet, raised her mirrored sunglasses to her forehead and settled in to wait in the sun for the bell to let the students out for the first lunch period. The warmth absorbed by her black garments relaxed her muscles, and the sun lit scarlet blankets behind her eyelids.

She was near sleep when the bell rang. Her sunglasses slid off her forehead to the bridge of her nose in an automatic gesture. She lazily sorted through the hoards of young people filing out the door until she found what she was looking for.

She stared purposefully at a lithe, delicate blonde that was poured fetchingly into designer jeans and a white leotard top. About her neck a soft pink scarf enhanced her exquisite, high-boned cheeks.

The young girl noticed Ryan a moment later and squealed to her friend walking beside her. Together they hurried to greet Ryan. A contented smile crossed Ryan's face as she watched the graceful way Christine covered territory in high heels.

Bubbling with joy, Christine stood before her. "Hi Ryan!"

"Hi Chris." Ryan's voice had shifted downward to the octave that accompanied her kindled desire. Just the sight of Christine sparked a twinge in her groin. "Who's your friend?"

"This is Pam." "Pam, this is Ryan. Remember, I told you

about her?'' Christine's excitement punctuated her speech.

Ryan appraised Pam slowly. Overdeveloped for that age and too hippy, not her type.

Pam blushed, seeing her reflection in Ryan's glasses, knowing she was being given a once over.

Ryan turned to Christine. "Come home with me and make lunch. I'm hungry.''

Christine gave her lips a subtle lick; her blue eyes twinkled in response to Ryan's request. She knew, in her childish wisdom, exactly what Ryan was hungry for. "Where's Sanji?''

"She split. So that makes you,'' Ryan ran her gloved finger from the top of the white leotard in a line between the budding breasts, over the taught tummy, to the top button of the jeans and hooked her finger inside, "my leading lady.''

"Really?''

Ryan held up her helmet to the anxious blonde. "Really.''

Christine didn't hesitate. She handed her purse to her awed friend, put the helmet on and took back her purse. "I won't be back today, Pam.'' She waited for Ryan to start the motorcycle and straddled the seat behind her. Ryan squeezed her knee, sending overpowering rushes through her that kept perfect time with the vibrations of the massive machine beneath her. They roared off, leaving Pam standing in a daze, choked with envy.

Little compared with the exhiliration Christine got from riding on the back of Ryan's motorcycle. It heightened her senses, and never failed to dampen the fabric between her legs. With studied concentration, she locked her hands on her thighs, resisting the temptation to distract Ryan's driving by encircling the firm waist before her. Her shoulder-length hair escaped the confines of the helmet and stung her face. She edged closer to Ryan's back to avoid the chilly wind, which brought Ryan's billowing jacket in contact with her tender nipples and sent shots of sensation through her.

Tilting and accelerating into turns afforded Christine opportunities to revel in her admiration of Ryan and the powerful ease she lent to the machine. Her joy exceeded her limited capacity to contain it when she watched Ryan's hair being swept back in the wake of the wind. When they came to rest at a traffic light, she caught the reflection of Ryan's lusty smile in the rearview mirror. Her cheeks reddened.

When they passed through the gate, Ryan knew that the guards would keep their improprieties to themselves until she was out of sight. Her longstanding reputation for maintaining a steady supply of attractive females was a source of scorn and thinly veiled jealousy among them.

When she pulled into her drive, she was considering skipping lunch and getting on with dessert. She was still thinking about it when she followed Christine in through the back door. Christine put the helmet and her purse on the table and turned for the refrigerator.

Watching her charge out of the corner of her eye, Ryan took her gloves and glasses off and laid them by the helmet.

Christine inspected the contents of the refrigerator carefully. The exotic fruits and odd concoctions were gone. All that remained were the basic staples the housekeeper arranged for. "She really is gone!"

"Seeing is believing, young one. Do you want to look in her room too?" Ryan teased.

Embarrassed, Christine shook her head. "There isn't much here to work with."

"I trust you." Ryan unzipped her jacket and leaned over the refrigerator door and withdrew a beer. She rubbed the cold bottle against Christine's nipple. The chill hardened it. The condensation on the bottle moistened the leotard and exposed the rosebud beneath. "Here."

Christine hissed through her teeth. Her soft, dainty hand reached up to take the refreshment. She twisted the cap off and drank deeply, buying herself recovery time.

Folding her arms across her chest, Ryan leaned against a chairback to watch Christine assemble the ingredients for crepes, knowing that the real talent in the kitchen went beyond cooking. Christine excelled in making the chore of cooking erotic. Every move was designed to incite passion. She delighted in having Ryan as her willing audience.

Ryan still had her keys in her hand. She began taking two of them off the ring. "Still having problems at home?"

"The same." Christine finished preparing the cheese and looked around to Ryan.

139

Ryan stepped over to Christine and held up a key. "This is for the alarm," she held up a larger one, "the back door. If things get bad," she slipped them into Christine's front pocket, "you come over here."

Her clear blue eyes widened. She could barely answer. "God, Ryan, do you mean it?"

"Will you stop looking at me like I was a soap bubble. I'm not going to pop and disappear. Of course I mean it." She bent to kiss the surprise from Christine's face. Their lips met in a shy embrace. "Cook, you sweet thing."

With tingling nerves and wobbly knees, she forced herself to open the jar she needed. "Bottled mushrooms, jeez Ryan. If you had some fresh food around here, I could cook a proper meal."

Ryan opened a drawer and sorted through its contents, produced a pen and pad, wrote the housekeeper's name on it and handed it to her childlike chef. "Write whatever you need on this, and Bonnie will pick it up."

Christine was beginning to feel more comfortable with her new status. "Okay, I will." She took the pad and set it on the counter, then turned her attention to the crepe batter.

She was so intent on heating the pan properly and pouring the first crepe, she didn't notice Ryan was standing directly behind her. To her surprise, Ryan reached around her and unbuttoned her jeans. "Ryan, I'll ruin this," she whispered.

Ryan turned the heat off under the pan. "I don't care. I haven't had a piece of ass in three weeks." She further expressed her urgent need with paced grinding into Christine's petite orbs, bracing the tiny pelvis with her bony hands.

Christine's heels didn't quite compensate for the difference between her height and Ryan's five foot ten inches. Ryan had to spread her feet outside of Christine's to thrust her burning groin into the firm rear.

Christine placed her hands safely on the stove to maintain her balance against the force of Ryan's need and give her the leverage to answer with her own insistent rhythm. Mastering the skill Ryan taught her, she flexed and relaxed the muscles of her buttocks, rotating her hips down and back in time with Ryan's grinding.

"That's right, Chris. You know how to make me want you." Ryan's hot whispering sent chills down Christine's side.

Ryan separated for a quick moment to slide the denim over the undulating hips and partway down the healthy thighs, leaving the cotton leotard the only obstacle between her and the milky skin beneath. She joined her partner again, but slower, like a dance. Her hands followed the rocking motion of the hips to the bare thighs, allowing her thumb to skim the surface of the love lips.

Christine's breathing got harder and deeper, encouraged by the tender touch. Ryan's hand coiled back, and the first two fingers disappeared inside the legband, traveled downward and out, deftly pulling the cloth away from her ultimate target. Her other hand left its station to find the switchblade that was housed in the deep recesses of her jacket.

The distinctive jumping click it made upon entering the scene drew Christine's attention to it. Mesmerized, she managed to continue her soft rocking as the knife parted the fabric gathered in Ryan's hand with ease. The quiet hiss Ryan gave when the leotard shrunk away from the golden pubic area was music to Christine's ears.

Ryan tossed the knife on the stove recklessly. She began to feel her passion getting away from her. Acting quickly, she stopped her hips and grabbed Christine about the waist and telegraphed her need to stop. She threw her head back and closed her eyes. Even the feeling of their combined breathing threatened to be enough to make her come. Three weeks had been far too long for her to go without release. Her extreme need struggled to overpower her, but her self-mastery won out and her breathing eased, her color lessened. Once again under control, she turned her attention to her fragile lover, to urge her back up the scale of sexual plateaus.

Ryan's hand traveled back to the golden palace, touching the silky hair with a kiss of a breeze, sending shockwaves through Christine's body.

"Oh Ryan," she panted, "I want you inside me."

Not one to ignore a request made in the throes of passion, Ryan obliged. She invaded the delicate pink lips with her middle finger, slowly at first, then harder as she began to be swept away by the sweet perfume of Christine's sex.

"Ohhh, ohh." Christine's moans became trembling

whimpers that blended with the moist orchestra Ryan was directing in her nether regions.

Ryan spoke directly into Christine's ear with throaty, broken tones. "I'm hungry, Chris."

"Eat me," she hissed in reply.

Without disturbing her finger nestled in Christine's womb, Ryan turned her around, bent her own knees and lifted the frail, weightless form over her shoulder and took off for the bedroom. Christine's astonishment at being handled in this fashion was doubled by the sensation of Ryan's finger plunging deeper into her helplessness with each step.

The bedroom was lit solely by the subdued northern rays sneaking through the vine covered window. Marshalling her patience again, Ryan placed her knee on the bed, cradled her nymph to the mattress and extracted her digit from its burning home. She lay next to Christine and brushed the tresses away from the expectant face. She explored Christine's moist lips and inner mouth with the gentleness she reserved for the very young.

The contrast between the unbridled passion and this soothing courtship was what Christine loved best about Ryan. She floated like a petal on a pool into the secret world Ryan had shown her. Here she would stay for the duration of their lovemaking.

Ryan greeted her there with a knowing glance, her jade eyes penetrating the depths of Christine's soul. She never abused this gift, as she did with other women. Here trust was an honor, not a right and she respected it accordingly, not overstepping the boundaries.

In her trancelike state, Christine cooperated fully with the removal of her clothing. Ryan left the scarf and replaced the shoes. Before easing off the bed, she stopped to pay homage to the flushed points atop the lemon sized breasts. Christine's quickening heartbeat shook them like miniature earth tremors. Kissing, yet not, Ryan's regular breath raised the tips higher. Christine's breathing accelerated in an attempt to bring them nearer Ryan's thin, talented lips. The lips she sought disappeared as fast as they had come.

Ryan stood, walked around to the foot of the bed and took in the view. Christine's legs were parted slightly, her hands were caressing her aching breasts and her face was sculptured longing.

Ryan's even expression masked her desire in a calculated effort to drive Christine mad. She took her cigarettes and lighter from her pocket and dropped them on the end of the mattress. With ritualistic calm, she removed her jacket and hung it on the door knob. The zipper and snaps struck the oak door, breaking the silence.

The warm morning sun had relaxed the stiffness from her ribs, making it easier for her to move about. She undid the top two snaps on her shirt, then she turned her attention to the gold, diamond shaped cufflinks at her wrists. She took the first one out, watching Christine's eyes follow each careful move. The cuff fell open and dangled freely; the second link let loose the other cuff.

Ryan stepped to the dresser and returned the links to their alabaster chest, along with her watch. After running a comb through her windblown tangles, she stood at the foot of the bed to retrieve her cigarettes. She lit one and dropped the pack and lighter on the bed.

By now, Christine's hips were digging into the bed, and her breathing was audible. Half through rolling up her left sleeve, Ryan inquired through the cigarette dangling from her lips, "You want it, baby?"

"Ounn Ryan, you know I do."

Ryan took the cigarette from her mouth and pointed to Christine's golden crotch with her middle finger. "Prove it to me then. Play with yourself, sweet thing. Spread that icing around, make me *want* to eat you."

Christine complied willingly, spreading her lips with the first two fingers of her hand. Her middle finger of her other hand deftly scooped the creamy icing out and spread it over the hard node on top and around her pink softness. She couldn't control the movement of her hips or the delight noises escaping from her depths.

Ashes fell unnoticed from the tip of the cigarette to the carpet as Ryan rolled up her other sleeve. Without taking her eyes off Christine, she unhooked the Lear Jet belt buckle and slid her belt through the loops. She rolled it up on itself and turned to the dresser, where she deposited it and her cigarette. When she turned toward the bed again, Christine's pace quickened in anticipation.

Ryan joined her young goddess on the bed. Their eyes locked, the blue followed the jade downward toward the soaking gold. Neither of them could refrain a second longer. Christine's pearly hands made way for Ryan's love-starved tongue.

Ryan stretched out diagonally, wedging Christine's fragile ankle into her own desperate cunt. She grabbed Christine's rocking hips and lost herself in the power of their mutual need. She tasted and gorged herself on the saccharine goodness, swirling her tongue around every pore and crevice, greedily consuming everything Christine had to give.

Christine ran her long fingers through Ryan's springy black hair and pulled her deeper into her love snare. She dug her ankle further into the wedge of Ryan's smouldering tension. Between her own fitful sobs she could hear and feel Ryan groan in a regular, patterned escalation of arousal. She was overwhelmed by the sight of her lover taking her. Her sobs became uncontrolled begging. "Take me, oh god, Ryan. Please, oh please take me. Take everything. Ohh. . .Ryan. . . Oh, oh.''

Later, she would make Christine wait, but now, it had been too long. Her excitement had soaked through her jeans. The sensation of Christine's ankle pressing the seam against her clit combined with the heady flavor and aroma of the golden casing around her mouth. It was too much.

She tightened about the captive ankle, held her breath, pinpointed her tongue, and made tiny, intense strokes on Christine's clitoris. She felt Christine stiffen to her touch and her breathing halt. Skillfully timed, the contractions began in earnest. Ryan matched Christine's each for another. For an ecstatic second there was silence. Then with throbbing zeal, they let loose the pent up frustrations and tensions, washing away in a primordial sea of womanly utterings.

Their bodies collapsed in panting heaps. Sweat covered Christine's body and Ryan's brow. Ryan released the instrument of her pleasure and rolled on her side. She put Christine's legs together and pulled the slippery body down, even with hers.

Protectively, she gathered up the delicate form in her arms, holding tight the feeling of contentment. Christine sought Ryan's lips and her own lingering spice. Sandwiched between affectionate kisses, Ryan praised her softly and caressed her hair.

Being less than half Ryan's age, Christine regained her strength first. She slid off the bed, handed Ryan her cigarettes and lighter and turned to the closet for the robe.

"Don't."

Christine looked back at Ryan; confused.

"Open the other closet. There are some silk shirts. Take one of them." Ryan checked the undercurrent of crossness in her voice. She wasn't willing to let someone else other than Leslie wear her robe.

Christine found one of the black silk shirts and put it on. The tails reached her knees, and her arms were completely lost in the sleeves. "There aren't any buttons," she laughed.

Ryan sat up on the edge of the bed, an unlit cigarette wedged between her fingers. "Come here."

She came close and watched Ryan roll up the sleeves to a manageable length, Ryan stood and walked her over to the dresser. With great fascination, she looked on as Ryan produced a diamond stud and fastened it in the opening between her breasts. The feel of the soft fabric on her skin didn't match the specialness Ryan made her feel with that simple act.

Ryan leaned on the dresser and smiled; satisfied. "That," she opened the lower part of the shirt, exposing the golden curls below, "is the only button you'll ever need."

Christine put her arms around Ryan's neck and kissed her hard. "Thank you."

Ryan answered her sincerely, "You're welcome. Now where's my lunch?"

Christine released her grasp on Ryans neck and ran her fingers slowly down the Northern white skin of the neckline, to the vee between the breasts no larger than her own, stopping at the first snap to cross her path. She knew this was where all inquiries stopped. "Right away, old lady. Got to keep your strength up."

She received a mischievious grin in reply to her teasing. She squealed with laughter and dodged Ryan's grasp, then disappeared to cook the forgotten meal.

March finished, cold, wet and windy. April opened, warmer and drier. Ryan grew more relaxed, profitting from her arrangement with Christine. Each day, she returned from work and found Christine's bicycle parked on the back terrace and Christine singing happily to herself in the kitchen.

Christine coaxed Ryan into unlocking the china hutches and letting her use the Wedgewood and Waterford. She arranged the family silver on fine tablecloths with reverence for their meals together.

Ryan enlisted her housekeeper, Bonnie, to begin a spring cleaning program on the neglected home. Bonnie agreed eagerly, thrilled to see Ryan take an interest in her home again.

The gardeners were brought back to mount a full-scale assault on the neglected trees, shrubs and gardens on the nine acres surrounding the Tudor home. Ryan stoically accepted the tempermental scoldings of the head gardener for allowing the property to decline so pitifully. She gave him carte blanche to replace anything he saw fit, and he settled down; pacified.

Evenings were spent at the cleared dining table, peacefully working on Christine's studies. Ryan's soul took nourishment from helping Christine learn and explore the world of education. In the short year since they met, Christine had moved from failing all her subjects, to tenth in her class.

It was because of this progress that Christine's parents unwittingly allowed the relationship to flourish. They accepted without question that Christine's scholastic improvement was due to Ryan's tutoring. Their pride in their daughter's accomplishments kept them from interfering with her time spent away from home.

Their work came easier now that Sanji wasn't around to make them tense. One evening, after a history lesson, Ryan felt a wave of nostalgia flow through her. She looked into Christine's restful eyes. "Would you like to see where I did my studying?"

"I would love to," Christine answered with a mature warmth.

When they reached the top of the stairs to Patrick O'Donnell's apartment, Ryan was better equiped to handle the emotions she would have to process. She took comfort in Christine's closeness. She had not, however, adequately prepared her young friend for the haunting difference between the abandoned apartment and the rest of the house.

With the door opened and the chandelier turned on, the

power and presence of the wood paneled room gave Christine a faint heart.

Ryan held her close and looked into the timid eyes. "It's a bit overwhelming at first, but you get used to it." Together, they stood in the doorway, taking mental excursions around the room. Ryan could sense her father in the room. She straightened her shoulders; this was her declaration of independence. She was finding her way in life, without her father, and was beginning to feel good about it.

Christine's mental tour disembarked on the portrait above the mantle. "Is that your father?"

Ryan escorted her across the room and stood before it. "Yes. It is. Patrick O'Donnell." The pride was evident in her voice.

"How long ago did he die?"

"Six years ago, last month."

"I can see where you got your handsomeness." She coughed slightly from the dust. "You haven't been up here since, have you?"

"Once. Pretty pathetic, isn't it?"

"Just dusty. I could clean it for you."

Ryan held Christine away to look at her. After a long, serious appraisal, she hugged her tight and kissed the soft blonde head. "You're incredible. Do you know that?"

Christine squeezed her reply.

"It does need cleaning, but I'll let Bonnie do it. She's used to handling my father's things."

Christine's shoulders slumped in disappointment. Ryan took the firm chin in her hand and lifted the sad face to hers. She kissed the eyes and then the mouth. "Don't be sad, little one. I love it that you offered, but think of Bonnie for a moment. She's sad over the loss of my father as well, and she needs the chance to put things in order for herself. Is it alright if we let her?"

Christine was thrilled by being asked for her permission and being included in the decision. She forgot about her mood. "Sure."

"Thank you. This is where I did my studies." She shifted the tone to a happier time, and directed Christine to the cluttered desk and turned on the long dormant study lamp.

Christine's attention was drawn to a stack of photos on the

bookshelf connected to the study desk. There were black and white pictures of various types of small aircraft. None of them yielded an image of the young Ryan, as she had hoped. "None of these have you in them."

"It's a good thing, too. I'm not feeling *that* nostalgic."

She set them down and looked at some of the titles occupying the massive shelves before her. "God, you must have read a lot!"

"We both did."

"Then you finished school early, too?"

Ryan rested her hands on Christine's shoulders. "If I hadn't been quite so busy flying and had some small amount of ambition, I might have. Nobody could get me out of the air long enough to buckle down and finish early. Just lazy I guess."

Christine rubbed her cheek against Ryan's knuckles. "Once you get used to it up here, it's very peaceful. It sounds like you had a good time when you were young."

"I did. My father and I cared for each other a great deal We spent as much time as we could together. He would have liked you, Chris."

Christine turned halfway to look Ryan in the eye. "Honest?"

Ryan smiled and turned her around the rest of the way. "Yes, my dear. As a matter of fact, if we were closer in age and if he were still around, he would have pushed for me to marry you."

A gasp accompanied the somersault in Christine's heart. When she recovered from the jolt, she asked, "Would you have?"

The question brought Ryan back to the present. Like the past she had been running from, it confronted her full force. She looked to the floor, hung her head and whispered, "You deserve better, Christine."

"How can you possibly say that?" Christine's voice was filled with shock and disbelief. She had fought against falling in love with Ryan for months, as she had been warned to do. Their close association in recent weeks made it impossible.

"When you get older," Ryan forced herself to look at the youth, "do yourself a favor. Find someone who isn't already married to her job. I lost one woman because of my passion for flying. It isn't a pleasant feeling, for either party."

Christine tried to answer, but Ryan stilled her. "You have too many wounds to heal. Although you have been very therapeutic for me, in the long run you would grow to hate me."

"Never, Ryan. I couldn't."

"I know you feel that way now, honey. I hope you never have to find out that I'm right."

"This hurts, Ryan."

"That's because you fell in love with me, didn't you?" Ryan felt the strength of her compassion well in her heart. She held the young girlwoman tight in her arms.

"Please don't be mad at me." Christine began to cry.

Ryan pulled a handkerchief from her back pocket and gave it to Christine. "I'm not, I couldn't do that." She held Christine's face between her hands and searched for understanding. "You are so special to me. You are the main reason I'm still alive, and I will never be able to repay you for that gift."

"You've taught me that love exists," she paused to swallow the lump in her throat, "and that sex can be wonderful instead of ugly. You've shown me the world of learning. I'd say the score is pretty even." She saw evidence in Ryan's concerned expression that they were both getting what they wanted. She was glad to give Ryan something of herself. She cleaned the tears from her face and blew her nose. "I'm alright now."

"Come here." Ryan led her through the apartment, back to the heavily masculine bedroom. She suppressed the difficult emotions the room evoked and made her way, Christine in hand, to the night stand next to the bed. She opened the walnut door below the drawer and took a small brown leather case from it.

Christine's hand was cradled lightly in hers. She opened the case and took out the diamond set gold band from inside. She dropped the case on the bed behind her and turned to Christine. "This was my mothers. I never knew her, but she had to have been the kind of lady you are. I can't marry you, for reasons you wouldn't understand, but I will never forget you, never." Ryan pressed the ring into the tiny palm and folded the long fingers over it.

Christine looked up at Ryan, her lips quivering; speechless.

"Don't ever, ever let your parents find this. They would take it from you and that would be the last either of us would see of it. One day, something will come between us, it's inevitable. When it does, I want you to remember that of all the girls I've

149

had, you are and always will be, the best."

Christine broke down in uncontrolled weeping. Ryan held her and soothed her quietly.

That night, after Christine left, Ryan removed all but one of the pictures from her bedroom wall and put them in the trash. She knew that, in Christine, she had found all that she had wanted in a young girl and that she would never know that special quality again. She lay on her bed and wept for lost innocence, Christine's, Leslie's and her own.

12

After work the next evening, Ryan asked the son of a neighbor to help her push her Rolls Royce out of the carriage house into the drive. She had grown comfortable with the idea of driving it, but it required some work before it could be used.

The following Saturday, she turned her full attention to it. Christine joined her outside and sat on the partially green grass to enjoy the warm sun. She handed tools to Ryan with little concentration and was glad Ryan wanted her for the company she provided and not any machanical know-how. Her attention wavered between smelling the hyacinth bouquet Ryan picked for her and lazily admiring Ryan's crotch.

Ryan was lying on a creeper, knees up and a foot to either side of the creeper. The balance of her torso was obscured from view underneath the jacked-up car.

A vehicle pulled into the drive. "You've got company," Christine informed Ryan.

"What kind of car?" came Ryan's muffled inquiry.

"It's a Bronco."

"Does the driver have red hair?"

"Yes."

Ryan seemed to be expecting the guest, or so Christine thought. She didn't move from her place under the car. Christine turned her attention to the new arrival. She contained her surprise quickly when the stranger's full body came into sight after walking around the car on crutches.

The stranger favored her with a cursory smile and addressed the knees she stood above. "I don't believe it."

"Believe what, MacSweeney?" Ryan rolled out from under the car.

The tall woman shook her head and smiled. "You. I didn't think I'd see the day when you'd care about this car again."

"Oh."

Brigid poked Ryan's thigh with her crutch. "Manners, O'Donnell."

Ryan braced the creeper with her heel and leaned over for the grease soap. She lathered up her hands and replied abashed, "Pardon me. Brigid, this is Christine Latham. Christine, my cousin, Brigid MacSweeney."

Brigid shook Christine's fragile hand reverently. "My pleasure."

Christine felt the controlled power in Brigid's handshake and saw the honest goodness in the eyes. She blushed deeply, "Charmed," then smiled in reply to Brigid's quick, almost flirtatious wink.

Ryan finished cleaning her hands and lit a cigarette. She shielded her eyes from the intense high altitude sun with her sunglasses and followed the line from Christine's gentle smile to her friend's peaceful face. "What brings you out of the hills on a weekend, buddy?"

Brigid pried her gaze from the beautiful youth. "You. I need to talk. Alone."

Ryan regarded her friend with a raised eyebrow. She maneuvered herself off the creeper and stood. Christine stood also, taking her cue politely. Ryan kissed her cheek. "Go check on dinner, babe. We'll be in later." Christine obeyed silently.

Brigid watched Ryan let the car down from the jack. "What year is this?"

"It's a '57 Silver Cloud," Ryan answered, not without some pride.

"She's a honey. Patrick sure took care of her."

"You got that right. I don't have to do any restoration at all. The body is in excellent condition and except for the driver's seat, the interior is mint."

"How does she run?"

Ryan answered with a "you know better" look.

"I'm sorry, I don't know what came over me."

"When I'm done with her, she'll run like a dream," Ryan added rhetorically.

"And ride like one if I remember."

"Like glass."

Being a fair mechanic herself, Brigid admired Ryan's talent for fixing and maintaining anything that had moving parts, whether it was an airplane, motorcycle or car. She shifted the conversation to something else she admired Ryan for, her ability to attract women. "That heartbreaker in there has trouble written all over her."

"You're undoubtedly right, but she's worth it."

"Is she?"

Ryan took her coat off the mirror of the car and put it on. "Brig, the only ground level reality I have right now is the soft touch of that young girl's hand."

With a resigned sigh, Brigid dropped the subject. She reached out and lifted the sunglasses to scrutinize Ryan's eyes. The clear gaze brought a smile to her face. She replaced them and took Ryan's hand and held it flat in front of her, then let go. The hand remained still, rock steady. "Damn, you look good. I'm impressed."

Ryan took her hand back and rescued the cigarette dangling from her mouth. "I haven't had a drink in six weeks. I'd forgotten how good it could feel."

Brigid nodded her head evenly with approval and looked about her. "Isn't that Bonnie's car? She doesn't work on Saturdays."

"She's cleaning father's apartment."

Brigid was wide-eyed with joy. "This is too good to be true, Ryan. My prayers have been answered for sure."

"You and Bonnie and your prayers. Bunch of damn Irishwomen." Ryan mocked Bonnie's heavy accent, "Glory be lass and you're on the mend then." Her teasing was in good nature and released the tension she felt about the response her recovery was bringing.

"Are you?"

"I'm not entirely sure what it feels like to be on the mend. I guess so."

Brigid took a sweeping glance of the whole picture. "Leslie is having a better effect on you than I thought."

Ryan felt like she had been punched in the stomach, short of breath and queasy. She sat on the fender and closed her eyes against the pain. She experienced a momentary bout of anger for being caught off guard. It hadn't occurred to her that Brigid knew Leslie. They hadn't talked since she met Leslie.

She started when Brigid touched her shoulder with concern. "Are you alright?"

Ryan ran her fingers through her hair. "I wasn't aware that you knew her."

"We need to spend more time together. Then you would know things like that. Leslie has been a close friend of ours for quite some time. I can tell you, she isn't taking any of this well at all."

A tormented groan escaped from Ryan before she could suppress it. She threw her cigarette out, buried her hands in her pockets, and said nothing.

"This is getting out of hand, Ryan. She's lost weight, she can't sleep and her law practice is suffering. She can't last much longer. You have to do *something*. Go to Rags and explain it. Get her to let up."

"I can't."

Brigid regarded her, unsure if stubborness was a factor. "For god's sake, Ryan. She can't still be mad at you."

Ryan gave her head a defeated nod. "Yes, she can."

Brigid's tone grew serious and her eyes narrowed. "Just what did you do to Sanji?"

The conversation was becoming more uncomfortable for Ryan. She crossed her arms over her chest and stared at a point in the distance. "I ripped her back to shreds."

Brigid knew the answer, but asked anyway. "With?"

"A bullwhip."

Brigid was a sensitive woman. She had the heart of a peaceful, hermetic artist trapped in the body of a passionate, fiery thoroughbred, not unlike Ryan's. It was times like these it was hardest to be friends with her childhood companion. Other people's pain charged through her like a burning rapier and made it difficult to maintain her balance between her warring personalities.

Ryan's pain was broadcasting on all channels and made it close to impossible for Brigid to concentrate.

"I thought you stopped using that."

"Only because Rags told me I couldn't use it on Sanji."

"God Ryan! What were you thinking of?" Brigid knew that, more than anything, Ryan's flagrant disobedience was the primary cause for the trouble at hand.

"Murder," Ryan replied candidly.

Brigid looked toward the sky, unable to cope with the flood of feelings.

Ryan was in the past for a short time. Her voice was acidic and hateful. "I've never been so angry with someone in all my life. I was going to kill her."

A sorrowful lump formed in Brigid's throat. "Was what she did to you that awful?"

"It's clear I thought so. I had already lost my ability to reason when she did that. I tried to hit Leslie the night before. You know better than anyone that I do *not* conduct myself that way."

"No, you don't. What kept you from killing Sanji?"

"I collapsed."

"You what!?" Brigid was horrified.

"I think we'd both like to forget the last time I had that much to drink."

"My god. Did you stop breathing again?"

"I must have. When I came to, Rags was asking me if I knew where I was and was checking my pulse."

"I had no idea you were in that much trouble. Why didn't you call me?"

"If I thought for a minute that you or anyone else could have helped," her thought trailed off in a sigh. "Brig, I had to hit rock bottom before I could climb out of that pit."

"No matter who you wasted along the way down?" Brigid began to relax a little. She was certain that this was the first sign of health she had seen Ryan show during the six year hell that seemed to be drawing to a painful close.

Ryan stood and looked into her tall friend's eyes. "Be practical. Somebody always gets hurt on the way down. The trick is not to do it on the way up."

Brigid nodded her head in the direction of the house. "She's headed for a fall."

Ryan stepped out of the confines of Brigid's crutches and

leaned over her tool box. She took out a meter and other tools and opened the door to the driver's seat. She leaned into the car and opened the passenger door, inviting Brigid to join her. Then she lay on her back on the floorboard under the steering column and began sorting through the morass of wires under the dash. Brigid settled herself in the rich leather seat and stretched her leg out near Ryan's head. Ryan tossed her sunglasses on the empty driver's seat. "There's a short somewhere in this mess."

Silence.

"I know it Brig, and that will be my fault too. So, you tell me what the hell I do about it."

"You got me there, buddy. Does she know about Les?"

"Ho no. Does Leslie know about her?"

"She asked about her because she heard Rags mention her. I'm damn glad I didn't know who she was."

"Me too — I don't need that right now."

Brigid rubbed her temples in slow circular motions, imagining what Ryan had been through. "I don't suspect you do with all this hatred you're dealing with."

Ryan stopped looking at her meter to scowl defensively at Brigid.

"Don't look at me that way, O'Donnell. You know damn well you hate Rags, and it's her you're lashing out at."

"I do not hate her. I want free of her, but I don't hate her."

"It's hard to imagine anyone going through what you've been through in the last six years and not hating her. I've prayed daily for something to happen to help you get free of Rags. I couldn't bear it if Anara succeeded in breaking your will or destroying your soul. What changed?"

"The turning point came when I realized that killing Sanji would have played right into Anara's hands. She could get two birds with one stone. I would end up in prison for premeditated murder and that would split Leslie and me up for good. Then Rags would be deprived of her reason for living too. Seeing that made me decide to fight back. I will not let Anara get the better of me."

"I wasn't aware that Anara wanted to hurt Rags."

"Not hurt her especially, just make sure she's never happy to be here. Anara doesn't care about anyone but herself. She never has."

"It's the hard way to go about it, but I believe you're stronger now. Anara and Rags can be beaten — I can feel it in my heart. My money is on you."

"I appreciate your confidence, but I'm still not close to being a match for either of them. There you are sucker." The elusive short revealed itself. "Hand me that clip." Ryan marked the wire for future reference and pulled herself off the floorboard to the seat. She rescued her shades before she sat back. Before she put them on she looked closely at Brigid's eyes.

Suddenly, Brigid's pain came rushing into her like water from a broken dam. It was overwhelming, but more so, it surprised her that she hadn't felt it sooner.

Brigid saw, as she had many times before, her own pain reflected in Ryan's face. She, too, was amazed that it was the first Ryan knew of it. All their lives, Ryan had felt, to the last detail, all her pain — immediately. They shared a private look of understanding.

Ryan didn't need to pry the reason from her cousin — it was volunteered, readily. Brigid slumped into her seat wearily. "I kicked Star out about a month ago."

"You what?" Ryan tried to picture the scene and couldn't. She shook her head, appalled at herself. This was the first she realized how out of touch with herself she had become in the last six years of hell.

"I had to. I told her that I wouldn't put up with her boycotting Cary's, but she did it anyway."

"Boycotting Cary's?" Now Ryan was confused.

Brigid turned her head slowly toward Ryan. "You didn't know she mounted a boycott against you and Rags?"

"I haven't talked to Rags, and I haven't been anywhere near a bar. So, she found out who owns it. How did that happen?"

"Oh, Les asked me what you did with your money. All I said was you had some Gay bars, and she figured it out in a second."

"She's quick."

"Mind like a steel trap if she's paying attention to what's going on."

"She told Star?" It didn't sound like something Leslie would do.

157

"Star was sitting right there. I should have kept my mouth shut. I'm sorry."

Ryan lit a cigarette and waved it. "Hey, I don't care what happens to that bar, but I'll bet Rags isn't too happy about it."

"I wonder if she even knows — no one has seen her for weeks."

"She's in love, so that doesn't surprise me. You look like hell. I'm worried about you."

"God, I miss her. It's hell without her. I'd buy that fucking bar myself if I had the money." For a moment, Brigid felt very near tears.

Ryan was deeply touched by her friend's loyalty. "If it was mine to give, I'd give it to you." She smoothed her hand over the anguished face. Brigid relaxed to her touch, as did everyone. Ryan carried with her an unrealized power to heal that affected people without her making a conscious effort. "I'm honored that you would go to such extremes to protect our friendship." An idea formed in her mind. "Would Star come back to you if you did buy the bar?"

"Probably. Rags won't sell though. That place is her home, and the patrons are her family."

"No, she wouldn't put up with a real sale, but she would go along with a sale on paper."

Brigid sat up straighter; intrigued.

"I could have Barbara and my banker make it *look* like you mortgaged the farm to buy and redecorate the bar." Ryan raised her eyebrows speculatively. "Let Star give it a new name and a facelift? Would she come back for that?"

Brigid warmed instantly to the idea. She was desperate. "Pretty shrewd, O'Donnell. She'll check it out."

"I'd be two steps ahead of her the whole way."

"What about Rags? How would you get her to go along with it?"

"Barbara can handle her. Rags can't afford to object; she's not in good shape financially. Her victim restitutions cut pretty deeply into her income — losing money at the bar would put her behind, and that's a parole violation."

"You sound pretty sure of yourself."

"Always."

"Go for it, then."

"Consider it done."

Brigid sighed heavily. "Thanks. I didn't come down here to ask for your help, you know. I came to plead Leslie's case."

"I know. Damn, I want to see her so badly. We're quite a pair without our womenfolk, aren't we?"

"Real morbid."

"You will tell her that I love her and to hang in there. Things have got to get better."

"I will. I'll be most happy to tell her you're getting well. That should do her some good. Now, if I could just get Del to come around."

"They're partners, aren't they?"

"In this very small world, yes they are."

"I'd like to knock some sense into that bitch."

"You're a fine one to talk. Your grudge runs as deep as hers."

"You're right cousin, we are morbid. I believe my little slice of heaven is in the house cooking Cornish Game Hens. Can you stay?"

Brigid licked her lips sensuously. "With waterchestnuts?"

"What else?"

"I can stay."

By Tuesday, the boycott was called off and the bar had a different name: A New Leaf. Star moved back with Brigid, and Brigid settled in to wait for Rags to relent. Leslie took heart from Ryan's message and started to eat better, although her sleep remained troubled.

13

The house was quiet, the kind of quiet Ryan preferred when she was reading. Nursing a tepid cup of coffee, she tried to remain awake while she poured over her quarterly financial report. She knew it was unwise to stretch out on a comfortable couch with such boring material.

She looked at her watch and considered retiring when she heard a car pull into her drive. The hair on the back of her neck stood on end. She put her coffee down and got up to look out the front drape.

The lights on the patrol car turned off and two officers were getting out of it.

"Shit." She walked back to the couch and picked up her jacket. From the jacket pockets she removed her switchblade and amyl nitrate and handcuffs. She put them next to her half-empty coffee cup along with her wallet, money clip and watch.

When the doorchimes rang, she sighed and walked to the front door. The porchlight came on, the red light on the alarm went out, and the door opened.

She leaned against the open door and refrained from greeting her guests. On the porch before her was a young officer, sporting a moustache, and an older one, clean-shaven.

The older one addressed her. "Ryan O'Donnell?"

Ryan nodded her head; her eyes bored into him. She was disgusted.

"Will you come with us, please? You are under arrest."

"For what?" she demanded crossly. Her attention was momentarily diverted by a light coming on across the street. She was grateful that the officers had shown some discretion by not using the lights atop their car and causing a scene. Even so, she knew that everyone in her neighborhood would know she had been arrested before the night was out. Very few secrets stayed secrets for long in her clicquish neighborhood.

"Child Molesting and Corrupting the Morals of a Minor," the officer supplied in a distasteful tone.

Ryan snorted and closed the door behind her. She locked the deadbolt and the alarm, then turned to stare into the younger man's eyes. "Let's get this over with."

He read her her rights and pulled his handcuffs from his belt. He fastened them on Ryan's wrists. "This way ma'am."

—◦◦◦—

Ryan lay on the striped mattress with her hands under her head and her feet crossed at the ankles. Her mind was blank with anger. She detached herself from her surroundings — the voices outside her cell, the scrawlings on the walls, the interminable passage of time. She refused to sleep when she was in jail or use the facilities. On one other occasion she had been held long enough to refuse a meal. It was a point of pride with her to cooperate as little as possible without actually resisting what was required of her. Her pride won her no friends or favors with the guards or the nightwatch. They purposely held her for hours before they allowed her to make a phone call.

When the guard did come to let her use the telephone, she complied automatically, but her jaw clenched and released visibly in anger. They gave her no privacy for the conversation. She ignored them and dialed.

"Law Offices." The operator had a soothing voice.

"I need Barbara McFarland. This is Ryan O'Donnell."

"Miss McFarland is in the Bahamas this week. Can someone else help you?"

Ryan looked at the clock on the green tile wall beside her. "No. I'm down at City. Will you dial another number for me?"

It had been eight weeks since she last spoke with Rags. The middle of the night was hardly the time to resume communica-

162

tions, but she only had one phone call and didn't have time to waste it.

The voice that answered was sluggish. "Yeah."

Rags was tangled in Sanji's limbs — she had been awakened by the phone call as well. Rags pulled her tight and was brought to full awareness by the surprise voice coming over the phone. "Ryan?" She rubbed her eyes and kissed Sanji reassuringly. She rolled over to look at the clock. "It's three god damned thirty. What do you want?"

"I'm in City and Barbara is in the Bahamas. Can you find someone to get me out of here?" Ryan struggled to keep the anger out of her voice to prevent aggravating Rags.

"You're where? City?" It finally made sense to her. She laid on her back and settled Sanji's head on her shoulder. "Mother in Heaven, when did they pick you up?"

"Five hours ago."

"And they're just now letting you call. Assholes. Yeah, I'll find someone, hang tight."

"Thanks."

Rags hung up the phone with her finger and let the receiver button up to dial. "Just a minute, love. I have to find someone to bail Ryan out of the slammer."

Sanji was unaffected by the mention of the name. She appeared not to acknowledge it.

Rags dialed from memory.

"Hello." The soft voice was clear and alert.

"Leslie, this is Rags. I need your help. Sorry to bother you so late."

"Rags! I wasn't asleep anyway. Whats wrong?"

"Ryan is in City Jail and her attorney is out of town. Would you go down and get her out for me?"

"I'll be glad to. What happened?"

"I don't know, but she'll tell you."

"Fine. Rags, does this mean that I can see her now?"

Rags looked into Sanji's abyssmal eyes and read the love in them. "Yes."

Rags set the receiver down slowly, lost in Sanji's shining smile. "Come here, you." She gathered Sanji in her eager arms to make love to her for the third time that night.

The clanking metallic sound of the cell door being unlocked interrupted Ryan's thoughtless meditation. Her attention was drawn to the muscular female guard standing in the doorway.

"Your attorney is here to see you."

Ryan swung her feet to the floor and stood in one fluid motion. She buried her hands in her jacket pockets and followed the uniformed woman down the hall. They halted in front of a wooden door. Ryan looked about her and noticed someone she recognized from the bar being fingerprinted.

When the door was opened, she walked in defiantly and waited for the door to be locked behind her. She stood by the door, feet apart, strong and proud. Her eyes were hard and relentless as she looked across the near empty room at Leslie.

Leslie was standing next to the grilled window that looked out on the hallway. She was draped in the palor of weariness. Ryan was a vision of arrogance and defense. The scene was not what either of them hoped for when they met again.

Ryan was mindful of the helplessness of her situation. She would have preferred to spare Leslie the knowledge of this side of herself for awhile longer. Leslie was ill at ease with the official capacity she was forced to serve in. She wanted her reunion with Ryan to be more than a business transaction.

She compelled herself to speak first. "Hi."

The struggle Ryan was involved in to subdue her contumacious attitude was evident to Leslie. She knew it wasn't her that this stony silence was meant for. She stepped closer to Ryan, slowly, intent on the jade eyes burning into her. She summoned every shred of her courage to take the last step that brought her less than a foot from Ryan.

Ryan pulled her hand out of its pocket and cupped the back of Leslie's head. She pulled her close and their lips met in a fierce kiss. Then she brought her other hand around to the small of Leslie's back and pressed their bodies together.

The power of Ryan's greeting took Leslie by surprise briefly, but she was quick to answer it. She hooked her arms about Ryan's

164

ribcage and put the full force of her desire into the kiss.

It was Leslie who remembered where they were, and she ended the kiss abruptly, resting her chin on Ryan's shoulder to catch her breath. The feel of Ryan's strong body next to hers after so long made it even more difficult to recover.

Ryan closed her eyes and began to relax. "You feel so good. Damn I'm glad to see you."

"If only you knew how badly I have wanted to hear you say that." She pulled her body away while she still could. "I have to play lawyer while I'm here. Please don't make it hard for me."

Ryan let go reluctantly. "That's fair. Let's sit down." She took a moment to admire the tailored black suit and white blouse Leslie was wearing before joining her at the metal table where Leslie had left her purse and some papers. She took the delicate wrist and looked at the time on the slender gold watch. "Four fifteen. You got here quickly. Can you always pull yourself together so attractively on such short notice?"

Leslie blushed. "I didn't even put makeup on, Ryan. Can we get serious for just a moment? Please?"

"I'm sorry." Ryan lit a cigarette. "Go on."

"They are holding you over until a nine o'clock arraignment. The judge will set bail at that time."

Ryan put her elbow on the table and rested her head on the heel of her palm. "Who's the judge?"

"Your name appears on Judge Hendricks' docket."

"He'll let me off on PR."

"How do you know that?"

"He did last time."

Leslie looked down at the papers on the desk. Mention of this incident not being the first made her nervous. "These are pretty serious charges, Ryan."

"The judges in this town tend to let people with net worths in excess of a million off on their own personal recognizance." Ryan waited for Leslie to meet her eyes.

She did, with a determined professionalism. "Just how in excess are we talking about anyway?"

"Thirty or so. We can look when we get home."

"Then I guess you can afford my fees." Leslie tried to sidestep her amazement. Ryan's flippant modesty about her wealth disarmed her. Ryan's comment about her home being "their" home didn't go unnoticed. She remembered Brigid telling her once that it took more than courage to love Ryan. Scanning the arrest record again gave her a clue to what Brigid meant. "You have been accused of Child Molestation and Corrupting the Morals of a Minor by the parents of Christine Latham in her behalf. What plea do you want to enter?"

"Not guilty," Ryan answered calmly, leaning back in her chair.

Leslie made notes on her pad. Ryan watched the comely hand direct the gold pen across the yellow lined paper.

Leslie's bangs fell into her eyes. She jerked them out of her way when she looked up at Ryan. Her feminine face was steeped in anger. "Did you sleep with her?"

Ryan was beginning to see that her lover was as excitable as she was. She smiled to herself and thought about the very interesting relationship they would have. "I did."

"Sweet Diana, Ryan. She's only fifteen!"

"Leslie," she countered, "I have been sleeping with fifteen year old girls for twenty years, since I was eleven. You tell me if it isn't a bit odd that for the first few years no one thought a thing of it. Then, suddenly, it was illegal? Yeah, not guilty."

"I'm not being judgmental. I'm jealous. I've been going through hell these past weeks, and then I find out that you've been shacked up with a girl half your age."

Leslie's righteousness was cut short by the intensity of Ryan's response. "We will talk about that later."

Leslie backed down. She was beginning to sense that she always would, no matter how angry she got. She took refuge in the papers before her. "You have two prior arrests. No convictions?"

"None."

She sought Ryan's eyes again. "How did you manage that?"

"Let's just say that everyone has their price."

"Huh. I don't know why I didn't think of *that*. Is that what you intend to do this time?"

"Yes, but in reverse."

"I don't follow."

"I've been blackmailed before, Leslie. This time I'm going to do the blackmailing. Those charges will be dropped within a week."

"Well, what do you need me for?" Leslie asked sarcastically.

"More than I want to admit," Ryan revealed. "For now, will you enter my plea later, then give me a ride home?"

Leslie got up and rang the bell for the guard. The door opened noisily. Before leaving, she turned to Ryan, "Yes, I will," and walked away.

—◆⁍❀⁌◆—

"You're one prideful woman, Ryan. I've never seen anyone stand so straight and tall with handcuffs on. I don't know how you do it, but you manage to make even a court appearance exciting."

"I was just being myself." Ryan watched the rain on the windshield as they drove through the residential area near her home. The trees were leafing out in a shimmering edge of green. The air felt fresh on her face. She kept her window opened slightly to take the edge off the feeling that clung to her from the jail cell.

"Tell me why it was that you were the only one wearing handcuffs."

"I got in a little tiff with my cellmate. Just blowing off steam. They didn't trust me after that." Ryan relaxed to the feel of the grey leather seat of Leslie's 450SL. Sleep started to overcome her until she noticed the outline of a garter under Leslie's skirt where the trench coat fell away from her leg. "Well, counselor, you didn't look so bad yourself, standing there so calm. I told you he'd let me go."

"I was very tired last night, or I would have known that." Leslie smiled with contentment. It was good to have Ryan's attention and to be alone with her after weeks of stressful separation. "You are one for fighting, aren't you?"

"I have a very bad temper and little reason to keep it under control." Ryan rested her eyes on the blonde feast at the wheel. "You look splendid in linen. It suits you."

"The way leather suits you. We make quite a couple." Leslie looked at Ryan quickly, then back to the road. "It seems that fighting isn't the only passion you don't bother to control."

167

"I have my eccentricities, and I'm a woman of powerful appetites. Not even Rags expects me to go long without female companionship."

"If you need a piece of tail, go find Christine," Leslie mocked angrily. Her gloved hand tightened on the steering wheel, and she turned the corner hard.

"She didn't want me going across the street from work to pick up flight attendants to bring home." Ryan pulled her right knee toward her chest and rested her wrist on it. Her head eased back in the seat and she turned to look at Leslie.

Another angry glance. "What's the difference?"

"She knew I wouldn't drink around Chris, and if I was chasing flight attendants, I would."

Leslie thought back to what Rags had told her about Ryan's drinking being deadly. "She didn't seem to think making you stop drinking would do much good. She said you were hell bent for leather to kill yourself. What kept you from getting that bad?"

"Nothing. I got that bad. But, I'm better now."

"Oh, Ryan. I'm sorry. It's hard to keep it in perspective that Rags cares about you. I'm glad that I didn't know you were that bad off. I never would have been able to stay away from you."

"Let's just say Rags wants me alive. She isn't always particularly interested in what shape I'm in."

"It sounds like she *wanted* you to have female companionship. You need it that much?"

Ryan rolled her eyes skyward and sighed. "Pull over."

Leslie maneuvered the car next to a curb at the corner of the street and turned off the engine. She could feel her heart race, worried what Ryan might do.

Rain gathered on the limbs above them and dropped loudly on the roof. Ryan sat up in her seat and shifted sideways to look at Leslie. "Listen to me. I have a lot to thank Rags for. I wasn't too happy about her saving my life again. I've since done a lot of soul searching, and I've decided to stick around and stop running from life.

"We both have a great deal to thank Christine for. Yes, I needed her that much. How many times do you think I wanted to call you, send cables, flowers, anything to hear your voice again, see you, touch you? I tried to drink myself to death because

I was so afraid of loving someone again. It was Christine who kept me alive while we were apart. She was there when wanting you got so bad I couldn't stand it."

"Couldn't you have sent me a note, anything, to let me know you still cared? I was half out of my mind thinking I wouldn't see you again." The strain ravaged her expression.

Ryan took the gloved hand off the steering wheel and caressed it. "No darling, I couldn't. Don't you see? If for one second I had given in to one of those impulses to contact you directly, the next second I would have been on your doorstep. Do I have to remind you what would have happened next?"

"No." Leslie closed her eyes for an instant, remembering the terrorized evening in Ryan's kitchen.

"Do we understand one another?"

She gazed into the passion filled eyes and knew, finally and completely that Ryan loved her. "Yes."

"Well then, drive on woman before I rape you right here and now."

Leslie started the engine and pulled away from the curb. "You would too, wouldn't you?"

"Damn right I would. I spend a good deal more time screwing than I do fighting. Now's your chance to bail out if you're not up to it."

Leslie teased Ryan with a protracted silence; then she placed her hand on Ryan's thigh and squeezed it. "I can handle it." She stepped on the accelerator, and the Mercedes surged down the street in response to her need.

Ryan splashed water from the kitchen tap on her face and shook the jailcell memories from her mind. Refreshed, she mopped her face with a dishtowel. "I'm a lousy host. You're pretty much on your own in this house." She opened a cupboard door and took out a glass container and walked over to the dining room table where Leslie was sitting. She broke the seal on the container and opened it. Their senses were awakened to a luxurious bouquet of fresh, ground coffee.

"Umm, where did you get that?"

"Columbia. My father discovered it the last time he was there. I've been having it imported since. I could use a cup, how about you?" Ryan smiled and coaxed Leslie into the kitchen with her to make the coffee.

"You're a temptress, Ryan O'Donnell."

Ryan laughed quietly. "I've been called many things, my dear, but never that. Have you had breakfast?"

"I can't face a courtroom on an empty stomach. Didn't they feed you in there?"

Ryan's "are you kidding" expression revealed in finer detail to Leslie the extent of the pride that motivated Ryan's every move. Leslie turned her attention to filling the coffee maker in silence.

Ryan produced a bagel, butter, and cream cheese from the refrigerator. While the bagel was browning in the toaster oven, she located some oranges. She halved them and squeezed their sweet nectar in a juicer.

Leslie found herself fascinated with the dispatch Ryan applied to simple domestic functions. It was clear Ryan pointedly hated every minute of it. She wondered why there was no employee around to perform such tasks. "Ryan, why don't you have a staff?"

Ryan handed a crystal juice glass to her. It brimmed with foaming orange juice.

"I dismissed everyone but Bonnie when father died. I wanted to be alone."

"To die?"

"Yes."

"Then why didn't you let Bonnie go?"

"I guess I didn't have the heart to ask her to leave. She's been with the family since I was born."

Ryan held up her juice glass in a toast. "I will make up for last night." Their glasses rang, and Leslie knew that this was Ryan's way of saying she would make up for the last eight weeks and possibly the last six years. She sensed that this simple citrus offering was a foretaste of the nourishment Ryan had to offer.

Ryan ate her bagel silently and watched Leslie prepare and serve the coffee skillfully. She tasted and nodded her approval. "You do nice work, lady."

"Thank you. This is delicious. You look better already. Rough night?"

"I've had worse. I hear you haven't been sleeping well." She set her cup down and stretched.

"Looking at you now, it was worth it."

"People worry about me too much. Oh, damn." Ryan walked over to the phone and picked up the receiver. She winked at Leslie and pushed the buttons hard, disgusted with herself. She cradled the receiver between her shoulder and ear and walked back to Leslie, stretching the cord behind her. She rubbed Leslie's neck as she talked.

"Is Phil there?"

"Phil, I'm sorry I didn't call sooner, but I just got out of jail."

"No. Girls."

"Yes, again. Listen, I'm not coming in today." She squeezed Leslie's shoulder. "Yes, I'm in love."

"Call if you need me."

"*Goodbye* Phil." Ryan closed the conversation with good humor and returned the receiver to the phone.

"Does he know you that well?"

"He should, after all these years."

"I would like to know you that well."

"Stick around."

"I intend to."

Ryan smiled and picked up her coffee. "Let's sit on the couch."

Leslie relaxed in the softness of the receptive cushions and watched Ryan return her wallet and other items to their proper places. The sun began to break up the rain clouds and lighten the room Ryan joined Leslie on the couch, leaned over and took Leslie's ankles and placed them in her lap. She rubbed the tops of the ankles softly.

Leslie sighed contentedly and relaxed to her touch. She drifted with the feeling of vulnerability and allowed it to penetrate her inner being. Here was safety; peace. She thought of a fresh mountain stream and released the rigid facade of aloofness she hid behind daily. Trusting Ryan gave her a sense of security. "Have you always been able to work this kind of spell over women?"

"Yes," Ryan replied sincerely, without boast.

"You must have loved uncountable women," Leslie speculated.

171

She was fishing.

"You're only the second," Ryan provided.

"But you are never alone."

"Leslie, I need women like other people need food. I have cared deeply about one or two young girls, but love is another matter. You are special."

The penetrating, almost painful expression on Ryan's face told Leslie that she was indeed special. A mercurical warmth flowed over her, terminating in the stimulated area of her ankles. "I feel special. I've never been in love. If this is what it feels like, I've been cheating myself."

"You have some catching up to do." Ryan was amazed that this vision of loveliness could have held out so long.

"Will you help me?" she asked, returning Ryan's knowing smile. Her attention was drawn to her ankles. "Do you have a foot fetish?" she teased.

Ryan ran her fingers over the champagne heel of the shoe and answered seriously, "Shoe."

Unexpectedly, Ryan's candid answer torched a spark within Leslie. A tiny gasp was forced out of her. "You want to marry me for my shoes?"

"A shoe is just a shoe, my dear, without a beautiful, well-formed foot, such as yours, to animate it." Ryan penetrated Leslie's arch with a firm stroke from back to front, eliciting another gasp from her lover. Ryan contained her excitement and put the lovely legs down. She got up and left her lover to ponder her words.

The financial report beckoned Leslie's attention. She picked it up. After reading part of the page it was open to she looked up for her mate.

Crouched by the mantle, Ryan was opening the floor safe. Leslie looked on, wondering if she should. The cylindrical top lifted out easily, and Ryan set it on the hearth, then pulled out a manilla envelope. She stood and placed the envelope on the coffee table, saying nothing about it. She noticed Leslie holding the financial report. "I said we were going to look at that, didn't I?" She sat next to Leslie and took it from her. She thumbed through the pages of the listed assets and liabilities and stopped at the final column, then she held it open for Leslie without comment.

"Thirty-two million, nine hundred fifty thousand. Oh, Ryan." Leslie was stunned. She had no idea that this modest-living individual was so affluent.

"Uncle Sam and my accountant are the only other people who know that. I'd like to keep it that way. I do *not* flaunt my wealth," Ryan cautioned.

"You go to extremes to keep it quiet. You could have a great deal of influence in your position."

"You need ambition and lots of patience to do that, love. I have neither."

"Don't you think that's irresponsible?"

"I don't care." Ryan stilled Leslie's protests. "Marry me and I'll put you on any Board you want to be on. Fair?"

"You are full of surprises."

"Get used to it."

"I don't need to be bribed to marry you, but I would like to get to know you better first."

"That could take time, and as I said, I'm not very patient." Ryan was concerned.

"Learn." Leslie picked up the report again to animate her question. She had no intention of letting Ryan rush her. "It would seem that you could easily afford to sell Cary's to Brigid. How did you talk Rags into it?"

Ryan sat back in the cushion behind her. She gauged Leslie and the extent of her knowledge before answering, "I didn't. Barbara did. The first time I called Rags was last night."

Leslie abandoned her misplaced suspicion. "I'm sorry, I wondered that if you had been talking to her before this, you could have ended our separation sooner."

"If Barbara hadn't been in the Bahamas, we might be apart still."

"Again, I am in her debt."

Ryan reached for the envelope on the coffee table. "We both are, in more ways than one." She opened it and took out one of the black and white enlargements and handed it to Leslie.

It was a photograph of three couples, males and females engaged in sexual activities. In the foreground of the picture, a young girl was scantily dressed in a French maid costume and stood with

173

a tray of drinks in her hand, watching the proceedings.

The photo trembled slightly in Leslie's hands. She fought the nausea threatening her stomach. Ryan pointed to the youth. "That's Christine." She pointed to one of the couples. "Her parents."

"Where did you get this?" Leslie stared with perverse fascination at the picture.

"Barbara hired a private detective to take them from the outside." Ryan coaxed the picture from Leslie, no longer able to look at it herself. She returned it to the envelope and dropped it on the coffee table; disgusted.

"How did you know this was going on?"

"Christine told me. I told Barbara. It was a simple matter to get the pictures. Barbara is ruthless. I couldn't have brought myself to invade Chris' privacy that way. That is why she's my attorney."

Leslie leaned back into the cushions. "Blackmail. You would really do that?"

"I have to."

"She could be in danger. Her parents might retaliate." Concern etched lines across Leslie's brow.

"I'm hoping to avoid that. If I have to hang onto these until she is an adult, I will. I can apply a sizeable amount of pressure on them to not only drop the charges against me, but to leave her alone too. This may be the best thing that ever happened to her."

"You can only go so far with a few pictures."

Ryan shifted in her seat and forced her hands deep into her jacket. "I can be ruthless too. I'll stop at nothing to protect her."

Leslie reached over and ran her fingers through the fierce black hair. "She really got to you, didn't she?" The proud head nodded under her touch. "I love you for that. How do you think they found out about your relationship?"

Ryan sighed, then answered, "I don't know. In the past it's been a diary or a jealous girlfriend." She sought the comfort of Leslie's receptive face. "It means everything to me that you understand so well."

"Let's change the subject for a while. You need a break." Leslie trailed her hand down Ryan's tense neck muscles. "Do you always wear this coat?''

"I have to be real relaxed to take it off." She pulled her hand out of its pocket and placed it firmly on Leslie's thigh. The light brown linen fabric yielded to her touch.

"One of your hardened layers?" Leslie speculated that Ryan had several, obscuring her inner self from the casual observer.

"Hmm." Ryan's thoughts had turned elsewhere. Under her palm a garter enticed her. With her little finger she explored the fine ridge made by the top of the chocolate stockings. Leslie's eyes closed contentedly when the curious hand reached up for the silky bow gathered at the neck of the sable blouse. A slight tug tumbled it over her quivering bosom. "You're right. Let's change the subject."

Leslie's grip tightened about Ryan's neck. She dug her nails into the fragile skin.

Ryan allowed herself to be drawn into kissing range. She slid her hand behind the slender back and hovered over the glossy lips. Withholding hers, she chose instead to hypnotize her lover with her jade glare. Leslie's response was immediate. She was subdued easily and willingly. Her eyes beseeched Ryan to take what was hers. Assured and confident, Ryan possessed the begging lips and rewarded them for their compliance.

Emboldened by her success at pleasing her lover, Leslie's hand ventured to the shirt snaps she longed to part, indeed had in her dreams a thousand times. The top snap gave way, the second, the third jerked open in her grasp. The following instant her wrist was encircled forcefully and plucked from its task.

Ryan emerged from the kiss. "Try something like that again and you'll find out what handcuffs *feel* like." Her low-pitched warning aroused a vague challenge within Leslie, but she gave no hint of it. A part of her held out against Ryan's determination to follow through with the treat. Her hand went limp, transmitting her feigned willingness to comply.

Ryan guided the offending hand inside her leather jacket and placed it safely on her back. She drew Leslie near and resumed her desire-filled kiss, slowly beckoning her lover to join her in the mounting heat of passion.

When Ryan seemed lost to her ardor, Leslie found her chance. Her hand traveled down the lean back, around the writhing hips and sought the button-fly barrier to Ryan's moist vagina. Spurned on by Ryan's inaction, she reached under the belt buckle and began freeing the buttons on her way to the elusive prize.

Ryan shifted her weight. Leslie believed the shift was to facilitate her progress. Her own excitement kept her from noticing that Ryan had reached into her pocket for the promised handcuffs. With only two buttons remaining, Leslie felt the ominous steel enclasp her wrist. She heard the well-used tumblers crackle into place, effectively halting her advancement.

Her hand was brutally yanked from its treasure hunt. Ryan grabbed the hand from her neck and by exerting her advantage of strength and position, she trapped it behind Leslie's back. Leslie was taken off guard by Ryan's swiftness. Before she could gather her wits to resist, Ryan had joined her appendages in a metal prison.

Ryan's next move was to stand, roughly bringing Leslie's weight and struggle off the penned wrists. "Don't. They'll tighten up and cut you."

Leslie answered her with wide eyes and a heaving chest. Her defiance withered in the face of Ryan's fixed stare. In Ryan's mind, Leslie's blatant challenge gave tacit consent to the use of handcuffs and forfeited any right to rebel.

With a mind to perfect the sculpture of helplessness, Ryan bent a knee to the sofa cushion next to her lover and calmly unbuttoned her blouse, slowly pulling it away from the heaving tits. She reached around to adjust the cuffs for comfort, then she locked them into place with the small key she took from her jacket. She squeezed the bracelets together to assure her captive she was safe, but totaly at her mercy.

Before returning the key to its home, she paused to tease the unprotected nipples. Leslie shivered and moaned to her touch. More temptation came when Ryan brought her pelvis close to the beautiful face. Stray black hairs escaped the confines of the jeans and shirttails.

Leslie tried to kiss them, but Ryan moved away at the last second. She stood again, and planted her feet apart, arrogantly. The taunted grey eyes rose to the astonishing whiteness of the skin between Ryan's breasts.

Knowing Leslie was focused on her bare flesh, Ryan lit a

cigarette and casually snapped the shirt together. She took the crestfallen chin in her hand and held it up to her wicked gaze, then bent to kiss the shining lips.

Leslie moaned under the caress, knowing she was being asked to give up control of herself. She gave it willingly in exchange for the heights Ryan would take her to. The unfathomable reaches of lust would be spread before her like an ocean, hers to explore and float upon: an excursion into ecstasy.

Ryan straightened and placed her aroused lips around her cigarette. She inhaled deeply of the smoke and the heady impulses she was getting from looking at Leslie sitting helplessly on her sofa. "I thought you were beautiful when you were angry. There's no comparison to how you look when you're powerless."

Leslie relaxed into the cushions behind her and hissed through her teeth with delight. Her eyes were caught by the action of Ryan unfastening her beltbuckle. A twinge of hope stirred in her. All for naught. Ryan proceeded to purposefully rebutton her pants and redo the belt, laying to waste all Leslie's efforts. "You're getting off easy this time. Try that again and you'll be asking for real trouble."

Leslie's response to the naked threat shot through her like an electric wave. It startled her with its intensity. In her heart she acknowledged that the time would come when she would try again. She wanted to see what Ryan meant by real trouble. The thought excited her because provoking Ryan brought thrilling results. The command in the voice, the self-possessed expression, the thinly veiled sexual menace answered needs in her that she hadn't been aware of until this moment.

Ryan extinguished the cigarette in the ashtray on the coffee table. She tired of preliminaries easily. She reached down for one of the immobile elbows and turned her lover on her stomach, perpendicular to the sofa.

Leslie felt her knees slide to the floor and her exposed breasts mash against the seat cushion. The fabric was rich and textured and roughened her nipples. Her position intensified her awareness of the handcuffs that rested on the small of her back.

Her breath quickened when she felt Ryan's knees straddle hers. Her skirt and slip fell in a puddle about her knees.

Ryan sucked in her breath to the feel of the shapely rear,

framed by a soft, champagne lace garter belt and panty. Rubbing her denim pelvis against it, "Ohn, sweet mama, I want you."

The lace hips answered her fervently. Ryan smoothed her hand around them and found the burning clitoris. She rubbed it in concentrated, penetrating circles, and sensed it was about to explode. Not wanting to prolong its imminent release, she caressed it all the harder. Leslie cried out, urging her exploiter on. Ryan's free hand cupped a breast and crushed it with her firm grip, forcing joint moans from both of them.

Ryan's own tension was building to a peak, made worse by the rasping response of the woman she was bringing to a fever pitch. Leslie was moaning and tightening; her feminine fragrance was driving Ryan wild. "Come on baby, give it to me." Ryan's command pushed Leslie over the edge. Her orgasm began in earnest.

Ryan acted fast and refused to allow her to finish and recover. She pulled her finger from the love nest and forced Leslie's confined hands into the inferno between her own legs. Leslie's response was alert and dexterous.

Ryan pulled her up by the shoulders to make it easier for her to reach the target. She abruptly abandoned the shoulders and assaulted the breasts. Leslie wailed with pleasure. Ryan brought her mouth close to Leslie's ear, kissed it and spoke with a thready hoarseness. "I'm going to fuck you so hard, baby."

"Ohh." Leslie almost fainted from the excitement. She signaled her readiness through her fingers and forced a moan from Ryan.

Ryan released all but the most important of her internal controls and allowed her savage self loose. The handcuffs dug into Leslie's softness. She barely felt it; the pain was masked by her sexual arousal. She concentrated on keeping her fingers rigid against Ryan's merciless humping. Her own need accelerated, making her reach heights she had never known before.

Leslie's physical body began to rebel. It was becoming increasingly difficult to hold her fingers stiff against her imperious sex partner. She seemed tireless.

Ryan sensed her lover's flagging endurance. "Stay with me, lover. I need you." Thin, bony hands exerted their incredible strength as they mauled the luscious breasts.

Leslie was again reminded that Ryan was to be taken seriously at all times. Her lover's passionate entreaty pushed her beyond pain into the realm of sheer pleasure. She was being taken, completely and wholly. No doubt remained in her mind.

Happily, and to her surprise, she was able to go the distance. Her reward came with the fierceness of Ryan's release. No sound was more beautiful to her than the gutteral, near screams erupting from Ryan's being. Her own release was triggered by it. She was overcome by the waves of muscle contractions conquering her nether regions. Her fingers tingled — paralyzed by the spasms inundating Ryan.

Before Leslie knew what happened, she had been freed from the cuffs and was restored to the comfort of the cushions. Ryan was massaging her bruised wrists and gently soothing her psyche with words of praise. "Oh lover, you're a natural. Damn, you were good."

Leslie floated back to reality in gradual stages. When she realized where she had been and what she had done, her heart thrilled to it. Never before had she submitted so completely or willingly to anyone. The freedom and security were new experiences for her, totally different from the tight restraints she placed on herself during every waking hour. Ryan had freed her, but she knew that she would be forever and always in bondage to the love she brought.

She smiled peacefully and knowingly at her happy, satisfied lover. They had sojourned to the palace that only lovers who can abandon themselves may enter. They returned with a special wisdom about each other that would serve as their catalyst for continuing passion and buy them return passages. Leslie learned that day that Ryan was a master of passion, and she was eagerly looking forward to learning all that she could from her.

•

14

Leslie arranged her nerves before knocking on the doorframe of David Martin's office. The door stood open, a general welcome. She scanned the organized bedlam of the aging office and felt like she was walking into a B movie.

She tapped the metal frame with her umbrella. The grey head of the occupant rose from its vague interest in a notebook. The blistery red face, framed in clouds of whiskers, appraised her shrewdly. "Miss Serle." His voice sounded livelier than one would expect of a sixty-one year old man.

She walked into the small office, crammed with books and plants. "Leslie please. Thank you for seeing me on such short notice." She looked warily at the backless couch competing for space under the barred window. David invited her to sit in an ancient wooden chair. She loosened her trench coat and laid her purse and umbrella on the floor next to her.

"I make time for anyone who wants to talk about Rags." He dumped the ashes from his pipe into an overflowing ashtray and flashed a yellowing smile at her.

She was taken aback. Charlotte had made the appointment for her, so there was no way he could have known she desired to learn more about her lover's nemesis.

"How do you know I planned to discuss her?"

"You're the young lady Ryan O'Donnell is seeing?"

Leslie's cheeks reddened. She was prepared for a businesslike meeting with Rags' parole officer. She was not prepared for him knowing about her. She hated being the subject of unknown conversations.

"Pardon me. I'm embarrassing you. The nuances of social graces escape me sometimes. I know of you, but I don't know you. Can we start over?"

"There's no need. I'm learning how to recover quicker when people throw me like that. I should have expected Rags to mention me. Everyone around her seems to expedite life and do away with amenities."

"She does have that effect on people." David rustled his thinning hair. "Only a small part of this is really mine. The rest of it is a gift from Rags."

Leslie smiled at his tender wit. "How long have you been her parole officer?"

"Seven years."

"That is quite a while. Isn't that somewhat unusual?"

David leaned back in his highbacked leather chair and regarded her pensively. "You don't know anything about her do you?"

"Very little. I've seen her court record, courtesy of a well-meaning friend. I have seen a side of her that I'm in no hurry to see again, however." Leslie took a cigarette from her bag and began to relax a little.

David reached over to light it for her. "Far too many people have I'm afraid."

"Why *isn't* she in prison?"

"Because," he paused to fill his pipe with fresh tobacco, "I'm selfish. I want her alive. I can't bear the thought of her committing suicide in some dingy prison cell. So," he puffed hard on the weary pipe as he lit it, "I call in my debts to keep her out of those hell holes. Some say it's unwise to leave her on the street, but it really is the lesser of two evils in my book."

"She doesn't strike me as the type to end her life that easily."

"Don't be fooled. Both Rags and Ryan have a fragile hold on life. Either of them could check out with the smallest provocation."

"I think Ryan has become more committed to staying alive."

"Has she? It's probably because of you then. Rags mentioned that Ryan has fallen pretty hard for you."

Leslie savored the sweetness of his words. She was proud of the effect she was having on Ryan and enjoyed having it recognized. "Rags seems to have fallen in love herself."

David shifted in his seat and stared out the foliage curtained window. "I'm not happy about Sanji moving in with her. It may prove to be her downfall."

His solemn mood made Leslie doubt the wisdom of her fact-finding mission. Perhaps ignorance was bliss. She would never know because she couldn't contain her curiosity.

"Why does that bother you?"

David inhaled thoughtfully, then let out a pained sigh. His broad, muscular shoulders seemed to deflate. "She's a loner, the sort of person who has no business sharing the intimacies of marriage with anyone. Much less someone as sensitive as Sanji. It's mellowed her, but I can see her edges wearing thin."

"I should think that would make her a little more human."

"She can't afford to let that happen." He turned his wise brown eyes on Leslie, making her shift uneasily in her seat. The perilous depths of his gaze reminded her of her first encounter with Rags. The inescapable penetration was the same. The parallels between this imperturbable man and Rags unnerved her.

"Maybe we should start at the beginning so I could be more clear about what you mean."

"That's fair." He began to recall his first experience with Rags with a wistful nostalgia. "Her case was dumped in my lap as a desperate act of the court. The authorities were at a total loss for what to make of her. I was more than surprised when I got it too. All my parolees are male."

Leslie's eyes widened, an eyebrow rose.

"Precisely my reaction. I agreed to meet with her because my curiosity was piqued. To this day, I'm glad I did. I was expecting a tough rebellious individual, someone who was going to be difficult to manage. I was only partly right. She's tough — as tough as any of my male parolees. That alone surprised me, but what I didn't expect to find was a severe case of despondency."

Leslie moved closer to the edge of her chair. "Rags?"

"Seems out of character, doesn't it? When she walked in that door for the first time, the thing that struck me hardest about her was that she was at the end of her rope. I've never seen the prison experience hit someone so hard and see them live through it."

"Behavior like that puts most people in psyche wards, not

out on parole," Leslie observed.

"Fortunately for her, they didn't see it. I saw it because we don't pose any threat to one another. All they could see was how to get rid of her the fastest way possible."

Leslie blinked and tried to imagine it. "That doesn't make sense to me. What sort of trouble was she causing that they couldn't handle?"

David settled into his seat, more relaxed. He derived a vicarious pleasure from considering Rags' prison behavior. He appreciated the poetic justice of it and felt certain someone like Leslie would also. "There was very little she didn't do except get involved in drugs. First off — no one there ever discovered that she could read their minds, so she had a field day with that."

Leslie smiled. She was beginning to see it from a different angle.

David went on, "As you know, they play Lesbianism down at most prisons. They're always trying to make it look like it doesn't exist. Well, Rags put an end to that. She literally went on a sexual rampage from the very first day she got there. She was so promiscuous, she even bedded some of the guards and a couple of civilians."

Leslie had to laugh. Although she wasn't attracted to Rags personally, she could feel the sexual power Rags had, a power that made it easy for Rags to get what she wanted. Rags' approach indeed had a delicious poetry about it that she savored, despite herself.

"They didn't think it was funny." David was smiling at their mutual pleasure.

Still chuckling slightly, "I don't imagine they did."

"Well, their applecart was upset so badly that they didn't see the real person or the real problem. Rags was coming apart at the seams. What that did for me, given her history of violence, was make me want to know why she was so upset. What makes someone like that tick?"

"How difficult was that? She's pretty complex." Leslie was intrigued.

David brightened. "It's been the biggest challenge of my life, replete with roadblocks. The hard roadblock was establishing a pattern to these attacks, a reason as it were. It's very common for people to black out when they attack someone, and Rags is no different."

"I've heard that hypnotism works well in cases like that." David motioned toward the couch. "You heard right. I use hypnotism in all my cases, but Rags wouldn't agree to it."

Leslie looked from the couch back to David. "Surely it was within your jurisdiction to compel her to submit."

"That's true, but you can't approach someone as psychically talented as Rags is in that fashion. She knows her own mind, Leslie. There was something she didn't want revealed, something she was protecting. Above all else I had to gain her trust, and that took years, instead of the months it usually takes," David supplied warmly. He relit his pipe absently while he listened to Leslie's next question.

"I wouldn't have had that much patience. Couldn't anyone figure out her pathology?"

"No one else had the patience either. That is why I succeeded where no one else did. I had plenty to do in the interim. Just tracking down and interviewing her victims took a considerable amount of time in itself. I got a pattern to develop, a flimsy one. So flimsy, in fact, that I had to resort to hypnotism with them. But then the answers started to come, and I knew I was getting close."

Leslie wanted to shake the information out of him like a fat pillow out of a pillowcase. She knew she was being skillfully manipulated to pry the information out of him, and it frustrated her. She waited silently for him to go on.

"Because none of her victims, apart from Ryan, recognized her on a conscious level. I hoped someone would on an unconscious level. It took awhile, but someone surfaced who gave me the information I needed."

"And?" Leslie inquired; lightly perturbed.

"She recognized her from a past lifetime." David waited for an inappropriate response to signal to him that Leslie was not going to be able to handle more information. Leslie was still waiting to find out more.

"And?"

"Three thousnad years ago."

Leslie sat back in her chair. She felt winded suddenly. The idea wasn't preposterous to her, as David had hoped. She simply wasn't prepared for it. Speechless, she signed for him to go on.

"Well, I knew better than to confront her with it until I had her in a compromising position. That happened when she attacked Ryan. Ryan wouldn't press charges against Rags, but the attack was none the less a major parole violation. A violation for which I could easily have sent her back to prison. I blackmailed her into submitting to hypnotism and I got my answers."

Leslie was more recovered. "Mr. Martin, will you please just tell me?"

It was clear to David that Leslie was going to stick it out, no matter what. He continued, "I was introduced to an obscure Pagan Priestess. Her name is Anara. She lived three thousand years ago and controlled a very powerful, highly esoteric, if small in numbers, clan. This clan was incredibly wealthy, and Anara's spiritual powers were awesome and finely crafted. Rags was her handmaiden. Ryan was her lover. Somehow, I don't have the details, the clan turned against Anara and killed her. Rags was the sole holdout. She remained faithful to Anara until her death. And beyond. She committed suicide to be with Anara."

"Who killed Anara?" Leslie's voice was shaky. She hadn't expected Ryan to be included in this unreal scenario.

"Someone from outside the clan, but they all plotted it."

"Ryan too?"

"Yes. I'm not sure, but it's possible that it was her idea."

"Was Ryan a woman then?" The color left her face and her palms began to perspire.

"The entire clan was female. The frightening part is that Anara is reaching out from beyond the grave, three thousand years later, to taste revenge. Her vehicle is Rags. She gave Rags a mission — to punish and break the wills of everyone who participated in the coup. Rags has found fifteen of them so far — and Ryan."

"Why did she wait this long?" Leslie knew she had to believe. She listened as though her life depended on it.

"Two reasons. One, time doesn't exist in the spirit world. Three thousand years is really nothing to someone like Anara. The second reason is that apparently this is the only time each of them reincarnated at once. For some unexplained reason, within a time span of five years, the entire clan reappeared and Anara was waiting for them."

186

"Ryan's will hasn't been broken."

David blew out smoke hard. "Damn near though. When Rags finally got around to Ryan, she put her in the hospital for three months. It got to the point where Rags had to choose between letting up or killing her. She hasn't killed anyone yet. I don't think that would serve her purpose. Or should I say Anara's purpose. Ryan has a formidable will, and her life being in peril was no threat to it."

Leslie winced against the sadness of it. She reached down and found the courage to hear the rest. "Does this mean that Ryan is in for another beating?"

David raised his hands in dismay. "I have absolutely no idea. She's one tough broad. She's clever as hell and has so far managed to keep Rags from succeeding in her effort." He appeared to talk to someone else, as though there were another presence in the room. "Ryan was amazing to hypnotize. She is clearly Anara's equal. Or so I believe from what I have found out about her. But Anara can't possibly be sated yet. My guess is that she has something more in mind for Ryan. Rags has been trying to subdue Ryan for years. As much as I admire Rags' ability, I don't think she'll make it."

"Ryan looked awfully frightenend to me."

"Frightened? Maybe. Outsmarted? Not a chance. Anara is severly limited by her use of Rags as her vehicle of revenge. To best Ryan, she is going to have to show herself. So far, she hasn't done that."

"So Ryan knows about all this?"

"Yes," he replied flatly, trying to subdue his anger.

"That doesn't sit well with you?" Leslie perceived.

"She's playing a waiting game with Anara. At Rags' expense. I've told Rags about it, but she's getting too human to protect herself."

"Too human?"

David hesitated, doubtful of the reception he would get if he revealed any more information. Leslie's clear, impatient gaze made the decision for him. "Rags wasn't born. She had no childhood or adolescence."

"I beg your pardon?" Leslie had a vague idea of what he meant, but it was too incredible.

187

"When I said that Anara's skill was awesome, I wasn't exaggerating. Rags incarnated at the age of eighteen."

"Oh, my..."

"I discovered it when I digressed her into her past life. She has no past beyond the age of eighteen and no incarnations anywhere along the line. Her most recent lifetime is with Anara. Ryan's last lifetime was with Anara also." He waited quietly for Leslie to recover from the enormity of the admission. He was pleased with her pluck. Her face showed a reserved acceptance of the information. Doubt began to creep into his mind when he watched her jaw set with firm resolve. He questioned his judgment in revealing such secrets to someone with the determination Leslie clearly had. He could see a challenge brewing, a stormy purpose coalescing in the intelligent grey eyes.

"Is there more?" Her voice was tight and constrained.

"Only a warning that you would do well to take. Leslie, this is a high stakes game. Don't put your money on the table unless you can afford to absorb your losses, because lose you will. You have a distinct look of challenge about you, young lady. For your own sake, is Ryan worth it?"

"I think you know the answer to that, Mr. Martin. I thank you for your time and openness. I really must go now." Leslie picked up her purse and umbrella and vanished. She didn't wait for a reply or the lingering, uncomfortable pauses that were sure to follow.

David stared after her, contemplating retirement.

That evening, in Leslie's home, Ryan lazed on one of the sofas. She was content and full. Leslie dispatched with the dinner dishes and joined Ryan with a brandy.

Ryan closed her eyes and savored the sweet amber drink. "These have been the happiest two weeks of my life. I am so comfortable around you."

Leslie sighed. She was pleased with herself. Doubly so because Ryan was relaxing more all the time. She had taken off her jacket the moment she arrived, which was a good sign.

Ryan preferred the comfort of Leslie's domestic expression

188

to the dispassionate emptiness of her own home. After the first week of their renewed romance she began lobbying for them to find a new home together and do away with their separateness.

Leslie found herself warming to the idea, despite her natural reluctance to disrupt her living arrangements. What she had learned earlier in the day served to convince her that it was more wise to resist the temptation to let Ryan rush her. She knew Ryan could be persuasive. Ryan spent barely less than an hour each of the last several nights enticing her. Then passion would supplant their domestic plans, and she would be granted a reprieve from making a hasty decision.

Neither of them had been to work, but Leslie was beginning to sense the irritation creeping into Ryan's nerves. Twice she tried to convince Ryan to get airborne again. Ryan was loath to leave her. She stopped short of suggesting that they go together. She wasn't confident about where she stood in relation to Ryan's first lover, the sky.

She was secretly jealous and wanted it to be Ryan who suggested that she join her and meet the competition. Instinctively, she knew that the subject was sensitive to Ryan. She was burning to know why, but asking questions sometimes brought her more than she cared to find out.

She chose another subject. "I went to see David Martin today." She spoke quietly, hoping to soften the impact.

Ryan's eyes opened suddenly, vaguely disquieted. She turned to look at Leslie. "You don't give up, do you?" An unsettling hostility penetrated her voice.

"I can't, Ryan. I have to know what I'm getting myself into. I don't like surprises."

"You got more than you bargained for from him then." Ryan put her brandy down and lit a cigarette. She settled into the sofa again and ran both her hands through her hair. She regarded Leslie through the triangle of her arm.

"He isn't at all happy with you." Leslie was beginning to feel somewhat vexed herself.

Ryan snorted. "Rags is his pet project. He devotes everything he has to it. Anything that comes between him and his lab experiment isn't real well liked."

"I thought he seemed to care a lot about her," Leslie pleaded.

189

She wasn't sure why she was defending him.

"Like hell he does." Ryan sat up suddenly, making Leslie flinch. "He wants to write a book. A damn sensationalist book. All he cares about is looking good in front of those parapsychology cronies he calls friends. I've been to the mat with him in court two times keeping him censored."

"Is what he told me even true?" Leslie was outraged.

"Just what *did* he tell you?"

Leslie watched Ryan's face darken as she covered the points David Martin revealed to her. Her stomach did a slow roll as she realized that all that she had heard was fact, not fiction. It was beginning to fade from the spectre of bizarre and absorb the shades of frightening reality. "He warned me to stay out of it."

"He's a wise man."

"Are you telling me not to worry about you, even when Rags might make another attempt to break your will?"

The sorrow in Leslie's plea softened Ryan's heart. The thought of an ally touched her unexpected. Until now, she had not known how lonely her fight had been. "It isn't my will I'm worried about. The stakes are higher for me than the others. Anara is after my soul."

Leslie was silent — shocked.

"Believe me, I'm tempted to accept your support. Your safety may be at risk even if I don't. No one knows how long Rags' hitlist is. Your name could be on it too." Ryan put her cigarette out and reached for Leslie's hand. She sheltered it between hers. "It hasn't been fair to you for me to keep quiet about this. In a way I'm glad you went to see him today. I wanted to tell you. I've wanted to tell you everything about me and not have you take it full in the face every time it hits the fan. Anara is very real and serious. I'm asking too much of you to stick by me in this." Ryan's head hung low, painfully aware of her solitude. Her despair penetrated every molecule of the atmosphere.

Leslie inhaled it, and it filled her bloodstream. An infected teardrop fell on her breast. She blinked, sending another tumbling down her front. Her eyelashes shimmered, dampened by her grief.

Ryan raised up, hopelessness scoring pathways down her cheeks.

190

"I couldn't live with myself, Ryan, if I made you go through this alone. David asked me today if you were worth it." She swallowed hard. "You are."

Ryan pulled her close and cradled the courageous blonde head on her chest. Together they held each other, silently forming a covenant and forging their individual strengths into an unassailable force.

Neither of them knew how long they remained absorbed in their communion when the phone chimed into their consciousness. Leslie answered it, subdued; "Hello."

"Is Ryan there?"

"Yes, she is. May I say who's calling?"

"Phil Peterson."

She handed the receiver to Ryan. "Phil."

Ryan smiled and took the call. "Hi, fella."

"Hey, stranger. Is she as pretty as she sounds?" Phil teased.

"Prettier." Ryan winked at her lover. "What do you need, guy?"

"I'm in a bind. I've got some hot shot oil czars coming in tomorrow morning. They want to take a Lear Jet up to Crested Butte for a meeting. You and Jerry are the only ones who know how to handle these guys with kid gloves. Jerry just called me. He has the flu real bad. Help me out. I wouldn't call you away from your hot romance if it wasn't important." He sounded hassled.

"Sure. What time?"

"Ryan, you're a life saver. Six A.M."

"I'll be there."

"Great. Give her a kiss for me. Remember, your father said you couldn't marry again unless I approved. So, you better bring her in soon."

"He never said any such thing," Ryan laughed.

"He would have. Do I have your word?"

"Yes sir. As soon as she agrees to marry me, I'll bring her in for inspection."

"Tell her to hurry up and accept. See you in the morning."

After Ryan hung up the phone, she planted a juicy kiss on her lover. "That's from Phil." She got up and put her jacket on. "I have to go, gorgeous. I really do prefer to be well rested before

I fly."

Leslie's cream-colored lounging gown clung to her as she stood. "Don't go. Sleep here, I'll be good."

Ryan gathered her up in a crushing hug, followed by a lingering kiss. She held Leslie away from her. "I won't. Let me go while I still can." She made for the door and let herself out. She closed the door behind her, almost slamming it to put a barrier between her desire and its object.

Long, determined strides brought her to her motorcycle. She drove home through a soft drizzle. The temptation to turn back only lessened when she walked into her bedroom and collapsed into her bed, damp and fully dressed. She slept dreamlessly and hard.

15

May continued unpredictable. There was a sense of hope in the clean and fragrant air. Ryan imposed a routine on herself and returned to work on a regular basis. She insisted on rhythm and balance in her new life.

Leslie had mixed feelings about the time they were forced to spend apart. Ryan was more relaxed and easier to be around, but Leslie found her loneliness difficult to manage. At times she caught herself blaming Ryan's need to fly for her loneliness; then guilt consumed her like an illness and she abandoned the idea.

She returned to her law practice reluctantly, but quickly saw that work was her best medicine. All was in good order, for which she thanked Susan effusively. Relations in the office were varied and unstable.

Leslie lived for the weekends, when she could have Ryan completely to herself. Completely, that is, except for the times when Ryan would disappear early in the morning. Leslie resented this too, for Ryan would go home to shower and change clothes. The time had not yet come when Leslie was allowed to see Ryan unclothed.

Ryan's neurotic need to stay covered worried and angered Leslie. She saw it as a betrayal of trust: a secret denied her that she believed she had a right to. She approached Ryan about it only once and was quietly, but firmly told, "When I'm ready." Nothing more was said.

It was Friday and promised to stay a warm, comfortable day. Leslie was dwelling on the problem of Ryan's privacy when she entered the reception area of the law offices. At the same time,

Ryan walked in the front door of the office. Leslie let out a tiny gasp, followed by an enthusiastic greeting, "Hi!" For a time, they stood gazing into each other's eyes as only lovers can.

Ryan greeted her. "Will you have lunch with me?"

Charlotte stared at the slender character standing casually before her desk. She was curiously amazed at what she saw. Ryan's charm was infectious.

Leslie remembered where she was. "Yes, I'd love to." She introduced Ryan to Charlotte and, in turn, to Susan Benson who walked into the reception area on her way to lunch. Each received Ryan's deliberate handshake happily, relieved to finally meet. Ryan was warm and friendly to them both.

She was cool and restrained when Delores walked in on the scene. "Del."

"Ryan," she answered bitterly. She didn't bother to contain her hot gaze.

Leslie cleared her throat to interrupt the encounter. She slipped her arm in Ryan's and headed for the door. "I'm starved. Let's go to the Tea Room." She ushered Ryan into the elevator before the ensuing storm could gather strength.

Walking down the sidewalk, she quizzed her lover. "What is it with you two anyway?"

Ryan cleared her mind with a heavy sigh and returned to the present. "Nothing important. A silly grudge that we have both been hanging onto out of habit. We just touch each other off, that's all. Some people do that."

"I guess that hoping you two could be friends is just a pipe dream."

"I'm afraid so." Ryan slowed her pace to accomodate Leslie's slower stride.

"Do you feel the same way about Star?"

"I have nothing against Star. The feeling isn't mutual however."

"If she got to know you better, I think she would change her mind. I would so like it if we could be on good terms with *them* at least." Leslie's voice carried a note of sadness.

It didn't go unnoticed by Ryan. "I'm willing to try. For you."

Leslie brightened. "Would you? Oh, Brigid would love it too. By the way. Did you send her a card?"

"We have never gotten in the practice of sending each other birthday cards. I called her this morning."

"I like phone calls. I prefer the special effort behind a card. Do you do things like that?"

"Send cards? With other people I do. It's just redundant with Brig. We aren't likely to forget one another's birthdays."

"Why?"

Ryan smiled indulgently at her luncheon date. "Because they're on the same day."

Leslie stopped dead in her tracks. Ryan laughed. "Baby, don't be mad at me. I just don't like to make a fuss about it." She cupped Leslie's cheek in her palm. People on the sidewalk dodged them.

"Ryan, you could have told me. I want to get you a gift."

"What can you get the woman who has everything?"

"Do you?" Leslie was curious if Ryan thought of herself that way.

"I have you, don't I?" She locked Leslie's eyes in a loving trance.

Leslie smiled contentedly. "You are incorrigible. And full of surprises, as usual. To what do I owe this pleasant surprise?" Leslie indicated Ryan's unexpected arrival for lunch.

"The late dinner you're going to have if you agree to go on a date with me tonight."

"You're going to spoil me. I'll start expecting you to ask in person all the time."

Ryan urged her to walk along again. "My dear, I have every intention of spoiling you thoroughly, but no intention of doing what you expect."

They reached the restaurant. In line, Ryan advised, "I want you to eat well, dinner will be quite late."

"I haven't said yes yet," Leslie teased.

Ryan smiled privately to herself, knowing all the while Leslie wouldn't refuse.

—·◦⊰❊⊱◦·—

After lunch, Ryan returned to work and approached Phil with a flight plan. She laid it on the desk before him. "I'm taking the jet tonight."

Without looking up he asked, "Who do you want for a copilot?"

"No one."

At that, Phil picked up the flight plan and looked at it. "The FAA and your insurance company won't be too..."

Ryan looked at him sternly.

"I know, I know. It's your jet."

"That's right, Phil."

Like everyone else, Phil couldn't say no to Ryan. He relented and made the arrangements for the jet. He did so happily. Ryan's renewed interest in life delighted and relieved him. He said as much to Ryan with a paternal tenderness.

Few people claimed intimacy with her. Phil's long standing as a surrogate parent made him the only male close to Ryan's heart. They understood each other. Their common love of flying brought them closer still.

Phil had devoted much of his life to Ryan, more than to his own children. It was times like these when he was most glad he had. He grew impatient to meet the author of her happiness. "She hasn't said yes, even still?"

"She will. Be patient, Phil. I respect her for waiting until she is sure this is what she wants."

"I didn't know the word 'patient' was in your vocabulary."

"I haven't ever had anything worth being patient for, until now. Anyway, I'm having fun courting her."

———✦❦✦———

Leslie arrived at Ryan's home at six thirty, dressed semi-formally, as she promised. Ryan greeted her at the door in a tuxedo.

At first, Leslie was speechless. The spectacle of Ryan in a perfectly tailored tux and unadorned white shirt with black studs entranced her. Ryan gently urged her into the foyer and closed the door behind her. She had grown accustomed to drawing stares wherever she went. She bore Leslie's incredulous expression gracefully.

"You look fantastic!" It was a whisper of what she wanted to say, but couldn't. A moment passed before she realized the disparity between her outfit and the formality of Ryan's apparel. "Why did you ask me to wear this?" A hand came to her chest with annoyance.

"Trust me. I wouldn't embarrass you that way. I have a surprise for you if you'll indulge me." Ryan put her arm around Leslie's waist and lead her toward the bedroom.

"It *is* your birthday, so I suppose I could." Leslie enjoyed teasing her lover.

Ryan didn't respond verbally. Instead, on the bed was a gold and white sequined gown, matching shoes, and bag. Leslie's hands came to her cheeks. "Ryan! It's beautiful."

Without hesitation, she picked it up and held it to her front.

"Please say you'll wear it." Leslie's fierce pride and independence made Ryan uneasy about giving her gifts. She'd felt fanciful in the past week planning this evening and she wanted Leslie to be pleased. She had nothing to fear.

Leslie loved to dress up. That was part of her attraction to modeling. She gave way to a drunken laughter and abandoned her careful reserve. She reveled in the luxurious feel of the outfit. She submitted to Ryan's watchful eye as she pulled the gown over her underthings. She wasn't surprised when it fit; snugly but comfortably. Her figure was highlighted in a way none of the clothes she owned ever made it. The simple lines sparkled with her every move. She felt Ryan's eyes caress her in newly discovered places. She slipped into the shoes. They fit as well.

She had been resisting being the object of Ryan's generosity, but from the first moment of it she felt as though she were born to such extravagance.

Ryan handed her a glacier mink stole. She hissed and purred when she felt it about her shoulders. She shivered when Ryan fastened a diamond choker around her neck and brushed a tiny kiss on her ear. A small sound arose in Ryan's throat that warned her that they might not get out of the bedroom. "Ryan." Her breathing grew labored. "Neither of us has an ounce of willpower. If we are leaving, perhaps we'd better go now." Her plea was half-hearted.

Ryan pulled away reluctantly. "You're right." She pulled a pearl dinner ring from her pocket and slipped it on her lover's finger. While Leslie was admiring it in stunned silence, Ryan transferred the contents of Leslie's purse to the evening bag and handed it, along with the formal gloves, to her. She handed the earrings to Leslie. "Put these on in the car. If we don't get out of here *this* instant, we never will."

In a daze, Leslie followed Ryan to the carriage house and allowed herself to be placed in the Rolls. She remained silent halfway to the airport. "When did you get this?" The rich smell of the Conolly hides brought her back to earth. She smoothed her hand over the luxurious seat.

"The Rolls? It was my father's."

"It's beautiful." Pause. "You haven't looked at me since we left the house."

"I know."

"Why not?"

"You are far more lovely than I imagined possible, Leslie. I'm afraid to look at you; we might end up in a ditch."

She realized that she hadn't looked at Ryan either. She had never seen Ryan drive a car before. Ryan looked splendidly relaxed and suave. She was so in control of the monstrous vehicle as she steadily guided it down the freeway.

The light of a passing street lamp caught a stone in her earring and flashed. She looked down at them in her hand and smiled. Three diamond teardrops, each larger than the one above it. She remembered what Ryan had told her about wanting her to know who she was without getting it full in the face. Apparently, Ryan didn't know how to do anything in a small way. Ryan lived hard and loved hard.

She put the earrings on and touched Ryan's thigh lightly. "I love you."

Ryan's words caught in her throat. Her hand left the steering wheel and squeezed Leslie's.

The airport came into view. Leslie asked, "Where are we going?"

"To dinner and a show," Ryan answered cryptically.

When they arrived at Peterson's Flight Service, the gate was open and a light was burning in the office. Leslie's heart began to pound as Ryan turned into the parking lot and parked next to Phil's car. Ryan laughed. "He just couldn't wait to meet you.

198

If we don't humor him, he'll never speak to me again. Do you mind?" She finally looked at Leslie. "Jesus, you look ravishing."

They walked in together to meet Phil.

He was speechless at the sight of them. He had forgotten how sophisticated Ryan could be if she wanted to. Leslie was, by far, the most attractive woman he could remember seeing. He rose instinctively and walked around his desk and blurted, "Ho-ly man."

"Phil," Ryan hissed, bringing him to his senses. He realigned his sense of propriety, under Ryan's baleful gaze.

Her voice remained charming as she introduced her lover to her mentor. He dragged out his rusty decorum and kissed Leslie's hand.

Ryan was anxious to be off. "We haven't had dinner yet, Phil."

Phil answered her without looking in her direction. His eyes continued to devour Leslie. "She's out back. Got her ready myself."

"Let's go." She escorted Leslie out the door. "Thanks. Good-night, Phil."

He called paternally after them, "Have a good time."

As they walked around to the back of the building, Ryan apologized for her friend's behavior. Leslie said she understood and asked again where they were going.

"Vegas," Ryan replied. They rounded the corner and a shining white jet came into view.

Leslie felt as though she would swoon. At last her desire to fly with Ryan was about to be fulfilled. It was like a dream, yet at the same time excrutiatingly real. Pleasure and excitement suffused her. She floated into the plane, all the while determined to watch every move Ryan made.

After removing the blocks from the front wheel, Ryan joined her in the jet. She smiled and shook her head. "I forgot to ask you if you get airsickness."

"Oh no, I'll be fine."

Ryan reached across Leslie's lap and fastened the seatbelt, then did her own. "I think I'd better hurry and get this honey off the ground. I want to be as high as you are. Damn, you look good. I don't know if I want to take you out in public if everyone is going to drool over you like Phil did."

"You love it," Leslie bantered.

Ryan turned her attention to the task at hand. Leslie settled in to savor each detail as Ryan ran through her checklist and began to taxi to a runway. She listened intently to the conversation between Ryan and the control tower. It sounded like a foreign language to her, but Ryan spoke it fluently and provocatively.

They took off, sandwiched between two commercial airliners, and headed west. They were in the air fifteen minutes before Leslie was able to put her emotions in order. This too, was Ryan's way. She introduced Leslie to her competition in grand style, a night flight in a Lear Jet. Her jealousy melted in the face of the otherworldly expression that had taken over Ryan. "I can see why you love it so much. It's glorious up here. You are marvelous to watch. Now I know that you're in good hands when we aren't together."

Ryan stared hard at the vision next to her. Love welled up and threatened to overflow the banks of her heart. All she could say was, "*You* understand."

The rest of the flight was accomplished in near total silence, each absorbed in her private thoughts. Once on the ground, Ryan resolved to be happy and carefree on their date. She began by molesting Leslie against the outside of the jet, which reduced them to giggles.

She arranged in advance for a chauffered limosine to meet them. It took them to the Strip where they dined ravenously on steak and lobster. As promised, they took in a show: Diana Ross. From there, on a dare from Ryan, they maximized their heterosexual appearance and went dancing in a straight nightclub. To their mutual surprise, they enjoyed themselves tremendously. Each was enormously proud of the other.

On the path up the Strip toward the airport, Ryan had the chauffer stop at the MGM Grand.

"Do you play Blackjack?"

"I understand the game, but I'm not lionhearted enough to gamble. I'll watch you."

Blithely cashing a personal check for twenty-five thousand dollars brought pleasure to Ryan because Leslie enjoyed it so thoroughly. Ryan took her chips to a vacant table and engaged the brunette dealer's eyes. Leslie sat down beside her and looked on as the dealer paled slightly and turned to her pit boss to say something Leslie didn't catch.

Ryan turned her confident stare on the balding, cruel-looking man. He accepted the challenge and raised the limit on the table.

"Is the lady playing?"

"I'll play her hand."

The cards came in fast succession, followed closely by more chips. Twenty minutes of Ryan's relentless winning brought about an early shift change for the dealers. The brunette was replaced by an Italian man; tall and cool. Ryan knew she had pulled their best dealer, he started winning immediately.

Leslie began to squirm in her seat. She accepted the cocktail she ordered gratefully. Ryan refrained from drinking. Not because she wanted to keep her wits about her at the table — the money meant nothing to her. Night flying carried with it its own set of hazards.

She did tire of the dealer winning because of her pride. She lit a cigarette and relaxed. Her attitude changed and she began to win easily again. She tipped the dealer heavily. He was moderately polite, but soon beads of sweat formed on his forehead. The pit boss was talking on the phone behind him and rubbing his chin in choppy movements. A small crowd gathered to watch, but were held at bay by an armed security guard.

When Ryan noticed another dealer heading toward her, she looked at her watch. "It's three. Let's go. I want to miss the vacation traffic." She turned to the frantic pit boss and said, "I'm done here." To the security guard, "I could use your assistance, please."

He nodded quietly and accompanied her to the teller to cash in the chips. She accepted their offer of a check and walked out with Leslie's arm resting regally on hers. The valet whistled for their limousine.

Inside, enroute to the airport, Ryan could contain her laughter no longer. She handed the check to Leslie. It was for one hundred-fifty thousand dollars.

"This is incredible!"

"Damn that was fun. I needed that. Took those suckers for a hundred fifty Gs in an hour! I love it."

"The rich get richer." Leslie felt a flood of laughter emerging

201

from her as well.

They did get caught in traffic. Ryan let loose her restraints and tensions that built during their madcap evening and took Leslie on the floor of the jet before taking off for Denver.

By Sunday morning they were both sufficiently revived to think about doing something besides sleep and make love. Ryan left to change and retrieve her cycle. When she returned, she found Leslie dressed in jeans and a flannel shirt.

"Ryan, I want to go for a ride on your motorcycle."

Ryan was taken aback. "You do?" To her, nothing was more incongruous than her sophisticated lover on the back of a chopper such as hers. She laughed at the request and was treated to Leslie's first pout. Her heart melted into a waxy pool in the pit of her stomach at the sight. She could not bear to see Leslie refused anything she asked for. She gave in.

Over breakfast Ryan quizzed Leslie about her riding experience, which was none. Leslie headed off all Ryan's objections with the cool purpose she saved for the courtroom. Her final and winning argument came when she produced the helmet she had purchased the week before. Ryan smiled at her determination. After their meal they took off, Leslie with her heart in her throat, Ryan shaking her head in amazement.

They took the Turnpike to Boulder. She sped the entire way and raced between traffic. From Boulder they took off for Nederland. The clean mountain air intoxicated Ryan and her passions built in pressure between her legs. She started searching for a side road that might be dry enough to navigate this early in the season. She spotted one on the opposite side of the road, but passed on. It was best explored on the way down. They stopped for coffee in town. Leslie was radiant with excitement which did little to assuage Ryan's growing need.

The road she picked was steep but dry and had several potential places for one in search of privacy. She settled on a small grassy area behind a large boulder. She guided the bike into a position that suited her purpose.

She left the engine on, letting it idle in slow, powerful throbs beneath them. She took her helmet off and laid it on the ground. Leslie followed suit. Ryan braced the weight of the machine between her legs and lifted slightly. She unfastened her belt buckle

202

and ripped open her fly. She reached behind her for Leslie's hand and plunged it into the burning recesses of her jeans. Leslie's hand was cold and willing. Ryan leaned her head against Leslie's shoulder and whispered hoarsely, "Touch me."

Leslie's heart all but stopped. The sensation of her finger gliding into Ryan's vagina for the first time was beyond power. But, touch her she did. Ryan came to her again and again, hastened by the rhythmic surges of mechanical might beneath her.

When Ryan could function again, she squeezed Leslie's hand, returned it to its owner, took off her gloves and refastened her clothes. She gave Leslie a small kiss and put her helmet back on. Leslie did the same, unsure what would come next.

Ryan put her gloves back on and headed slowly back to the hiway.

The way home lead them through Boulder and once more, recklessly down the Turnpike.

Ryan was relaxed and calm. Leslie boiled, as they waited on the side of the road while the officer wrote out the speeding ticket. Ryan had been doing one hundred miles an hour, bringing Leslie's desire to an uncontrollable pitch.

Ryan aggravated her even more by rubbing Leslie's thigh, getting dangerously close to her anxious crotch. The officer pretended not to notice what was going on, even as his own excitement threatened his concentration. Ryan took the ticket and shoved it into her pocket. She sedately drove off at half her previous speed.

In Ryan's living room, Leslie lit into her. "Damn it, Ryan. He could have taken us in for going that fast. Then you had the nerve to tease me like that, right in front of him!"

"What's wrong angel?" Ryan asked sweetly, feigning innocence. "You hot?"

"You know I am, and in more ways than one."

"Well, let's take a shower and cool off then."

Ryan was halfway down the hall before Leslie registered what had been said. She dashed after her.

Ryan was sitting on her bed removing her boots and socks. "Are you going to wear those into the shower, or are you going to strip?"

Absently, Leslie began removing her clothes — her eyes fixed on

Ryan.

Ryan ignored her and went about taking off her clothes. First the cufflinks tumbled onto the dresser, then the belt was unfastened. She faced her lover, deliberately enticing her with a nonchalant striptease. She opened the snaps of the shirt one by one and revealed her downy white flesh.

Of all the contrasts in Ryan's style, this struck Leslie as the most dramatic. The wild black hair and garments, set off strikingly by the brilliant skin. Spellbound, she watched the shirttails pull free of the jeans, the shirt ease over the shoulders, the slight, perfectly contoured breasts exposed. She controlled her urge to reach out for the chestnut areola and nipples that stood as defiantly as their owner. She thought better of any action save removing anything that would come between their nakedness after so long a wait.

The jean buttons lurched open in a flurry. The pants slid secudtively over Ryan's hips, glided over the muscular thighs like they had been greased. She stepped out of them casually and abandoned them on the floor.

A moan cut the silence. Leslie weakened at the sight of the raven womanhood. Her wrist was caught. She followed, intoxicated, to the shower.

The water was warm and relaxing. Leslie paid it no mind. She lost herself entirely to the sleek touch of Ryan's flesh. She resolved to explore every inch of it and had set about doing so when Ryan forced her back against the shocking cold of the tile behind her.

"Still hot?"

The combined sensations of the tingling chill running down her spine and buttocks and the searing press of Ryan's weight against her front focused and darted in cruel, insistent jabs to her genitals. "Oh. Ryan. Don't torture me. I can't take it any more."

Ryan sank slowly to her knees, leaving a trail of kisses intermingled with beads of water that dotted Leslie's pale landscape. She caressed her lover's need with her capable tongue, heightening and relieving it by turns. She pulled away and stood, leaving something for her lover to think about.

When Leslie could open her eyes, and her breathing subsided, Ryan was busy lathering her hair, damnably detached. Leslie took advantage of the opportunity to inspect her new treasure, uninhibited by Ryan's disturbing gaze. Her original survey hadn't revealed the numerous scars about the boyish frame. Long, thickened ones ran the course of the knees. An angry, pearly snake scored the abdomen. Smaller ones drew her attention to a variety of insults about the body. All residue of her passion rinsed away at the sight of it. She covered her mouth too late to keep Ryan from noticing her concern.

"What?"

Leslie's voice was edgy; near tears. "Did Rags do that to you?"

Ryan squeeked the excess water from her hair, stepped out of the water and traded places with Leslie. Compassionately she took the soap and began to caress Leslie's body with suds. She answered her with soothing care. "Yes, she did." She sensed the aching in her lover's heart. "Please don't. It's over now. Nothing hurts any more."

"How can you possibly still be friends with her?"

"I can't hate her for it. She's a pawn, caught in a deadly game. I'm alive. You're here. What more can I ask for?"

"You didn't know about Anara when this happened. How could you forgive Rags?"

"I knew. I've known all along."

"You have?"

Ryan handed the shampoo to her. "Sure. I was in the clutches of Death when I first met Rags. You see things."

"You're a better woman than I."

"Not by a long shot, my dear. You'll learn that one of these days."

"I doubt that. I hate to see such a fine body insulted like this. It's a shame."

"It would be a bigger shame if it happened to this fine body." Ryan ran her hands up the silky waistline and cupped the remarkable breasts. Less than a minute passed before the conversation was dropped and Leslie found her passion again.

—◦❦❦◦—

In the evening they took a quiet stroll about Ryan's property.

"It's lovely out here. I'm surprised you don't spend more time enjoying it."

"I didn't enjoy it until you came along." Ryan stopped at an apple tree and picked a blossom. She handed it to Leslie tenderly. "I didn't enjoy anything until I met you."

Leslie smiled shyly. She thought again about Ryan's scarred body. "Are your scars the reason you haven't wanted me to see you undressed?"

Ryan looked away suddenly. She knew the question would come. Knowing made it no easier. The fact that they were close and growing more so every day was due largely to Leslie's relentless prying. She forced the opening in Ryan's heart wider and injected herself into the new vault.

This subject was perhaps the most sensitive of all for her. She summoned her courage and met Leslie's inquisition head on. "No."

"I would like to understand why," Leslie encouraged gently.

Ryan leaned against the trunk of the fruit tree and gauged the trusting grey eyes. They were safe, as always. "I'm sure you do. This isn't easy for me, lady." She picked a piece of loose bark and toyed with it before going on. "I'm excessively private by nature. I always have been."

Leslie cocked her head and focused on the wavering jade eyes. The dusk faded them. "I was beginning to see that. It goes beyond that doesn't it?"

Ryan looked into her eyes. "The main reason now is because . . ." She turned her head toward the sliver of moon. It shone seductively near the skyline. She pulled her fingers through her hair. "I'm not very comfortable about being female." Once she had said it, she knew Leslie would understand and would accept it. "As long as I keep dressed around other people, I don't have to deal with it."

Leslie did understand. She had suspected as much for a long time. She was grateful to Ryan for sharing it with her. "Now? Wasn't it that way before?"

With the initial hurdle passed, Ryan began to relax. "I didn't realize I *was* female before."

"That's hard to believe."

"Not really. My father was no fool. He was determined to

have a son and damn anyone who got in his way. That's why we left Ireland. The Church and his family both hassled him about the way he was raising me, so he left. He decided to settle in Denver because the MacSweeneys invited him.''

"Brigid's parents?''

"Yes. Brig is my cousin." Ryan smiled at her surprise. "Didn't she tell you that?''

"No. She must have thought you did. I think that's wonderful. How close?'' Leslie was intensely curious about families in general and Ryan's in particular. She missed her own a great deal.

"Her great grandmother and my great grandfather were brother and sister. The MacSweeneys sympathized with my father. They convinced him that in America he could raise his child as he wished, so he accepted. So, thorough man that he was, he founded the school I attended to keep my environment so tightly controlled that I wouldn't get any messages that I wasn't male. I never took an interest in television, so he didn't have to combat that brainwashing. Of course, the staff had to indulge the charade from the beginning.''

"He must have known that wouldn't last.''

"It was a sad day around here when Nature stopped cooperating with his game. I fought back by insisting on a hysterectomy. I wasn't going to go through life with a monthly reminder of life's little joke. I managed to make a token adjustment. The whole affair was more traumatic for my father's peers than for me.''

"Did they blame him?''

"Somewhat, but they were more upset about having to view me in a different light. Suddenly, I wasn't a prospective son-in-law, rather I was a possible mother to their future heirs. So, everyone settled in to wait for a delicate tearose to be grafted to the old world stock.''

Leslie smiled warmly. "They were disappointed. I'm not.''

Ryan started walking again. "Father still thought he had a son; the rest of society began to see me for what I was. They resigned themselves to the fact that several million dollars of inheritance had been withdrawn from the marriage market.''

"Did you have to cross the tracks for dates?'' Leslie asked half-seriously.

"No." Ryan had relaxed completely in the softness of her lover's compassion. "Becoming Ryan O'Donnell's love interest was still a lucrative pastime. There was a surplus of available young ladies back then, and gold digging wasn't beneath any of them."

"Oh, Ryan. That is disgusting." Leslie curled her lip in a darling gesture that made Ryan smile.

"But sensible. The point is — this gender confused adolescent who was just excessively private became compulsive about staying dressed in front of other people."

They halted to face each other in accord. Leslie smoothed Ryan's springy hair and brought her hands down to caress Ryan's proud face. "Do you think you'll ever become more comfortable with being female?"

"No. But I can get more comfortable with you."

"That's what I'm after."

16

Star looked up from her book. She thought she heard a car in the drive. Brigid was absorbed in petting one of her cats and didn't notice. The fire crackled peacefully, warming a mid-May evening.

Star rose to investigte and pulled the lace curtain away from the front window. The vehicle's outline contrasted against the murky dusk. Foremost was the distinctive winged hood ornament. She turned to Brigid. "Brig, who do you know that owns a Rolls Royce?"

Brigid stiffened slightly and regarded her mate warily. "Ryan."

Star jerked the window covering back. "By damn, it is her." She glowered at her lover. "Did you know they were coming?" Her tone was accusatory.

"No, I did not. Answer the door, Star," Brigid retorted.

Star yanked the curtain closed and swung the door open suddenly, startling her guests. She greeted them with silence and a fierce, blazing expression.

Brigid rescued the new arrivals by coming to the door and pushing the screen open with her crutch. "What a pleasant surprise. Come on in you two."

Leslie and Ryan crossed the threshold, openly abandoning caution. Before they arrived, they had discussed how to respond to Star's negativity and decided that taking the offensive stance would be their best defense. They greeted Brigid like a long lost friend and were received warmly. Leslie endured Star's insincere hug. Ryan fielded visual swords with dignity.

Brigid scooped up a cat from her chair. "Help me put these

cats in the guest room." Star grabbed the other two and follow-ed Brigid and her passenger, bouncing happily on her shoulders, to the guest room. The door was shut behind the indignant felines and Star turned on Brigid. "What the hell did you shut them up for?"

"Because Ryan hates cats."

"Oh, well. By all means, we can't have her be uncomfortable."

"Don't be a bitch, Star. It took a lot of courage for her to come up here. She knows how you feel about her, and you can bet she is doing this for Les."

"How noble of her."

"It's more than you ever did for me," Brigid replied acidly and returned to her company.

Star was transformed by Brigid's painful truth. Their recent separation had shown her how much Brigid meant to her and how unreasonable she had been. This was the first time her loyalty was being put to the test; she resolved not to fail. The trouble Brigid had gone through to get her back touched her soul to the depths. Their love was strengthened by it. She did not want her temper and convictions to come between them again. If Ryan had the courage to swallow her pride and subject herself to the scene that was sure to follow, she did as well.

Ryan and Brigid were talking quietly, and Leslie stared into the fire. Ryan had pulled a chair from the parlor and was sitting between Leslie, nearest the fireplace, and Brigid's comfortable seat.

Star marshalled her emotions. "Can I get either of you some coffee or a drink?"

"Coffee for me," Leslie answered with relief.

"Brandy," Ryan joined.

"Brig?"

"I'm fine, thank you." Brigid favored her with a smile and hoped she would have more reason to smile as the evening wore on.

Star returned with the refreshments. For herself she fixed a double scotch. She served everyone congenially and left the bran-dy decanter on the table next to Brigid.

Ryan opened the conversation. "How are things going at the bar?" She purposely directed the question to Star.

210

"Great. Haven't you been to see it yet?"

Ryan and Leslie shook their heads.

"Please come by some night. It came out lovely. I suppose I should thank you for selling . . ."

Her voice trailed off uncomfortably. She didn't want to let it show how it galled her to thank Ryan for anything.

"As long as you two are happy, that's all I care about." She smiled indulgently at her cousin. She knew Brigid felt guilty about the deception, even if she didn't. It had served a very important function, easily worth a dozen deceptions. Above it all, Brigid was grateful to her friend and pleased she cared about her relationship.

"Do you really care about us, Ryan? Or was it just expeditious financially?"

"Brigid is my best friend," Ryan answered, sensing no malice in Star's question. "It hurt her to be apart from you, and I don't like to see my friends hurt. I have always cared about your relationship. The money has nothing to do with it. I wouldn't put money before a friend, ever."

Leslie shifted in her seat, watching for signs of a storm. Out of the corner of her eye she could see Brigid's knuckles whiten on the arm of her chair.

"You do have values then," Star remarked sardonically.

Leslie gasped. It was clear that if Star knew as much about Ryan as she claimed, she wouldn't be courting danger in this fashion.

"What makes you think I don't?" Ryan was relaxed, her voice was even.

"The way you treat women," Star hissed.

"What do you know about how I treat women?"

"I talked with Beth for one thing. I've heard about others."

"Did you learn about Beth from Toni?"

"Yes."

"Tell me something, Star. When you tell people about Beth, do you tell them that your friend Toni had to change professions because she couldn't keep her counsel?"

Star took a long sip from her drink before replying, "No."

"Yet you think that what happened to Beth was wrong. It doesn't matter that no one in the medical community will have anything to do with Toni because she couldn't preserve sacred medical confidences." Ryan hadn't realized the vast disparity between her value system and Star's. It was inconceivable to her that anyone could condone the actions of someone like Toni.

Star was trapped and she lashed out, "There is no comparison to what you do! None at all. How can you justify tearing that poor woman's insides up like that?"

Ryan contemplated her empty brandy glass for a moment. She looked up at Star, her eyes narrowed slightly. "She wanted it."

"Oh. I suppose she wanted a broken jaw too."

"Rags did that."

"Same difference."

"Rags and I aren't joined at the hip, you know. Beth had a glass jaw. That blow wouldn't have raised a bruise on most people"

"When you were done with her she took off with a motorcycle gang."

"That was her choice."

"Oh, fuck, Ryan. Don't give me that. You ruined her. What else could she do?"

The light from the fire caught in Ryan's eye and gave Star her first portend of the emotions she was so glibly flirting with.

Leslie searched Brigid's grey eyes for a clue to a way to defuse the situation.

"More brandy, Ryan?" Brigid interjected the decanter to draw the fire in her direction. She knew it would lessen to a deadly coal if she could engage Ryan's attention. Ryan allowed herself to be disturbed and accepted the refill quietly. Brigid pleaded with her non-verbally and Ryan relaxed. She sat back in her chair and lit a cigarette. Leslie took one from her bag to get Ryan to look her way. Ryan performed the service for her lover then touched her arm reassuringly.

Star was still waiting for her answer.

"Things were going along just fine with her until she developed a death wish. Neither of us were interested in obliging her, so we dumped her."

"Just like that," Star imitated the action of dropping something into a garbage pail, "You dumped her."

"If it bothered you so much," Ryan interrupted, "why didn't

212

you take her in? Or to one of the safe houses?"

Star was stunned by the suggestion. Her sisterhood had never been questioned before, and she didn't know how to answer.

Ryan went on, "I realize I have developed an infamous reputation because of my sexuality. It has been created almost entirely by people who have no understanding of what goes on." They all knew Ryan was referring to Star without accusing her directly. "I have never bothered to combat it because I don't care what other people think about me. It does invade my privacy however, and I *am* getting tired of that.

"The pain, and the giving and taking of power involved in a sexual encounter with someone like Beth is always by mutual consent. She was not forced. She submitted to us willingly."

"Nobody could want that!"

"She did, and so do several other women I know."

Star shook her head violently, unable to acknowledge the possibility.

Leslie ventured into the conversation. "Not everyone takes their politics to bed with them, Star."

Star's hand came to her mouth in horror for a heartbeat, then she took it away to speak. "Sweet Diana, she's corrupted you too."

Ryan flashed an urgent look of warning to Brigid. Leslie laughed at the suggestion before Brigid could do anything.

"Don't be silly, Star. I'm not some brainless twit with a ring in her nose. I know perfectly well what I'm doing, and I trust Ryan implicitly. She has shown me things I had no idea existed and she will continue to do so, but only with my consent."

"I have never gone against anyone's will sexually," Ryan added crossly.

"I don't believe it."

"You're a fool." A definite storm was brewing. Even Star could feel it.

"A colossal one too," Brigid broke in. "Don't make her mad, Star, or we'll not get anywhere."

Star softened somewhat, at her lover's request. "I concede. I believe she hasn't forced anyone sexually, but only because you say so, Les." To Ryan, "But you have done your share of damage in non-sexual contexts." Star was unsatisfied with the direction the conversation was taking. She wanted to press Ryan further about her sex practices. Leslie's admission did little to dispel her curiosity.

"If you are referring to my temper, yes, I've had my share of fights. We both have." Ryan pointed to Brigid with her thumb.

"You act like you're proud of it."

"I'm not ashamed of it."

"She'd like for you to be. Then maybe I'd stop hellcatting around with you," Brigid laughed nervously.

Leslie rose from her chair with her coffee cup in hand. She could see nothing was being accomplished by this conversation other than to destroy forever any chance of becoming friends. "I need a refill. Come help me, Star. Want anything, Brigid?"

"No."

Star followed reluctantly. In the kitchen Leslie turned on her, "What in the hell do you think you're doing in there? Have you any idea how close you came to getting the daylights beaten out of you?"

"Les, I can't believe this is happening. I never thought I'd see the day when you would defend that vicious womanhater."

"Stop it, Star!" Leslie's words stung as hard as a slap. "Wake up and look past the end of your nose at what's going on around you, just once in your life. If Ryan lights into you, who do you think is going to stop her? Me? Brig? We have no control over her when she's calm, much less when she loses her temper." Leslie didn't allow Star to react. "I came here with her so we could start to be friends. You aren't using any sense at all. To you, there is only one side to Ryan, and in your incredible stupidity you bring it out just to prove your point. I honestly thought you were smarter than that."

Star came unravelled and began to cry. "Oh, Les. I'm sorry. I know I'm being an ass. It's just that I've hated her for so long. I couldn't stop myself from venting it."

Leslie put her arms around her friend and comforted her. "Sweet Star. You mean so well." When the sobs lessened, Leslie held her away to look into the moist eyes. "I know Ryan and Rags much better now, and I can assure you, you have the wrong person on trial out there."

Brigid appeared. "Are you alright?" She took her lover's chin in her hand and searched for a reply. Leslie handed Star a tissue and retreated a short distance.

"I'm fine."

"I hope so, because Ryan is getting drunk."

"Damn. That's the most she's had to drink in months," Leslie cursed.

Brigid warned Star sternly, "I don't know how to spell it out any clearer for you, but she can be very dangerous when she's drinking. Seeing you two fight like this is enough to make *me* want to drink. I can't take it, so back off."

Brigid's threat brought Star back to a sense of reason. It did more to frighten her than the potential of violence she was arousing within Ryan.

Leslie left Star in her lover's capable hands to seek out her intoxicated mate. "Maybe we ought to leave," she suggested gently.

"Sit down." Ryan knew full well that Leslie remembered the consequences of challenging her judgment; impaired or otherwise. Leslie took her seat and tried not to look worried.

Eventually, the pair in the kitchen returned with Leslie's forgotten coffee. They settled themselves, and Star continued, more reasonably. "Ryan, it has been pointed out to me, rather emphatically, that it's really Rags my anger is meant for, not you. I can see that now. Will you forgive me?"

Ryan regarded her thoughtfully. She replied, "We could learn to get along if you keep that in perspective, Star."

Star smiled wanly, vaguely pleased that Ryan wanted to improve relations. "Brig has always contended that you were different before your father died. I want to believe that."

"Ask Dana. She can tell you," Ryan provided calmly.

Star's eyes widened and darted to Brigid. Brigid's eyes were closed and she was shaking her head, doubting Ryan's sanity. Leslie felt her temples grey. She wondered to herself how many more bombshells Ryan had left to drop. Her mind made the connection. She remembered who it was that the Lautrec poster above their table on their first date reminded her of. She regarded Ryan pensively.

"How would she know?" Star asked urgently.

"Because, we were lovers for three years, before," Ryan emphasized, "my father died."

An image of Dana formed in Star's mind. The alluring, auburn, childbride of Leslie's partner Delores. She tried to connect the innocent beauty with Ryan and couldn't. She looked from Ryan to Leslie and marveled to herself. Ryan's charm was consistent and powerful. She was constantly in the company of attractive, intelligent women. Star had vastly underestimated this woman. Curiosity began to cleanse away her prejudice. She asked softly, with genuine concern, "What happened?"

The peace keepers breathed a collective sigh. The storm front had blown through, leaving no damage.

Ryan relaxed in her chair and put her booted ankle on her knee before answering, "There is a difference of opinion on that score. I say that she left me when I needed her most, into Del's very willing arms. Del's version is that I neglected Dana and she rescued her." The bitterness in Ryan's voice alerted Leslie that the grudge went far deeper than Ryan had led her to believe.

"Just what constitutes neglect?" Leslie asked.

"Air time." Ryan's cryptic answer meant nothing to Star. It brought back sad memories for Brigid. It answered numerous questions for Leslie. At last, she knew why Ryan had been so sensitive about the time they spent apart when Ryan was flying.

"I don't understand," Star said.

Ryan explained tenderly, with patience, "I was very young and very in love with Dana. I also spent the lion's share of my time flying. In those days, I couldn't get enough. Dana and I fought bitterly about it. She is the type of woman that requires a great deal of attention, and I was too stubborn to give it to her. When my father died, I was unbearable with grief. Dana couldn't handle that either, so she took off. She didn't have far to go. She had been sleeping with Del for months, and I had been too busy to notice.

"I have been mad at the world ever since. A lot of people got hurt in the process, including me. Hopefully now," she gazed lovingly at Leslie, "I can get over that."

For the first time, Star was touched by Ryan's humanness. Still, Ryan's reaction to the tragedy seemed out of proportion. "It must have hurt terribly to lose the two people you love most at the same time. Don't you think you went overboard reacting to that

216

pain?''

Ryan didn't answer, so Brigid answered for her. "Darling, Ryan isn't like most people. She loves and hurts far more deeply than either you or I could bear. It's true, she lashed out at the world, but if she hadn't, the pain would have consumed her alive. It was a small price to pay compared to the loss we all would have suffered if she had lost the battle." Her explanation was more for Leslie's benefit than Star's.

Ryan waited calmly for understanding to register in Star's eyes. She was not disappointed. Star wanted to console Ryan but knew it wouldn't be acceptable. Ryan simply shared a private look with Star and the possibility of friendship was born.

It was hot and close. Rags was sweating hard, but manual labor helped her keep her energy under control. She and two men were unloading heavy cartons from the back of a semi trailer. Her thoughts were occupied with Sanji as they always were. Thinking of Sanji made the day pass faster and more pleasantly.

A negative, angry presence penetrated her thoughts and, before she could recognize it, a terrific blow from behind knocked her off balance on the loading dock. She recovered quickly and blocked the next one.

Crazy Jess was a skilled fighter in her own right. She had seen Rags beat a man rather severely in the past and it was for that reason she had never let their frequent altercations come to blows. She would have kept the scales balanced that way for years to come had she not learned recently that the woman of her dreams, Sanji, was living with her much hated enemy. The time had come when she resolved to do something about it and tip the scales in her favor.

She was not prepared for the punishing force of Rags' answering attack. Rags let loose a fury she could not match. Criminally insane.

The jeering encouragement of Rags' fellow workers, gathered around to watch the fight, aroused Leonard Pace's curiosity. He looked away from his clipboard a moment, then suddenly he

217

realized what was going on. He dropped the clipboard and started running in the direction of the altercation. He called out to a giant, stupid looking man lifting a large crate. "Animal, drop that and get over here." The man obeyed without hesitation. The crate fell to the cement and cracked open, spilling packing peanuts all about. He ran after his boss to the scene of the fight. The foreman broke through the crowd and instructed animal, "Get Rags off her."

The great man responded immediately and pulled Rags and Crazy Jess apart. Jess disappeared the instant she'd been freed from the death trap. Rags fought against Animal's strength. "She strong," he said.

The angry foreman chastized his employees, "I told you never to let her fight anyone, ever. She could have killed that bitch. I don't want any fucking murders on my dock. Now get back to work. Jensen," he called out to a trusted employee.

The man came over. "What boss?"

"There's a number on my desk for her parole officer, David Martin. Call him and tell him to get over here, right now."

"You got it, boss." The man left to follow his instructions.

The foreman turned to the struggling woman. "Yo, Rags!" He snapped his fingers in her face and tried to get her attention. "Come back to earth, buddy."

Rags blinked out of her trance and ceased struggling. "What?"

"Are you with us?" He scrutinized the cooling inferno in the eyes and shivered. He never wanted to see that look on someone again, it was unnerving. "Let her go, Animal."

Animal did as he was told. Rags got her footing and winced against the bright sunlight. She tried to focus on her boss. "Jesus. What did I just do?" She held her head and stabilized her adrenalin.

"You just beat the holy living shit out of some black woman."

Rags sat down on a crate and shook her head. "Oh, damn. This has never happened to me before, Leonard. She hit me first and I didn't see it coming."

"You're getting too old for this kind of thing. Maybe you ought to hang up your gloves, kid. David is on his way over to pick you up. What the hell was that all about anyway?"

"A woman." Rags took the cool drink someone brought over

218

to her and chugged it.

"Goddamned deisels fighting over a fucking broad. Is it worth going to jail for, Rags?"

"I won't go to jail. Her arrest record is as long as mine — longer. She's on work rehab just like I am. There's no way she'd go to the cops."

"Haven't I seen her around here before?"

"Yeah, she works in the next block, at the fish market."

"Don't let it happen again, Rags. I can't afford any bad publicity. You got that straight?"

Rags nodded her head in defeat. David's car screeched to a halt next to the dock. She was relieved to see him.

17

A New Leaf was doing a brisk business during the pre-Memorial Day weekend. Word had spread rapidly and attracted clientele from other bars to sample the offerings of better music and more intimate decor.

During the afternoons the main attraction was the new volleyball pit and patio that had been created in the back where several parking spaces had been before. The facelift indoors created more room by retiring the antiquated kitchen and moving the pool table into it. The main bar was pleasantly cluttered with upholstered chairs and benches that surrounded the refinished dance floor. The old west look was gone. Now the walls sported wainscoting, attractive wallpaper, and posters of famous women.

Since the mock sale of the bar, Rags forfeited her view of the front door and made it a point to be less conspicuous. She and Sanji made it a habit to sit nearer the back of the bar on one of the plush benches that resembled a church pew with cushions.

She stepped up the pace of her psychic monitoring of the goings on around her. Her invasions into private thoughts of others picked up in frequency also. To remain comfortable with her beautiful lover, she found it necessary to be alert to the intentions of others toward her flirtatious mate. Sanji's incessant flirting posed no real problem for Rags. Very few people dared make any obvious response to her or any other woman Rags was seen with on a regular basis. Upon occasion, a woman who suffered from too much partying would forget who she was dealing with and make a serious advance toward Sanji. Rags would step in, remind her politely just what kind of trouble she was asking for and the interloper would back off.

Rags never took issue with Sanji about her flirtations. She was confident that the love Sanji felt for her was unassailable. Sanji needed to flirt; it was nourishment for her to have others notice and appreciate her beauty and allure. It was always Rags who benefitted at the end of an evening of dalliance. The newlyweds had yet to make it home from the bar without pulling into a dimly lit street to park and indulge in marital privilege.

The weekend began relaxed and promised to be enjoyable. Rags pressed her hand firmly into the small of Sanji's back and guided her off the dance floor to their bench. Sanji leaned over to converse with a neighbor and left Rags to her private thoughts. Rags was immersed in contentment. She was proud to have won the affections of the black goddess. Sanji's hip was teasing hers, reminding her constantly of the devotion that grew daily between them.

Sanji's recovery from Ryan's vicious attack had been slow and tedious at first. She formed an impenetrable mental block around the event. She forgot entirely who Ryan was and what happened that ill-starred night. Her emotional health suffered a setback of grave proportions. Her sense of rejection brought on despondency and severe depression. When it seemed she would lose contact with reality altogether, she made a sudden and happy reversal.

Rags had spent every free moment holding and soothing her with unfailing dedication. Sanji knew that she loved someone deeply, but was unable to recall who it was. Without realizing it, she woke one day and decided that the person who was holding her so tenderly was that lost love. Her well-being pivoted on that realization, and she transferred her love to Rags. Rags accepted it readily, knowing the ardor was, by proxy, intended for Ryan.

It was inconceivable to Rags how Ryan had remained unaffected by the hazy, entrancing appeal of Sanji's smokey eyes. Knowing the value of the moment, Rags indulged herself in the fantasy that the love was truly meant for her. Eventually, it took hold, and they both believed and lived it. Sanji thrived on the reciprocal affection she so richly deserved and had done without for the two years of her stay with Ryan.

Rags then, had mixed feelings when her probe alerted her to

Ryan's presence in the bar for the first time in months. She assured her mate that she would return shortly and made her way through the growing press of women to greet the newcomer.

Ryan stood with her back to Rags. She was ordering drinks. Beside her, Leslie was shaking hands with the cheerful manager/bartender. Ryan heeded the familiar hand on her shoulder enthusiastically. "Rags! Hey, buddy, how's it going?" Their hands joined soundly in a vigorous handshake.

"Just great, stranger," Rags replied. She appraised the couple quickly. Ryan's reclaimed strength far exceeded her expectations. Leslie's beauty outstripped her memory.

Leslie recoiled slightly, knowing Rags was assessing more than the tan cashmere sweater that revealed her braless condition. Her bronzed flesh hid the burning in her cheeks, but did nothing to conceal her thoughts from Rags' curiosity. She longed to obscure the windows of her soul behind the sunglasses nestled in the curls atop her head. She saw no way out of it. Rags would detect the unresolved feelings about her: the marginal hatred, the pity, the fear.

Rags regarded her steadily for a moment and smiled. She was determined to enjoy herself despite Leslie's ill will. She turned to Ryan. "Well, love looks good on you," she commented, referring to Ryan's improved color and clear eyes. She took in the bar with a sweeping gesture of her hand. "They did a hell of a job with this place." She took the couple on a guided tour of the bar. On the patio she pulled Ryan aside. "I'm going to have to introduce you to Sanji. She doesn't know who you are anymore."

Ryan looked perplexed and suspicious. "How did that happen?"

"She blocked the whole thing out, including your identity. She still has some rough moments when she catches sight of her back in the mirror. I tell her that it happened a long time ago and she seems to be okay with it."

Ryan pulled a cigarette from a pack with her teeth and offered one to Rags. Rags joined her in lighting up and waited for some sign of remorse from Ryan. Nothing. She changed the subject quickly when Leslie extracted herself from a meaningless conversation with an acquaintance who had cornered her.

223

Ryan explained to Leslie that Sanji was suffering a mental block and to follow her lead with the introductions. Ryan located two vacant chairs, and they sat opposite Sanji and Rags. Between them was a low-built coffee table.

Sanji withdrew from her conversation with the woman next to her and surveyed Ryan with great interest.

The introduction to her assailant went well. Rags' brief mental touch assured her that Ryan had not been recognized. Leslie, on the other hand, would only dignify the introduction with a curt nod.

Ryan sat back in her chair and countered Sanji's intrigued expression with a searching appreciation, delivered coyly over the rim of her glass. She was surprised by the grip of need between her legs. She was deeply aroused by the sensuous, phantom kiss telegraphed to her from the rich, full lips. A sideways glance toward Leslie told her that only she had seen it. Her lover was watching the rowdy crowd on the dance floor.

Sanji was draped in the midnight dress Ryan had bought for her when they first began to live together. It clung tenaciously to her shoulders and plunged sharply to the solar plexis, exposing fully half of the coffee colored globes. Ryan's palms ached to know the thinly veiled nipples that danced lightly as Sanji laughed at a joke Rags made about someone on the dance floor.

Ryan took her eyes reluctantly from her fancy to order another round of drinks when the waitress came by. She lit a cigarette and continued to peruse the queen thoughtfully. Twisted strands of silver, dotted with tiny cymbals, graced Sanji's neck and appeared again in a musical circle around her wrist. The chains gathered the alluring fabric at the waist as well.

In her mind, Ryan knew the cloth would be stretched taut over the muscular rear, and close scrutiny would reveal the absence of undergarments. A barely perceptible mound would pout in the front. She hoped Sanji wouldn't stand to prove it. But she did stand, to answer the call of Nature. Sanji made a point of walking by her admirer, bisecting the field of vision with her sex. Her rhythmic stride distributed her scent dangerously close to the object of her teasing.

Ryan exercised the greatest restraint to keep herself from reaching out to seize the hidden mound with her sweating grip.

She mentally glued herself to the chair and steeled herself for Rags' baleful gaze. The last thing she anticipated was smugness on the part of her friend. Rags was sitting with her arms folded easily across her chest, beer in hand, with an "eat your heart out" expression emblazoned on her face. Ryan laughed softly and tipped her glass in salute. Leslie had deserted her place and was purposely carrying on with a handsome butch on the dance floor.

The third drink came and Sanji accelerated her flirtations. Ryan was feeling less inhibited. Rags was growing concerned. Leslie fidgeted uncomfortably in her seat. It was clear to anyone who cared to look, that Ryan was encouraging Sanji more effectively than any other had been able to do.

The denim between Ryan's legs was bathed in preparation. Her own muskiness quickened her breathing. Sanji thrilled at the sight of Ryan's haunting eyes devouring her. She wanted more. For some minutes she had been easing the back of her dress over to one side. This had the effect of pulling her front away from one of her breasts. It was done in tiny, unnoticed moves. Finally and suddenly, her breast popped into full view.

For a few private heartbeats Ryan was the only one who saw. An agonized groan caught in her throat and wicked thoughts penetrated her consciousness. These Rags heard. She turned quickly to her lover.

Ryan grabbed Leslie's wrist savagely and yanked her to the dance floor. Leslie followed in a surprised flurry, having missed the exchange that precipitated Ryan's action.

To Sanji's delight, her lover's reaction to her blatant exhibitionism was not emotional, but sexual. Silently, with no outward signs, Rags had grown tremendously aroused watching Ryan respond to her wife. Rather than succumbing to a puritanical rage and restoring her dress to order, Rags captured the bared nipple in her mouth. Unmindful of her surroundings, she attacked Sanji's sex and forced the fabric of the dress into the willing tunnel.

Some of the onlookers nearby stole furtive glances. Others stared directly at the impassioned couple. None notified the management of the lewd act. Rags used her free hand to muffle the screams that would soon begin in earnest. Sanji mashed the close-cropped head into her pillowy womanhood and began to writhe to the insistent touch. The ravaging of her groin quickened and kept pace with her breathing.

The muscles of the brawny forearm then doubled the pace while the thumb occupied the place of honor with a penetrating massage. Rags vacated the aching tit and set to whispering her private command in Sanji's ear. To this Sanji stiffened, and every muscle and nerve obeyed their master. Even the casual observer could see that she was coming with such force that she might break and splinter like cheap glass.

The music animated the women on the dance floor. Their bodies gyrated to the constant beat. Ryan ignored the song. It was not one she would have normally chosen to dance to. She pulled Leslie tight against her in soft swaying motions and insinuated her desire.

Leslie spoke directly into her ear. "It's about time you started paying attention to me."

Ryan spread Leslie's buttocks and brought her pelvis closer. "You aren't jealous are you? You should know better by now."

Leslie felt her body betray her and answer Ryan's need with a mind of its own. She was angry with Ryan for her behavior and hurt by it. "It hurts...to...be ignored...Ryan, please." She tried to stop and be serious. Her lover wouldn't hear of it. She felt a bite on her neck and she knew she would have to go to work with a scarf on to hide the brand. "Ryan, cut it out. Oh...damn you." She had been drinking as freely as Ryan, and she could tell that struggle was pointless. She gave in and allowed herself to enjoy the feel of Ryan wanting her.

"Jesus!" Ryan gasped.

"What?" Leslie followed Ryan's line of vision and spotted Rags making love to Sanji. The sight was so powerfully erotic she felt her knees weaken beneath her.

"I can't stand it any more." Ryan took Leslie's hand and marched out to the back porch of the bar. It was dark and crisp with no moon. Empty tables greeted them mutely.

Ryan moved to the junction of the building and privacy fence and wedged Leslie's back into the crook. Leslie was breathless and excited. Ryan was singleminded. "I don't know why I let you wear this sweater."

"You said it accented my figure," Leslie reminded her with a sexy voice. Before she finished the comment Ryan had the sweater hoisted above her breasts. They were exposed to a mixture of the kiss of late Spring and the inferno of Ryan's body.

"What are you doing?" A touch of panic caught in Leslie's voice when her body willingly cooperated with the removal of the sweater. Ryan threw it to the ground and attacked the zipper of the white slacks. A startling moment later, Leslie's pants lay in a tangle about her ankles. She was otherwise naked in the night air. "Ryan, what if someone comes out here?" Her objection lacked conviction, but Ryan's reply didn't.

Ryan fanned the golden nether lips and thrust her denimed pubic bone against the moist receptacle. The burden of the impact was taken on Leslie's shoulder blades. Her buttocks were cradled securely in the hands of her near maniacal lover. Leslie could not deny her. She accepted the brutal rutting with a fire of her own.

The overpowering sensation of being exposed in a public place, where at any moment they might be discovered, rushed Leslie to the glorious place only Ryan could take her. She reveled in her abandonment and was transformed. All sense of propriety lay with her sweater, on the ground. Ryan made love to her mind as well, uttering inflamed encouragement, underlined with moans of urgency.

Ryan's middle finger sought the tight, circular muscle between the firm buttocks and began massaging it gently. It opened willingly for her. The digit was seized as it passed the threshold of the portal and was treated to the rigorous contractions of her lover's release. Ryan plunged her tongue into the depths of Leslie's mouth and swallowed her screams.

Ryan felt her own exclamations threaten to betray their activities as the scene sent her over the edge with her lover. She freed herself from the voluptuous lips, threw her head back and supplicated the stars. Her breath hissed through her clenched teeth as the orgasms wracked her body in tumultuous waves. Beads of sweat drenched her brow. As in everything she set her mind to, she succeeded in silencing herself.

Leslie's eyes were adjusted to the absence of light. She sought the supernatural look in Ryan's eyes. There it was, as she knew it would be. Any indignities her body was subjected to were always more than worth it to commune with her lover in this fashion. Ryan had shown her again and again how to soar with the angels and experience a meeting of souls in a timeless unity.

For several minutes they were lost in one another's eyes. Leslie was protected from the cool night air by their mutual desire. She knew her lover as no one had ever known her. Their intimacy was unique, beautiful. Through Ryan, she learned to blend her soul with that of her mate. Each time they came together, their spirits folded closer, layer upon layer.

Ryan spoke to her softly. "Each time, I think we can't get any closer. Then you open up to me more and force me to do the same. No one understands me the way you do, not even Rags. I love you so much it almost hurts." She kissed the small O formed on the lips she loved so well. "I never expected to find anyone as strong as you. My life looked like a desert at the height of day; parched and barren. Then you stole my heart and chased away my loneliness." She cradled the naked, feminine form in her arms, afraid it would vanish in the breeze.

Leslie nestled into the warmth of Ryan's chest and listened to the solid, regular heartbeat. Ryan's words played a symphony in her mind, orchestrating her love and pride. She stepped reverently into Ryan's inner sanctuary and beheld the overwhelming love, power, and devastating need. She relaxed there for a moment to savor the quiet and solitude. She was not alone. A face, a beautiful face, forged its image into her mind, startling her. The hair was black like Ryan's, but long. The skin shimmered like hoar frost at dawn. The eyes were silvery saucers with midnight pinpoints in the centers. Leslie had never seen white eyes before. She shivered. The salmon lips were patient, yet menacing. The image disappeared, leaving a stabbing pain in Leslie's heart as a calling card. "Ryan!"

Ryan lifted the trembling chin up and questioned her with concern, "What is it, babe?"

Leslie caught her breath and recovered from the darting ache. "A face. An incredibly wonderful, but frightening face!"

Ryan closed her eyes solemnly and called to mind the awesome vision. "White eyes?" She felt the chin nod affirmatively in her palm. "That's Anara." She opened her eyes to gauge her lover. "Did she hurt you?"

"Just a pain in my heart. It went away," Leslie managed to answer steadily.

"You're getting too close. Oh, damn. I can't let you go now, we've come too far."

"I'm not afraid of her, Ryan." Leslie sensed the struggle in Ryan's heart. Anara was dangerous. That had become painfully clear, but the gauntlet had been thrown before her.

She knew Ryan would never ask her to pick it up. The choice belonged to her alone. There was time, she knew. Ryan was playing a waiting game, and would go right on playing it alone if Leslie withheld her aid. About this, Ryan would not accept a hasty decision. Leslie would think and dream on it.

Ryan's reply shook her. "You will be." She let Leslie go and began restoring her clothing to order. Her mind snapped shut in a rush. It thrust Leslie into a kind of purgatory. The footing there was unsure and dismal. This was where Leslie would have to make her decision.

It was here that she would arise victorious and be readmitted into Ryan's inner world, or she would slide hopelessly into the emptiness she had known before meeting this amazing woman. The great require greatness about them. They have no room or time for mediocrity. It was a form of blackmail. Leslie knew that if she were ever again to experience the ecstasy, she would have to meet the stark terror head on.

Neither of them spoke more of it. They both knew what was needed. Time.

They concentrated instead on the feelings of the flesh. Ryan smoothed the flushed cheek. "I feel great, but we look like hell. Let's go freshen up." Leslie ran her fingers through her mussed hair and agreed enthusiastically.

When they exited the restroom a square-built woman in her early twenties bumped into Ryan. An accident with contrivance written all over it. Her voice was loud and gruff. "Well, if it isn't the Irish Executioner."

Ryan tried to walk past her. She was unwilling to acknowledge the challenge. The woman was slightly taller than she. She inserted herself between Ryan and Leslie, effectively blocking any retreat. "You're pretty tough with femmes aren't you? Why don't you try something with someone your own size?"

Ryan fixed the young tough with her eyes for a quick moment to distract her. The next instant her adversary was slammed against the wall by the force of a hard right to her chin. Before she could react, Ryan pinned her with a brutal forearm across the collarbone. Ryan's seasoned reflexes provided her with momentum and surprise. In less than a blink of an eye, Ryan produced the weapon she was loathe to use unless she wanted to end what was badly begun. The switchblade cracked open and was poised dangerously at her would-be attacker's throat. "Not tonight, ace. I'm not in the mood for a fight."

A thin angry voice addressed her from her right side. "Damn it, Ryan. I can't keep turning my back on your fights anymore."

Ryan looked askance at the manager, then back at the now frightened woman. "Am I done here?"

The tough was convinced and conceded. Ryan let her go and told her to sleep it off, allowing her a dignified retreat. She turned to the manager, folded the knife nonchalantly and replied, "What fight?" Before the manager could raise an objection, Ryan took Leslie's hand and disappeared into the crowd.

Returning to their table, they found Sanji curled in Rags' lap; content and sated.

Rags looked up. "What was that all about?"

"Just a young butch with too much to drink."

Rags smiled knowingly. Leslie took it all in stride as she was learning to do. "Does that happen often?"

"Not too. There aren't many hotshots left these days, and most of them already know better."

18

Ryan had grown edgy and withdrawn since Leslie's encounter with her foe. Their lovemaking missed the surrender and fulfillment it once had. Ryan kept herself sealed, cautiously avoiding any contact that would tempt her to let go or leave her vulnerable to her lover's charms. Her nerves were taught, her sleep disturbed. She thought nothing of spending an extra two hours, sometimes three at the airport. A confrontation was building, and she saw no way to prevent it.

Leslie found she was unable to purge her mind of the disturbing news of Sanji's inability to recognize Ryan, a woman she had lived with for two years. The cryptic words of her friends pounded in her ears: "In her basement! — You can bet Ryan made Sanji pay for that." What had happened? Why had Sanji blocked it out? Leslie had to know. She had never been in Ryan's basement. It had been purposely overlooked when Ryan had shown her the house. Her curiosity prickled on her skin, wanting satisfaction.

Her chance to satisfy it came on a Thursday night when she and Ryan returned from dinner. The phone was ringing when they came in, and Ryan stopped to answer it. Leslie was drawn to the forbidden door like an addict to drugs.

She opened it, found the light and descended into the sterile subterranean chambers. A dusky, unused smell assaulted her nose. The reflection of light from the brilliant white tile intrigued her. At the bottom of the steps she surveyed the area and thought to herself how unlike Ryan it was. Unlike the Ryan she knew.

She walked to the pool table and remembered briefly the first time she saw Ryan. Her eyes were drawn to the leather serpent, coiled casually on the green felt like a sleeping cat. She picked up the worn whip and felt its solid weight in her hand. The tip fell loose and flicked at her leg. A hungry snake, starved for its portion of flesh. She made a tiny jump inside herself.

The steel pole in the middle of the room caught her attention. She looked up and down it like a sculpture she couldn't comprehend. Her tour continued over to the expertly made bed and the solitary chair. On the chair she found the abandoned wrist cuffs. The fetters completed the picture in her mind. She worried the whip in her hand nervously. She had no way of knowing that Bonnie had cleaned the bloody evidence from the floor and replaced the linens on the bed. Everything was impeccably neat.

"Put that down!" Ryan's voice pierced her consciousness. She dropped the whip instantly and spun around to face Ryan. Her heart chilled at the sight of her.

Ryan's brows knit a tight canopy over her flintlike green spheres. Every feature was pinched with fury, seething on the surface. Her jaws and fists strained against the wrenching tension and restraint.

"Ryan, I . . ."

Ryan lunged at her. She ducked instinctively. Her wrist was scorched by Ryan's touch. Ryan held it up and pulled close to Leslie. She spoke in grinding acidic tones. "So you want to know what I do to little girls that humiliate me. You want to see what happens when I lose it. Alright, damn it. You will." With that pronouncement, Ryan yanked Leslie up the stairway, ignoring her cries of painful mishandling.

At the top of the stairs she grabbed Leslie's purse from the entrance table and let go of her wrist to find the keys. Keys in hand, she slapped the purse into Leslie's stomach. Leslie grabbed it before it fell to the floor.

Ryan opened the front door and pushed Leslie out on to the porch. She slammed the door behind herself with such force that the sound of it echoed sharply about the neighborhood.

Ryan dragged her to the Mercedes, then unlocked the passenger door. She opened it meanly and stared at Leslie. Leslie melted into the seat and opened the driver's door. Ryan slammed the passenger door hard, making the passenger flinch. Ryan took her place in the driver's seat confidently, turned the engine over, and squealed out of the drive.

In complete silence Ryan stewed and avoided looking at her companion. Leslie was fascinated by how Ryan was making her car do things she hadn't thought possible. She palmed the steering wheel, and screamed through corners, ran lights and stop signs whenever possible. Watching the angry woman drive was like watching a ballet. She'd become part of the machine.

On the Valley freeway, they headed north, faster than Leslie would have ever dared. She tried to pay attention to where they were going, but Ryan was too appealing to watch. Ryan was making love to the Mercedes. The erotic overtones compelled her to observe and experience the events next to her rather than those zooming by outside.

At the top of the exit, they turned west and drove through a suburb Leslie didn't recognize. Three more turns and two more stop signs brought them abreast of a small yellow house shrouded in pine and phitzer. Leslie recognized the black truck and green Volvo in the drive. A somber porchlight gave an insincere welcome. Ryan pulled in behind the other vehicles, then escorted Leslie to the door with a scathing silence.

Rags opened the door to the unexpected guests. She sensed the wonder and fear that Leslie was emanating. She turned to read Ryan and stepped away from the door to allow them in.

Leslie stepped timidly into the peaceful domestic setting. She was anxious about bringing to it the raw searing emotions in which she and her mate were embroiled. The living room smelled of Sanji's spicy scent and cigarette smoke. It was furnished with an assortment of unmatched antiques; dark and inviting. Blues and yellows picked up threads and weaved in and out of the upholstery and wallpaper. She knew she would be comfortable here under different circumstances.

Ryan stepped in behind her. It made the hair stand up on the nape of her neck.

Sanji walked in from the kitchen, wiping her hands from the dinner dishes. Her smile was pleasant; guiless. Rags closed the door quietly. She knew what would come next and dreaded it.

Ryan motioned sharply in Sanji's direction. "Show her."

Leslie and Sanji looked at one another; perplexed.

"Come here, babe," Rags entreated her lover with a protectively outstretched arm.

Ryan stood to Leslie's right with her hands shoved into her pockets and her jaws clenched forcefully. Rags positioned Sanji with her back to Leslie. With soft, murmuring tones, she hypnotized her spouse into a state of relaxed compliance. Then, slowly, she gathered the light cotton fabric of the blouse in her hands. She engaged Sanji's melted eyes and lifted the back of the blouse to expose to Leslie the ravaged skin. Sanji was unaware of the shock wave that stormed the room when Leslie saw, firsthand, why Rags had been angry enough to keep Ryan and her apart for so long.

She stood stock still, horrified. The lithe, well-formed back looked like a railyard from the air. Scored over and over again with punishing weals and ugly scars. She tried to imagine the pain and couldn't. Her mind blanked momentarily with terror. Her eyes brimmed over with salty moisture. She could see why Sanji blocked out the experience.

Her sorrow turned to white hot rage. This was permanent damage, done to another human being without just cause. Just cause. That was the crux of the issue for Leslie. Her life had been devoted to the pursuit of Justice. Here, before her, was a rape: spit in the eyes of Justice. Nothing Sanji could have done to Ryan would have been bad enough to deserve this.

She turned her fury on Ryan, but it fell short of its mark as did everyone's, save Rags. She couldn't match the intensity with which Ryan felt or displayed emotions. Her anger was impotent next to this tyrant, the tantrums of a child by comparison. Her only option, her only way to register her displeasure, was to flee. She forced herself to hold out her palm. Ryan dropped the keys in the trembling hand.

Leslie pivoted and walked out; dignified, but shaken.

Rags smoothed the shirt down Sanji's back and brought her out of her semi-trance. She led her rubbery mate to the velvet loveseat and comfort.

Ryan had not moved. Her eyes were fixed in a ghostlike stare. Rags could see the ether about the slender frame burn away like a funeral pyre. "You can't let this eat you up like this, Ryan." Getting no response, she ventured into the private thoughts, flinched and retreated. "Ryan, don't do this to yourself. You have to find an outlet for this anger. Don't turn it inward."

"Is she alright?" Sanji was concerned.

"No, not yet lover. You better go to bed." Rags guided her friend to an overstuffed chair and coaxed her to sit. She hoped Ryan would emerge, reborn from the flames of temper that were consuming her like a phoenix. It was her only hope.

Ryan's personal power had increased more than Rags had initially realized. She had been forcefully ejected from the tortured mind. She was worried and pondered the event thoughtfully.

Suddenly and without warning the voice, the knife-edged voice filled her mind. "STOP HER!"

Rags stumbled and reeled with the great force of it. She held her head to keep the agony from blowing it open. She didn't cry out verbally, but she knew that Anara realized what she had done.

Anara had commited a grave error. Her angry command carried such power and intensity that she defeated her purpose. In her vexation she had forgotten that her handmaiden was trapped in a physical body and could not withstand the might of her order. The pain of it rendered Rags useless and powerless to do her bidding.

Rags doubled over and fought against the heaves. An hour passed before she could think or feel anything but indescribable pain. Finally, after a tremendous struggle, she settled on her couch to recover from her searing headache and wait for Ryan to return to the physical plane. In her secret heart, she hoped Ryan would survive her Ordeal.

The smoke, the sickeningly sweet smoke. Her nostrils flinched and curled in response to it. Ryan blinked and adjusted to the softened light. At first she didn't recognize the smell; then it came to her. Birchwood. She was in a burning forest of birch. A teardrop slid partway down her cheek in sorrow for her beloved trees. It was insufferably hot there. She didn't know where she was.

A loud crack sounded behind her, and she whirled around

to see what caused it. Flashing, dancing prisms of light sparkled in front of her. She stepped backward and squinted against the brightness. Licks of flames danced about the hem of her robes. She paid them no mind. Her reflection circled a hundred different directions, shot, and bantered by the prisms.

She looked down at herself and began to recognize where she was. Long, charcoal grey robes draped her body. Swirls of black scalloping trimmed the edge of the hem and reflected the flames with a mysterious diamondlike clarity. Her sleeves were long and billowy and dangled on the murky ground below her. She felt her throat to make sure the stone was still there. A ruby, two inches in diameter floated and gleamed against her skin as protection.

She was not inside the physical body she had chosen for travel on her planet. This was her true form, condensed, for use in the higher planes that lingered nearby. Her face was pale and oval, with the illusion of frailty. Her eyes were clean, large and red with expandable pupils that allowed her to see in varying degrees of light. She remembered how to use them and gazed courageously at the spinning prisms. They disappeared instantly, unable to withstand her direct gaze.

Her hair matched her robe and hid under her full hood in long, heavy waves. She raised her hand and sighed softly. A tiny dove peeked out of the dark strands of its home and flew from her mane to her long, slender finger. "Greetings, my friend. You look well."

The miniature bird cooed contently and blinked its black jade eyes at here. She returned it to its home and walked up the burning hill toward what lay ahead.

The path was long and tiring. The harp music she was playing in her mind to keep her company was beginning to fade and sound distant. Replacing it, with increasing intensity, was a vague, cynical laughter.

The stones she walked on grew hotter with each step. She was sweating and breathing hard. Then, out of the corner of her eye, she saw a freshwater pool, surrounded by orchids. Their smell was cloying, and the water was extremely appealing in the heat. She walked over and knelt beside it. She bent to take some in her hand for a drink then sprang back like a spooked horse. The water turned into a hideous, three-legged creature with curled claws and six bloody eyes circling its head. It bared its slimy teeth and snarled at her.

Her eyes grew large with horror and her mouth tasted of sickness. She was standing in a patch of orchids and they began to reach their stinging mouths toward her.

Her first thought was to run and run. She wanted to retch. The heat was closing in on her throat. The laughter grew louder and more vile.

Her hand weighed hundreds of pounds it seemed, but she managed to raise it to the stone hovering about her neck. She covered it with her palm, and it began to glow. "Be gone thou stench and illusion." The creature and flowers disappeared silently. All that remained was the ferocious heat and the hideous laughter.

She walked on, parched and weak, to a crossroads. The power shimmered and played in swirling circles above it. There were no signposts. She stepped under the whirlwind and searched her heart for guidance. One path was empty and barren. The second was covered with flint and tinder. The third was paved with rufous colored stones. The one she was on disappeared, as if to say there was no retreat possible She listened for the laughter and tried to locate its source. She reasoned that the easiest path, the one that would lure her into the most perilous trap, would be the one where she could escape the mocking mirth. She chose the path where the sound was the loudest, the flint and tinder.

The way was sharp and cut her feet, and she was bleeding from little pinpricks on her soles. She had no more decided on this most treacherous path than a brilliant wall of yellow flames burst before her. The only way to her goal lay beyond that wall. Her heart pounded hard and fear began to well up inside her. Thoughts of a fiery end ran through her mind. The laughter grew louder.

If for no other reason but to defy the anonymous taunting, she marshalled her courage and walked through it. In a blinking of an eye it was over. She emerged on the other side; whole. She sensed her spirit was lighter than before.

An old hag was sitting beside the road looking at her curiously. She addressed the grey figure. "Woman of the Sunken Island, kiss me."

The idea was repulsive to the Woman of the Sunken Island. She knew it was a test of her pride and courage. She knelt next to the gnarled, scarred woman and took the ruined face in her hands. She bent her wine-colored lips to the withered lips of the hag and kissed them firmly and sincerely, as she would her own lover. The hag vanished in her grasp and there, where she had been sitting, was a glowing pitcher of cool water. She drank it and washed with it. The refreshment gave her strength. As she rose to go on, a red wall of flames burst out with a sultry steaming radiance.

Again fear, stronger this time, settled into her heart. The laughter sounded tinny and echoed from beyond the wall. She walked through it with resolve. It seared her skin and made her faint. She fought against crying out. When she passed through, she fell to the ground. Sweat was stinging her eyes. She wiped them clean and looked about her. Coming toward her, slowly and deliberately, were snakes, hundreds of them. She was too weak to flee, she couldn't even stand. They began crawling over her and biting her again and again. Her mind began to reel dizzily. She hallucinated. One of them swirled into her hair, in search of a more substantial meal. Her tender dove.

Her body swelled and expanded. Blackness threatened her. This was a test of will and power. She reached out for a diamond patterned snake and looked into its eyes. It was hypnotized by her red stare. She penetrated its mind and forced it to give up its knowledge to her. When all was taken, the serpents were transformed into a great, wise dragon. It addressed her. "Terranean Queen." The primordial voice shook her. "You are powerful indeed. Name your gift."

"I ask for your pyrope."

The dragon smiled at her wisdom and handed her the ring. She looked at the deep-red garnet and slipped the band on her little finger. She felt a familiar stirring on her neck and she was assured that the snake had failed to find her helpmate. She bowed graciously to the oldest of creatures. "I thank You, oh Great One."

The dragon laughed and vanished. A wall of blue flames arose suddenly. She stepped back slightly from the torrid heat. She did not feel fear as before, rather stark naked terror. The very marrow of her bones was scorched by it. How could she possibly pass through this when just the nearness of it was consuming her?

Then she recognized the laughter. It came from all around and inside her. The flames looked inviting by comparison. She stepped into them. Her screams were deafening, but she could still hear the laughter above them. She touched the ring to the stone at her neck and was forcefully thrown clear of the inferno.

She had been unconscious for some time. When she awakened, she was in a mirrored room. It began to spin. The rotation accelerated and her hearing returned. Louder than ever was the laughter. She did not call out the name of its owner, she would not give it power by acknowledging it. The mirrors did not reflect her image. Instead, all around her in swirling, haunting images, was Anara. She stopped laughing long enough to address her.

"Woman of Wings, how dare you enter my chamber unbidden. Go back from whence you came and trouble me no more. I enjoy your suffering. You are dying. I am winning. I will taste revenge and it will be sweet."

The Woman of Wings looked at the shining visage with compassion. She did not answer. Instead she waved her hand and the chamber was replaced with a wall of white flames. She relaxed and called out calmly, "Goddess of Fire. I humbly request an audience with Your Holiness." She prostrated herself and closed her eyes to wait.

The wall of flame died down to a flickering border. All about the Woman of Wings was a scintillating incandescence. The tiny dove worked its way out of her hair and flew toward the Goddess, landing on her fiery finger. She kissed it gently and put it in her white hair. "Rise and be welcome to the Land Of The Raging Peace," she proclaimed.

The Woman of Wings rose and approached the throne with respect and reverence.

The Goddess spoke again. "I thank you for your gift. I shall enjoy her company greatly." She smiled at the tickle on her neck. "You may speak. You have come far and done well. Sit, rest."

The Woman of Wings sat on a backless stool and smiled. "I am honored to be in Your Presence, My Lady."

"And I yours. Let us dispense with formality. We are friends here. You have begun to learn humility. I am pleased. The Contender does not know what she has done for you."

"It is hard. Dignity means a great deal to me," replied the grey beauty.

The Goddess was resplendent in the shimmering colors of flame. She couldn't be imagined in the limited terms of humanity. She appeared simply as silvery white flashes.

"I know it is a struggle. It is wise that you are learning. It will help you later. Teach it to others, Woman of Wings, and you will learn it better. I am much pleased with your progress. Your courage is greater than I imagined, and I am happy with the spirit and temper you show on the physical plane. It is good for you. It still controls you, however. This is something you *must* control and use it to your benefit. It will serve you well."

"I shall."

"Good. I have something for you. The Contender hid it well, even though she knew not that I was looking for it. I found it and wish to give it to you. Here." The Goddess held out to the Woman of Wings a burning necklace.

The Woman of Wings took it courageously and put it on. It did not burn her.

"Your true name. Your name of power is written on that necklace. It is yours now. You have earned it."

The Woman of Wings looked at the fiery letters. They read: BLAISE.

She spoke the name and the power rushed into her with a gale force. "Blaise."

The Goddess watched the red-eyed beauty transform and become a blaze for a short while. Finally, she returned to her original shape.

They smiled knowingly at each other. The Goddess continued. "Blaise, I have learned that The Contender does not know of your true identity. There are those who wish to see you serve who have contrived to keep that information from her. This is in your favor. Beware! Her camp is strong and powerful. They desire greatly her victory. When they discover who you are, your very soul will be in the greatest peril. For now, she is content to seek revenge, petty revenge, for your role in casting her from the physical sphere. Her power grows rapidly, yet she fears the One

Who Seeks Knowledge And Justice. I release you from the bonds of Fate and give you Free Will. From this moment forward, you have determination over this struggle. Its outcome is as much up to you as it is to The Contender. Go now. I bid you safe and swift conduct on your return."

The next breath she took was of earthly atmosphere.

19

The vigil lasted two days. During that time Ryan's body did not move. Her face held no expression and her breathing was shallow and less than half its normal pace. Rags stayed home from work and kept the living room dark and quiet and free of any outside interruptions. When she walked into the living room on Saturday evening, she found Ryan slumped with fatigue in her chair, casually smoking a cigarette.

"You're back. Good. I was going to start worrying about you in another couple hours." "Sanji, get Ryan some dinner, please." A flurry of activity began in the kitchen.

Ryan eyed Rags wearily. "Where is Leslie?"

"She left five minutes after you got here. Do you even know what day it is?"

Ryan looked at the date on her watch. Conscious memory of where she had been flooded into her mind. Her face darkened somewhat. "I'm exhausted."

"No small wonder. I'll take you home when you're stronger. Can you eat?"

"A little." Ryan looked deeply into her friend's eyes and they shared a private knowing. "I had forgotten how hard they were."

"Ordeals are just that. Ordeals," Rags commented sympathetically. "I wanted to spare you," Rags then lied. She was secretly glad that Ryan had survived the Ordeal and become stronger. They had become close friends, but Rags was unable to express her feelings for her Irish companion.

Ryan was catching glimpses of her last lifetime and recalling in greater detail the extent of her growth, bridging the gap of time. Her thoughts were interrupted by Sanji who was serving her some warm soup and wine. She looked up to her ex-lover and thanked her gratefully. After partaking of the sparse meal she felt stronger. She turned to Rags. "I've probably lost her for this."

"Leslie is a strong woman, but this might have been too much."

Ryan slept through Sunday and returned to work on Monday. The afternoon was still and pleasant. Phil had left the front door open to provide some sense of the outdoors to his desk-bound chores.

He looked up at the auburn mirage before him. "What are you doing here?"

She answered in the satin voice she was known for. "I want to see Ryan."

Phil scowled. "Haven't you caused her enough trouble? Get out."

His command came too late. Standing in the doorway, Ryan cut a dramatic figure draped in the ivory flying scarf Leslie had given her. Her eyes were hidden behind her mirrored sunglasses. "Dana," she breathed.

They walked toward one another slowly. Ryan could scarcely believe Dana was really there. Her heart pounded in her chest, and familiar twinges betrayed themselves between her legs. When they were close enough for Dana's perfume to work its magic, Ryan felt her knees weaken.

Dana had a curious way of looking like a photograph taken with a fog filter. She had no clear boundaries. Her face blended with her auburn mane, the hair blended with the atmosphere and her lips blended into her milky softness. Her indigo eyes opened abysmally, luring the unsuspecting to their perilous fates. She knew she had Ryan, as she always did, caught in her viscid web.

Phil was joined at his desk by another pilot and together they witnessed Ryan take the delicate face between her hands and kiss the receptive peach lips. "Damn, she always has the prettiest women I ever laid eyes on," the newly arrived pilot commented enviously.

Phil answered with vexation, "That's no woman — that is the She-Devil incarnate."

He continued to fume as he watched Ryan take the long scarf from around her neck and drape it over a coat rack. She escorted Dana to her Corvette, parked with a sultriness of its own, in the lot. Ryan held the passenger door open for her and closed it softly behind the seductress. She then got into the driver's seat and drove out of the airport confines in a westerly direction.

The journey lasted only a few blocks, terminating in the parking lot of The Clarion. They went into the lounge where Ryan ordered a double whiskey for herself and champagne for Dana.

"You look terrific," Ryan managed to speak. Dana was wearing a crepe suit, moss green pants and jacket over a beige chamisole top. Three lengths of gold chain disappeared into the crevice of her bosom to draw attention to their alluring roundness. The petulant nipples took center stage.

"Thank you, darling. Coming from you it's a real compliment." Dana had forgotten how completely Ryan could devour a woman and make her feel as though no other existed. She was quick to exploit Ryan's weakness for her. Her knee pressed against Ryan's under the table, making Ryan swallow her liquor harder than necessary. She moved in for the kill with one of the acts that got under the skin of several women. She reached up and began to play with her own nipple, rolling it and pinching it blatantly before her admirer. "I hear you're seeing Leslie these days. You can't be serious. She isn't half the woman I am. I've missed you Ryan, more than I knew." Her voice was polished, vixenish, and effective.

Ryan finished her drink and lit a cigarette. The alcoholic warmth relaxed her. She licked her lips in appreciation and desire. "I didn't realize I missed you until now. Come upstairs with me." It was a statement, not a request. She was well aware that Dana wanted her as much as ever. She was in no mood for long, drawn out, coy games.

The hotel manager winked at them when he handed over the room key. Ryan ignored him. She was involved in an internal struggle that was beginning to assert itself in her heart. An old, unsettling feeling was intruding itself between the shocks of desire and need.

She was silent but attentive to Dana on the elevator. The sensation grew. When she opened the door to the room, she could feel it lodge itself about her heart and begin to constrict. With the door closed behind her, it took on a life of its own.

She turned on Dana and pulled her close, savagely assaulting the surprised lips. She was taking from Dana what she had needed for six years. Power. The power to hurt.

Several minutes passed. The violent embrace involved the full body. Dana had ceased struggling. She found she enjoyed the rough handling. Ryan closed the kiss firmly and equalized her breathing. Her arms loosened their prey.

Dana rocked back on her heels. "Whew, where did you learn to kiss like that?"

"Take your clothes off," Ryan answered flatly.

Dana regarded her sensuously. "What's the hurry, sugar? We've got all night."

"I said strip!" Ryan hissed. She grabbed the blouse and ripped it off with one quick movement, making the naked breasts bounce indignantly.

Dana sucked in her breath; shocked. She squelched her urge to express her injured bitch routine. Instead, she found herself excited by Ryan's demand. She took her clothes off without seduction. "You've changed, Ryan. I like it."

"So have you, and I don't."

Dana wanted desperately to soothe Ryan and regain control over the situation. Ryan endured Dana unsnapping her shirt and watched her blankly as she knelt between her feet and unfastened her jeans. She allowed Dana to slide the pants over her hips as far as they would go easily, which was only far enough to expose her sex to the temptress.

Dana kissed it softly and was rewarded with a soft moan. Encouraged, she slipped her tongue into the inky cavern, seeking the seat of Ryan's desire. She flicked it gently at first, but Ryan's powerful fingers dug into her head and forced her closer, compelling her to intensify her efforts.

Without warning, something snapped inside Ryan and her erection went soft. She made fists in the auburn tangle and yanked the enthralled head away from her. Dana sat back on her heels; perplexed.

Ryan had finally realized she was no longer dealing with her first love, the innocent angel that had swept her off her feet at first sight. Someone else had been making love to her, a stranger. She looked into Dana's eyes. "You whore."

The rejected woman was a fast thinker. "Oh, *well*. What does that make you, O'Donnell?"

Ryan sent her sprawling on the floor with an enraged backhand blow to the face.

Dana came up on her elbow and yanked the tangled mass of hair out of her face. "You bitch!" She was shouting, "You won't get away with this."

Ryan laughed cruely and rearranged her shirt and jeans. "Bullshit, Dana. Are you going to make up some crap to explain this friendly call you made on me. Tell me. How are you going to explain that shiner to Del? Tell her the Irish Executioner attacked you? Then what? Do you think for a minute that Del is going to defend your honor? She's scared shitless of me and you know it. No baby, I already got away with it. You should be glad that's all I did." She threw the room key at Dana contemptuously and walked out of the room.

Dana came to her feet and opened the door to yell after her assailant, "You cunt. I'll get you for this." But Ryan had already rounded the corner.

She turned back into the room and slammed the door viciously. She didn't care if anyone had seen her naked, she was too angry. She threw herself on the bed, kicking the mattress and crying into the pillows.

247

20

The weekend closed in on Ryan like a shrinking room. Her experience with Dana had unnerved her. Never before had she lost her passion and not completed the act once it had begun.

Her thoughts and dreams were consumed with Leslie. Twice she had sought relief in the bar at the main airport terminal. She had gone there to pick up a flight attendant, but both times she changed her mind.

She ached for the knowing intimacy that Leslie alone could provide. She craved to know the flick of flames dancing about when they made love. Her need so disturbed her, it drove her out of the sky on Friday morning. Unable to concentrate, she brought her passenger back and didn't complete the flight.

Phil was walking out to his Stearman, intending to go up for some aerobatics practice. He stopped in his tracks when he saw Ryan coming toward him briskly, followed by an irate man in a business suit, yelling at her from behind. As she walked by Phil she tossed him the keys to the Cessna Cutlass. "Take him to Cheyenne, will you? I can't." She kept on walking and didn't wait for a reply.

The irate passenger caught up with Phil and started yelling at him. "Send me up with an amateur, will you? Get me a decent pilot."

Phil answered him crossly. "That is my best pilot, buddy, and she has never, in twenty five years, turned back a flight except under the most dire circumstances." He turned to follow Ryan to the parking lot, leaving the man behind sputtering with disbelief.

Phil caught up to her, grabbed her arm, and spun her around to face him. "What is wrong, Ryan?"

The sky was cloudless and getting hotter by the minute. So was Ryan. She was standing by her cycle, ready to mount it. She lashed out at Phil. "Leave me the fuck alone, Phil."

"Settle down, Ryan. Is there something wrong with the plane?"

Ryan's shoulder's loosened, and she tried to bring herself under some sort of control. "No, it's fine, It's me. I couldn't do it, Phil. I never should have taken off. I knew something was wrong when I got up this morning."

"Vertigo?" he asked, gravely concerned.

Ryan took off her sunglasses and gazed directly into his blue eyes. "No. I couldn't fly." Her eyes widened with disbelief. "I couldn't fucking fly." She put her glasses back on and straddled the cycle.

Her forgotten passenger appeared. "I demand to speak to the owner. I don't have to be treated like this."

"Yeah, what?" Ryan answered sarcastically.

"You're speaking to us," Phil answered. His patience was at an all time low.

"You? You two own this? No wonder. Mickey Mouse operation. Tell me how I'm going to get to my meeting on time?"

"Jesus." Ryan started her machine viciously.

"You'll get there on time." Phil was used to shouting over loud noises. His voice had a definite authority. His hand came up to silence the balance of the man's complaint. "No charge."

The passenger shut his mouth and waited.

Phil stopped Ryan from putting her helmet on. "Where are you going?"

"I'm not in the mood for a drink, if that's what you want to know."

It was. "Ryan, why don't you just call Leslie. She'll come around."

"No way. Hell will freeze over before *I* call a woman and ask her to come back to me."

"You and your pride . . ."

Ryan stopped listening. She put her helmet on and drove off.

Phil turned to her abandoned passenger. "Come on. I'll get you to Cheyenne. In record time."

Ryan returned home, got as far as the couch, and collapsed in a black mood. Several hours later the doorchime eased into her conciousness. When she realized she wasn't dreaming it, she answered the door.

Leslie crossed the threshold and set her attache case on the tiled floor of the foyer. Several heartbeats passed before Ryan registered her presence. Silently, she wrapped her arms around the apparition and held tight. Leslie rested her head on Ryan's shoulder. She too, was much relieved to be close again.

Their reverent welcoming into each other's hearts lasted a short while with neither of them speaking their gladness verbally. Then Ryan rubbed her cheek against Leslie's fragrant hair and sighed contentedly. "I don't want to be apart from you ever again."

"You don't have to be."

Ryan held her away and regarded her skeptically. Leslie loosened herself from Ryan's grasp and bent for her attache. She walked into the living room and set it on the coffee table.

Ryan joined her and watched her open it and pull out a thick, paperbound book. She recognized the multi-list book, and her heart quickened. Leslie thumbed through it, stopped midway, and showed the page to Ryan.

There it was, what she had hoped for these many weeks. Leslie's condominium was on the market.

"I promised my realtor she could have your listing too. Here's a contract."

Ryan felt as though the muscles in her face would tear from smiling so broadly. Her heart soared as it had never done before. She was speechless.

"I know you thought I was never coming back. I'm sorry to have put you through that. But I had to make sure I was doing the right thing. I actually put it on the market two weeks ago, but I wanted to surprise you." She put the multi-list book down and looked at Ryan. "What you did to Sanji was wrong, Ryan, but it's done. If you haven't learned from it yet, you will. I simply can't live without you anymore. Seeing you smile like that makes me the happiest woman on earth." Her own smile burst free of her serious intentions.

"Hold me," Ryan asked softly.

Leslie responded to Ryan's request willingly. This was the first time Ryan had asked, just asked for affection. She didn't take, demand, or entice; she asked. The rare show of vulnerability immersed Leslie in the warmth of Ryan's soul.

They remained entangled in one another's arms for several hours, peacefully exploring eyes; hands; lips. They joined in love without passion; tranquil and satisfied. In a thousand ways they gave themselves to the other, leaving nothing undone.

When the marriage was complete and solid, they began to stir. Ryan turned on the lamp behind them and they shared a cigarette. "I feel like celebrating. Let's get dinner and find Rags and Sanji."

"What about Brigid and Star?"

"They won't come out of the hills on a weekend. We can go up tomorrow if you like."

"That would be fine. I have something I want to discuss with you first."

"What?"

"How many women did you sleep with this week?" Leslie's tone was matter of fact and devoid of feeling.

Ryan didn't hesitate to answer. She knew that she would always answer this woman's questions, no matter how difficult they were. "A half of one."

"Who?"

"Dana."

Leslie closed her eyes against the admission, and fought off her emotions. She asked; now she had to deal with the answer. "Was it good?"

"Awful. I hated it. I couldn't finish."

Leslie opened her eyes; amazed and curious. "What happened?"

"She showed up at the airport on Monday, and I fell for her right off. Damn, I wanted her so badly. I didn't realize what a hold she still had over me."

"I've wanted her a time or two myself. I don't blame you," Leslie revealed.

"You?" Ryan shook her head. "It shouldn't surprise me.

252

She is out to conquer every holdout in town. Anyway, I took her for a drink and we ended up in a hotel room. When I got her there, all I could think about was hurting her, not loving her."

"Which you no doubt did."

"She got a black eye and a bruised ego for her trouble."

"That explains why Del has been so openly hostile this week. She probably thinks you raped her."

"Leslie, you don't need to put up with that grief. Quit that practice," Ryan pleaded.

"I probably will when I figure out what I want to do with my time. So, was revenge all it was cracked up to be?"

"It was an ending. I needed to know how I felt about her. I'm just glad it's over."

—◦⊰⧉⊱◦—

The bar crowd was in an upbeat mood all night. Rags had come alone to give Sanji some time to visit with a relative who was passing through Denver. The trio celebrated royally in her absence — dancing, laughing and sharing their good fortune.

The crowd began to thin around one o'clock. The happy trio decided to call it a night. By the door, Leslie stopped to chat with a friend briefly. Ryan and Rags left her behind.

Outside a crack sounded. Then another. Everything began to move in slow motion for Ryan.

A nauseating thump, thump reverberated in her ears. Bone splintered and blood splashed against the grey brick. Ryan looked in the direction that the bullets had come from. She saw a pistol disappear behind the red car door.

Ryan's voice split the night with a piercing curse. It rained down on the midnight head as it was carried away in the fleeing car, "Ceeeeeeee-Jaaaaaaaayyyyy!"

She turned instantly to Rags, whose face was impaled with a surprised, "not ready yet" look of agony. She had been thrust against the wall and was sinking down it, hastened by her own slippery blood.

Ryan tried to break her fall, as if keeping her standing would keep her alive.

Rags' leaden weight was too much. Ryan fell to her knees and Rags crumbled in a heap on top of her lap. The bullets had entered the chest area; her life was expiring fast.

Leslie opened the door and looked down. Her eyes widened with horror, but she was the sort that could keep her cool in a disaster if she had to. She pulled the door closed and hoped no one would leave the bar soon. She went to call the police and the paramedics.

Ryan cradled the mortally wounded form and rocked back and forth monotonously. Rags had always seemed so indestructable to her. "Please. Oh damn, please don't die, Rags. Don't leave me."

Rags struggled against her bloody breathing. It was erratic and she was choking on it. She summoned her last gram of strength to talk. Her request was made through painridden eyes. "Take . . . care . . . of . . . of . . . Sanji."

"Ohh. Rags, you know I will. How it must hurt to go this way." Ryan's tears fell freely on the heaving chest.

A crowd gathered around them. Leslie had to struggle to find her place near them. She knelt in the bloody pool and was painfully reminded that Rags was indeed human. She watched and listened.

The massive hand clutched Ryan's arm in the grip of death. She managed to whisper, ever so faintly, to Ryan's drenched jade eyes and grief inscribed face, "I love you."

Ryan felt the press of the wings, crowding her out. The dark angel fled, as quickly as she had come. Ryan cried out in anguish, "No! No, no no." She gathered the body close and wept openly.

Salty rivers formed on Leslie's cheeks, but she was not crying. Ryan needed her to be strong, and not fall apart. She reached down into her reserve account and found what she needed to stay composed in this insane scene.

The authorities arrived and pressed her into service. She rose calmly and answered their questions. They dispersed the crowd to a safe distance, more for their convenience than to preserve the dignity of the deceased and the grieving.

"Does she know who did it?" a tall blonde officer quizzed dryly, keeping his emotions in check.

Leslie bent to Ryan and pumped her gently. "Ryan, my love.

Who did this?"

Ryan's voice was metallic and hollow. "CJ pulled the trigger, but Anara killed her."

Leslie was stunned, but hid it. She turned to the officer. "It was a large black woman. They call her Crazy Jess."

He nodded. The name was recognizable to him. "We'll find her."

"She's dead too."

"What?" The officer heard her with his trained hearing.

"Ryan. What do you mean?" Leslie pushed, urgently.

"She's in her car. She drove off a bridge on one of the freeways."

"How do you know that?" he asked suspiciously.

"I know."

Leslie interceded with reason. "Just believe her. If you find CJ, you know Ryan had nothing to do with it. She's right here. People are sometimes aware of extraordinary events when they are under a lot of stress." Leslie's calm voice reassured the officer. Flashstrobes went off in rapid succession, gathering evidence.

"We need the body," a sympathetic paramedic urged.

Leslie knelt by her lover once more. "Honey, let them have her. You can't do anything now."

Ryan surrendered the discarded shell to the paramedics. The flurry of activity centered around the corpse leaving Ryan and Leslie to a degree of privacy.

Ryan spoke quietly and more reasonably. She was herself again. "I did do it."

"Do what?"

"Kill CJ."

Leslie looked anxiously around to see if anyone had heard. They were safe. "Ryan, how on earth did you do that?"

"With a curse."

"Is that safe?" Leslie was concerned for Ryan's soul.

"I didn't think. I just did it." She looked up at her lover. "I couldn't let her get to Sanji." Ryan dug her bloodied fingers into her hair and rested her forehead on her crimson palms. For the first time, Leslie realized that Ryan was soaked with Rags' blood. Her jacket and pants, it was everywhere.

"She's desperate, Leslie. She has to be. You picked up the gauntlet and within hours, she shows you what she's made of. Oh, how did I ever get myself mixed up in this? It doesn't pay to be on the receiving end of my love. Anara has destroyed, in one way or another, everyone I have ever loved deeply." She looked to Leslie again and very seriously warned her, "You're next, you know."

It was nightmarish, but Leslie could see that she wouldn't turn back. She would fight for as long as was necessary, side by side, with her beloved. "I told you once before that I am not afraid of her, Ryan. I will wade through the perils of hell to defeat her. We will," she took a bony, bloodsoaked hand in hers, "together."

"That is precisely where she'll make us go too. If we can get free of her, we can share a love such as the world seldom sees." Ryan was looking into her grey eyes, answering the challenge.